June 2009

WALK FREE

T. HOUSTON HAMILTON

(My friend Thelma)

Tybee News, Inc.

FIRST EDITION

This is a work of fiction. All characters, particular places and circumstances are products of the author's imagination.

A publication of
Tybee News, Inc.
2126 E. Victory Drive
UPS Box 184
Savannah, Georgia 31304

Printed in the United States of America

ISBN eps 89.5 KB

Chapter

1

Susan's real name was Shratt, but her adoptive name Sterne, and her married name Shields. She started what she was to think of as her public life in the eighth grade at age twelve—a year younger than her peers. Somewhere along the line a teacher, tired of Susan's too eager-to-excel attitude had advanced her a grade, a sobering experience for an already dismally solemn child.

When she was adopted (to everyone's astonishment including her own) she finished her last year of junior high as a Sterne. She blundered through that first year in the elegant suburb on the Main Line adjusting to the loss of the no-nonsense orphanage which had been suddenly and shockingly replaced by the snobbery of fellow pupils entrenched in their long-standing cliques.

By the time she entered senior high the next year, however, she had developed a solid image of herself as she wished to be perceived. She signed all her registration forms Suzi Sterne. She found a crowd of more dedicated scholars that she wanted to identify with, and introduced herself as the daughter of Reverend and Mrs. Chancellor Sterne, with never a mention of her recent adoption. That her so-called parents directed an old landmark church—well known to Philadelphians—and that she lived in the Manse, also a landmark, gave her a prestige she was quick to take advantage of.

She soon learned that from adults she could get more of the type of attention she required, and practiced cultivating them, learning to ask questions about things they took an interest in and beguiling them with her direct gaze and slow shy smile, a manner so habitual that there was no detecting the calculation behind it.

"You may call me Alice," Mrs. Sterne had said in the car, bringing Susan home with her from the orphanage. This jarred Susan's sensibilities. She had anticipated calling this somewhat formidable lady Mama or perhaps Mother. But—Alice?

There were other adjustments. She soon found that the work of keeping up the ten-room manse fell more and more on her strong but skinny shoulders. The beautiful room she had wonderingly taken as her own served as a place to store her clothes and to sleep. Alice utilized her at all other hours to cook, clean, launder and assist with entertaining.

Susan never complained. She performed all tasks with such intelligent speed and precision that Mrs. Sterne who worked beside her for a few months teaching her the ropes was moved to almost involuntary grunts of approval. In her mind Susan always addressed the large, stately blonde with her carefully painted face as "Miz Sterne, ma'am," mimicking the trace of Southern accent that lingered in Alice's voice after long years in the Northeast.

After six months any illusions that Susan might have cherished of becoming a tenderly nurtured daughter vanished on the day of her aborted return to her "own" room on the second floor. She'd cheerfully surrendered her place to a visiting big-wig when Alice told her to move her things to the little attic room to accommodate the guest.

Saturday morning after his departure, however, she threw her possessions into the small trunk she'd brought from the orphanage and started down the rather steep stairs. The bumping sounds must have alerted Alice because she appeared, flushed and heavily breathing, at the bottom of the steps.

"What are you doing, Susan?"

"Moving back to my room."

"That won't be necessary," Mrs. Sterne replied ascending the steps to confront Susan.

"Mr. Lee left already. That's my room."

"No, Susan. I've decided to keep that room as a guest room. Stay where you are."

"And let it stand empty most of the time? I have to climb up three flights to this dinky little place? Why can't I have my own room back?"

"My dear girl, I don't think I have to explain that. Do what I tell you and don't argue."

For the first and only time in her association with Mrs. Sterne, Susan lost her temper. "Why did you adopt me? You never wanted a daughter," she screamed.

"Stop that." Coldly furious herself, Mrs. Sterne turned abruptly and started down the stairs once again. Susan jumped over her trunk and pursued the lady. "All you wanted was someone you could work to death. Why don't you admit it?" she yelled. When no answer came she returned to the steps to the attic and hauled her trunk back, sobbing with anger.

Some time later she made a discovery that raised the worth of the despised room inestimably. One night after a particularly arduous day of preparation for a ladies' circle meeting, Susan lay in bed, too tired to sleep. An enormous tree stood outside the one small window of her room. And as she watched the branches move in the March wind she became aware of a low, not-quite-musical sound that had nothing to do with tree or wind.

Curious she sat up and strained her ears. Locating the sound in a far corner, she crept out of bed and moved closer and closer, identifying the sound as voices. There was a vent in the floor. Underneath it her so-called parents lay in the king-size bed in their massive bedroom. They were talking. Sue lay silent on the floor and suppressed a giggle. With her ear to the vent she could make out what they were saying.

The conversation had to do with a member of the church who had expressed discontent with Alice's plans to paint the recreation area in the enormous basement rooms below the first floor.

"I did my homework. That woodwork was painted when the church was first built," Alice complained.

"Even so—it never pays to quarrel. You know that," Rev. Sterne countered wearily.

"That dingy old mahogany varnish makes the place dark and gloomy," Alice insisted. "And it's not fancy woodwork, anyway. At least half the congregation agree with me on this. I don't see why we should have to give way to ignorance."

Rev. Sterne's sigh, heavy enough to carry upward to Susan's sharp ear, preceded what sounded like a final retort. "Can't you see that you're creating dissension again? But what's the use? You don't listen to reason. You'll keep on and on about this, won't you? So I'll say no more about it."

Susan who had no stake in the matter slid across the floor and huddled under her covers with a sense of satisfaction. She'd discovered a rich source of information.

Still wakeful, she compared the meticulous perfection of Alice's housekeeping with the slapdash, once-over that sufficed to keep the Orphanage livable. Much of that institution's cleaning she had become responsible for without knowing why. It seemed to her that she'd always done it.

At age five when distant relatives had dumped her at the shabby old building that housed twenty children and five or six staff, she'd hidden in the dormitory under her assigned bed for two weeks, terrified and disoriented. Dragged out for meals she ate obediently and escaped at the earliest possible moment.

No one gave her much attention until Sally, the cleaning woman, tried to get a dust mop under the bed and found her.

Sally exuded a sharp smell, had a red veined nose, bleary eyes and slatternly clothes garnered from the boxes of cast-offs left by church members. But her voice, though melancholy, had a comforting acceptance in it that reassured the frightened child cowering against the wall.

"Now, aint it pitiful, lost critter under there?" she demanded sitting down on the floor. "Come out and let me have a look at you." She waited, leaning against the wall and huffing while she examined the ceiling. Susie crept toward her cautiously, reassured by her inertia and sat down nearby.

Sally initiated a conversation, taking both sides. "Aint you a sight, dust all over your bottom? You can't help that, you say. Aint no place in this old Orphan's Home for a lonesome little kid that's lost her two parents in a wreck, you say.

"But sometime you gotta come out and start livin'." Susie crawled closer and when Sally raised a pendulous arm and offered to hug, she went to her sobbing.

After that it seemed perfectly natural to follow Sally around. Susan would vaguely remember that back before the fatal plane wreck that had left her here, and starting at age four, she had "assisted" her calm, serious mother with housework, standing on a chair to dry the already-dry dishes, pushing at the bottom of the vacuum cleaner and sprinkling cleanser in the sink. Not a syllable about getting in the way. Quite the contrary, she shared her mother's sense of accomplishment at the completion of chores.

Sally had an equal tolerance for the mournful infant who wanted to sweep and dust. It suited all concerned to have Susan thus occupied and seemingly happy.

They sent her to kindergarten. Before her first school day, Sally offered advice. "Don't never let anybody tell you you aint as good as everybody else. You're smart and a worker. Walk free, girl. Hold your head up." This counsel Susan remembered for the rest of her life. By the time she reached second grade she'd become adept in math and reading. At the orphanage her domestic assistance was no longer a myth.

Sally's progressive alcoholism impeded her efforts more and more as the months and years rolled on. Imperceptibly she and Susan changed roles. Gradually Sue became the initiator as they moved from room to room and up and down the long ramshackle building.

When she was ten Susan overheard some talk of firing Sally, whereupon she gave more critical attention to doing things well and quickly. When she heard anyone approach she'd wake Sally who frequently snored, leaning against a wall or even lying on the floor.

At sixty-two Sally retired on social security and a miniscule pension and Susan continued to perform the chores she seemed expected to assume. There was no way she could know that a sum for maintenance disappeared into certain pockets each month.

When she had a spare hour or two Susan at first walked the twelve blocks to Sally's one-room apartment to visit her. But as Sally's condition deteriorated she seemed scarcely able to identify the tall, rangy girl who dropped in out of the blue. Bereft, Susan called up her reserves of stoicism and pressed on. There had to be a better future for her somewhere out there.

The private Ecclesiastical Orphanage that sheltered Susan was a relic of a century-old approach to charity that no one knew how to dispose of. Its spry sixty-eight year old director managed to keep fifteen or twenty children in the run-down but adequate building. She also appeared regularly in churches and forwarded her cause with pastors and individual members who continued to budget its upkeep.

All proceeded without incident until a youthful reporter, beating the bushes for something he could term "investigative" zeroed in on the orphanage. It was antiquated and inadequate, he wrote, both in concept and execution. "Homes" nowadays resembled real homes with surrogate parents. The dormitories, mass dining and worn-out facilities should be closed.

Two things occurred as a result of this attack: First, a visit by a mission committee who put up new curtains and furnished a few rag rugs and lamps to make the place homier. And second, the adoption of Susan Shratt.

The Reverend Mrs. Sterne who prided herself on her interest in community affairs—those that might have a religious aspect, in particular—read the exposé with keen interest and made a point of visiting the institution.

Spruced up by the Committee and equipped with a set of defensive answers, the Orphanage disappointed her anticipation of finding an object for a crusade. But while she was there she saw Susan. The tall, angular and muscular girl with a long face and craggy profile interested her. This child wielded a vacuum cleaner with practiced ease. She learned that Susan was nearly twelve and that they no longer considered her a candidate for adoption. Not that she'd ever been much of a candidate. Her unsmiling and silent ways, her avoidance of visitors and her—well, sort of ugly looks—had not won any prospective parents' hearts.

It took Alice more than a week to persuade Rev. Sterne to agree to adopt Susan. "At our age?" She was only forty-nine, Mrs. Sterne reminded him. And at sixty-one he wasn't really old.

"But why? I thought you hated kids. I thought we agreed not to have any." This would be different. Susan wasn't really a child—more like a young woman. She could help with things around the manse.

"Oh—a live-in maid?" Rev. Sterne inquired.

"Not that. She's not to be salaried. We can do a lot for her."

"Such as?"

"We'll think of things," Alice equivocated.

In the end she wore him down as she knew she would. They went together to the Orphanage. He liked Susan who never giggled and chattered. They had to exert pressure to get the Orphanage to give her up. They could provide more advantages, could send her to college.

Mrs. Sterne sent a lawyer to explore legalities with the staff, and presently things worked out and papers got drawn up.

Susan had no regrets about leaving. With all its hardships, she much preferred life at the Manse. Figuring out how to bend the circumstances to suit herself occupied her mind while her body went through the necessary motions to keep Alice satisfied. After the fracas over the loss of her room she took a more distant attitude. She addressed Alice respectfully as "Ma'am," and treated her like an employer.

At first Alice had congratulated herself that the adoption had worked out successfully. Money previously budgeted for maid-service, laundry, and catering now provided certain cozy, tasteful items for the old place. Elegant it might be, but it had lacked a homier touch. Some of the antiques retreated to positions along the walls or went into nooks and corners where they could be displayed like works of art. Rich and comfortable sofas and warmly upholstered chairs appeared.

The informal dining room (once the servants' but now utilized by the family) had its scratched and scarred old table and battered chairs removed to the attic. A small round table and cushioned arm chairs replaced these, much to Susan's restrained satisfaction.

While feeling no particular affection for the pastor's wife, she recognized her abilities and, to an extent, emulated her manner of aggressive friendliness combined with unvarying dignity. There was something about Alice, however, that made the church ladies exchange looks behind her back, Sue observed. She cautiously added a slight diffidence to her own approach—a quality totally absent from Mrs. Sternes' confident and self-satisfied demeanor.

Middle school subjects required little in the way of study. Since she felt alienated from most of the students anyway, Susan often did her homework at the lunch hour. At home she had scarcely a minute to spare for anything but work.

Her stand-in parents had examined her first reports with anxious attention, relieved to find As and Bs. "I told you she'd do well in school and be a credit to us, didn't I?" Alice crowed, passing the report to her husband. He turned to Susan and in his formal way commended her for her performance. He signed the report and gave it back to her.

The next year they barely glanced at her reports, and by the second year of senior high school when she was fourteen, she often had to ask twice for a signature.

Chapter

2

After her fifteenth birthday in September went unobserved by her adoptive father and mother, Sue made a point of leaving the balloons and gift wrap from the celebration arranged by her three best friends at school in the hall trash basket. Alice, who wasn't given to apologies, said nothing, but Rev. Sterne managed to catch her alone, putting dishes away in the pantry.

"Sorry, Susie. I'm afraid we don't do too well—pinch hitting as parents. I still want to get you something. What would you like?"

Susan seized her chance. "I'd rather have the money if you wouldn't mind. All my pals have allowances and when we stop for ice cream or something on the way home I can never get anything. Sometimes Aggie offers to treat me, but I'm embarrassed to be always free loading."

Looking shamefaced, Rev. Sterne reached in his pocket and pulled out a couple of bills. "I'll see what I can do about the allowance. After all, if anyone deserves it, you sure do."

Thereafter, though with a grudging air, Mrs.

Sterne doled out an allowance every week as Susan had expected. In this, the Reverend (backed by the possibility of gossip about their stinginess) had prevailed. Alice handled the family finances and Rev. Sterne had limited pocket money, Sue realized, but whenever a genuine need arose she could get extra cash from him. By this point the relationship of the two females had so deteriorated that Susan would have suffered any ignominy rather than ask Mrs. Sterne for anything.

At thirteen Suzi had already successfully established herself at school and had fearlessly broadcast her alliance with the Sternes. At home she found life bleak. Rev. Sterne spent as much of his day as he could manage in his upstairs study. The formal study downstairs where he received occasional visitors and even performed a wedding at infrequent intervals was kept severely ordered. His upstairs study, strewn with books and papers, an old computer in the midst, was a different scene altogether. In that room not a paper could be moved nor an open book closed.

Rev. Sterne had published one heavy, abstruse tome, much admired in philosophical circles, and was at work on another. He hated interruptions and tried to get Alice to deal with the assistant pastors, the music director and members of the congregation who had problems. If she had nothing else on her agenda she organized matters and solved problems rather handily. But there were days when she abdicated and passed the daily cares back to Chancellor.

Sue, who had never stopped eavesdropping on their nightly discussions, grew accustomed to and rather bored with the tug-of-war over whose responsibility this or that might be. But when their remarks referred to her she listened with all her faculties alert. Recently Alice had begun to complain that Susan was "getting too big for her britches."

"I don't see it," Rev. Sterne objected. "She's perfectly courteous and obedient. I can't understand how you can fault her."

"You're never around. I'm with her all the time."

That's a lie, Susan thought, cautiously shifting her recumbent position to put pressure on the other ear. Alice was quite often away while Susan cleaned, washed clothes, ironed and cooked.

"Anyway, it's not anything she says. It's little things she does that I don't care for."

"Such as?"

"Nothing I can explain easily."

"Then why say any more about it?"

On this cue, as Susan started back into bed, careful to keep the springs from creaking, her lips parted and her teeth flashed white in the dark, bared in a wicked smile. She knew exactly what Alice was talking about.

What she'd learned was how to frustrate Alice's ongoing efforts to keep her in a servant's role. For nearly two years she'd remained in the background, inconspicuous, while she replenished tea tables, cooked and served Saturday luncheons, waited on guests at formal dinners until all these chores became second nature. Then at a tea one day a church member had stopped her as she passed a plate of cookies and asked, "Aren't you the Sterne's daughter?"

Pleased, Susan fell into conversation with the woman who seemed genuinely interested in her school activities. She even perched on the arm of the sofa and casually balanced the tray of cookies with one hand while gesturing with the other.

Glancing up she caught a look of involuntary disapproval and irritation on Mrs. Sterne's face, instantly wiped off when she met Susan's eyes. But now that she'd betrayed her intention Susan set forth systematically to thwart it.

Her services to guests took on an ever more pronounced air of gracious solicitude, conveying that her presence there was as a hostess rather than an automated domestic tool. None of this was lost on Mrs. Sterne. Sue sensed the exact degree to which Alice's impotent rage advanced and played on it, smiling slyly to herself as she cut cakes in the kitchen or chopped and mixed salads.

She made herself popular and appreciated. She remembered that old Mrs. Sanderson who couldn't get out of her wheel chair liked her tea with milk and two sugars. She remembered to ask attorney Brandt if his recently planted bushes had flourished.

Rev. Sterne, who avoided as much personal contact with the congregation as he could manage, expressed gratitude that somebody took an interest.

Then one night an obnoxious young woman was invited to dine. After a time, obviously unaware that Susan never ate with the family when guests were present, she announced loudly that Susan was driving her crazy, flitting around, and should give it up and sit down. At which point Mrs. Sterne was obliged to say that Sue had a test and would have to be excused to study for it.

In her attic room Susan collapsed on the bed and entertained herself with a vision of the majestic lady clearing her own table and bringing in the dessert. Too offended to call Susan back after the guest's departure Mrs. Sterne even loaded the dishwasher and cleaned the kitchen. Next day Sue gravely reported that she had done well on her exam and added that she hadn't realized that Alice knew about the test.

Mrs. Sterne, not to be circumvented, began to give Susan elaborate instructions about how to serve unobtrusively. Or she would catch Susan's eye when she was chatting with someone and nod toward the kitchen. Instantly responsive, always polite, Susan evinced no trace of overt opposition. But she was fifteen now, and tall and slim and attractive in a homely sort of way. Her thick blonde hair, tied back in a scarf or braided, hung below her shoulders. Her nose, too thin and too large jutted from her face and her chin—too long and square—detracted from her femininity. But she attracted attention, mostly favorable.

Alice's domineering ways, on the contrary,

had earned her numerous enemies who after the eighth year of the Sterne's ministry, began to unite against her. As Susan's star ascended, Alice Sterne's declined. Too perceptive to miss what was going on, the lady fumed and inveighed. She organized supporters in her defense and held her own. But it was humiliating to need justification. She began to count Susan with the opposition and to imagine that she complained to church members about her treatment. In that she was mistaken. Insofar as facts allowed, Sue tried to convey a subtle, consistent impression that she was indulged and cherished.

Even when Alice brought home a uniform and told her to wear it—to save her school clothes—Susan offered no resistance. Mrs. Sterne liked garments well cut and of fine materials and the uniform was basically "nice" Sue decided. She appeared before tea time in the new outfit and Mrs. Sterne greeted her with little grunts of approval.

Just before people started coming, however, Susan went to the bathroom, tied a bright scarf around her waist, stuck the apron on top of it, pulling it a bit off center, and wound the ties twice around her slender waist, knotting them in front. She unbuttoned the collar, folded and pushed up the sleeves. The effect satisfied her. If she had to, she'd tell Mrs. Sterne that it was too stiff and uncomfortable the other way.

Alice never brought up the subject and disguised her feelings when Susan even wore the uniform to school one day—sans apron, of course.

After Christmas the year Susan completed her last year of high school she detected an undercurrent of fear and tension in the house and a secretive scheming atmosphere in the church. Christmas preparations and festivities so exhausted Sue that she had fallen asleep night after night without listening to her "parents" talk. Now, impelled by a growing concern, she settled down over the vent without even getting into bed.

The tenor of the discussion she heard made her realize at once that some things were coming to a head in the congregation. Alice and Chancellor were discussing things like retirement, pensions and social security—alarming Sue with references to moving away! Not a syllable about herself. She went to bed and lay awake a long time fitting pieces together. For many Sundays she'd noticed that more people hung around in corridors of the church for longer periods. Men gathered in front after the service. If she approached they interrupted their talk and greeted her in a kind but perfunctory way.

Almost from the first she'd known that people had mixed feelings about their minister. They admired his tall, white haired distinguished looks, his famous scholarship and his gracious manners. But he closeted himself with his books and took minimal interest in the proliferation of church activities. So when Alice's friendship turned out to be superficial, her decisions incontrovertible, discontent with the pair deepened. They were deciding to ask him to resign, Sue thought. And he'd made up his mind to forestall them by announcing his retirement.

He was only sixty-three, but had never had an affinity for many of the chores involved in church work, Susan guessed. She could understand his decision to escape. But Alice?

She listened every night with fierce concentration. The pair took trips and looked at houses to buy and narrowed the choice to two. Rev. Sterne favored a rambling old-fashioned farmhouse outside Lexington, Virginia. Alice had her heart set on a compact but fully equipped house near a large retirement center in the city itself.

Chancellor argued for more privacy and independence and more room. "You know I have to have an adequate study."

"There are three nice large bedrooms in the other place. You can have one for a study."

"Then you'd have no office or hobby room for yourself," Chancellor demurred. "And you've always said you had to have one."

"We just need the one bedroom, and I can have the third for myself. That's no problem."

"Where would Susan sleep? There's no attic. Are you planning to hang her from the rafters?"

"Don't get sarcastic. No, I'm thinking of giving Sue her independence," Alice purred.

Susan's skin crawled as she sensed the vengeful satisfaction in Alice's voice. She felt sick and waited breathlessly for Rev. Sterne's answer which was a long time coming.

"It sounds to me as if you're intending to surrender a responsibility that we entered into as supposedly mature adults. We promised to take care of that girl and send her to college."

"If she'd stayed in the Orphanage, there would be no question of college. We don't have to feel obligated that way. She'll be done with high school and I'll find something for her to do."

"Good grief, Alice! She's just a kid. Sixteen. You'd turn her out to pasture just like that?"

"I didn't say that. I said I'd find an appropriate place for her."

"I don't like this. I want to buy the big house that has lots of room for everything. Let Susan attend the Community College over there—it's dirt cheap—and give her a chance. She's bright, she's worked hard. She deserves it."

Another silence ensued. Then Alice said, in that crafty way Susan recognized, that they didn't have to decide right then. They'd think about it. She could hear the click of the lamp turned off.

In bed with the covers pulled over her head Susan shivered uncontrollably. She knew who would win in the end. Alice would give Chancellor the lovey-dovey stuff and keep talking and insisting until she got her way.

She surveyed the wreckage of all her plans and dreams with a numb horror. If only she'd known! But it was useless to think she could have won Alice's heart. The woman had no heart to win. She had taken Susan in for expediency and would cut her out for the same reason. Oh, why had she taken all those college prep courses that prepared her for nothing in the real world that she was about to be thrust into? She should have majored in computer science, typing expertise, maybe even rudimentary accounting. What did she know of practical use except how to do housework? She could do housework all right—but for the rest of her life? Not if she could help it.

Despite this brief surge of bravado, however, Susan trembled with fear. She sat up in bed, hugging her knees and moaning softly, "What will become of me?"

Chapter

3

Mother's helper!" Susan thought, livid with anger as she passed through the modest house at ten p.m. relocating toys and clothing and dumping scattered food and contents of ash trays into a plastic bag. The stupid mother was no help to Susan and could not be straightened out, much as one might try.

Mrs. Klimpton might have been pretty before fat swelled her cheeks and puffed up her body. She spent the day on the sofa in front of the television, smoking and eating candy bars while Susan coped with the house, the baby (six months), the twin boys (four) and the snotty little girl, Millicent, who attended first grade.

Susan's fury wasn't directed so much toward the family, however, as it was toward Alice who had expressed smug satisfaction over this job, telling her husband that Sue would have a "lovely home in the suburbs" and a chance to "associate with other children" while she helped "such a sweet young housewife."

Rev. Sterne's protests that surely she could do office work, that they were obligated to find her a decent job and an apartment were vetoed. "She's only sixteen. No one would hire her."

"She looks a lot older than that. And acts like fifty."

"Her application would give her away. Trust me, Chancellor, this is best."

The baby, fed and diapered, had fallen asleep. The twins had dropped off from exhaustion and, in their respective rooms Millicent and her parents watched their last TV shows. In another hour Susan would sneak in on the snoring occupants and turn off the sets, but till then she finally had a bit of time to herself.

She picked up the newspaper that Mr. Klimpton had dismantled and strewn around his recliner. Most of it she folded into her trash bag, but she retained the classified ads and carried them under her arm, into the kitchen.

After sticking stray glasses and plates into the dishwasher and turning it on, Susan gathered the last of the garbage and put the bags into the can outside. Now she could endure the kitchen. It had taken months to get the sticky walls, floors and counters scrubbed down, the windows and curtains washed, the cupboards and appliances scoured. Actually, under all that crud, a rather decent and well equipped room had lurked.

She unfolded the employment section, found a pen that she kept on a top shelf, and began to read. She didn't know what she was hunting for, but her search was aimed at getting her out of this hole.

Her years in the manse had spoiled her, she

thought. She had become maybe the world's greatest housekeeper, but she had a painfully low tolerance for noise, disorder and sloth, the principal characteristics of the situation she now found herself in. Besides all that she missed the high leaded windows, arched doorways and magnificent curved staircases of her previous life.

She x'd through dozens of items for which she wasn't qualified, lingered uncertainly over "Receptionists" and "Clerks." She had the notion that a receptionist had to be glamorous. Her ugly face and schoolgirl wardrobe wouldn't do. Clerks had to file and run machines that she'd had no experience with.

Twice she'd tried answering ads for a "people-oriented individual, free to travel. Good salary. No experience needed." That job had been filled, crisp voices from employment agencies informed her. They learned her age and qualifications and got off the phone in a hurry.

Once more Susan reached the end of the ads without locating anything she wanted to do. Other domestic jobs looked more appealing than this one, but why make a complicated move for only a slight improvement? Hotels and restaurants offered little more money than she currently earned. How could she pay rent and buy food? Weary, she folded the pages. Maybe tomorrow's paper would offer something better.

Growing more discontented every day Susan labored on. The children who for a time had continued to pester their mother with shrill demands now stopped consulting her. Susan assumed full charge. When they screeched she ignored them. If they spoke quietly she listened and responded. They had to sit at the table and eat or get nothing.

Complaints to their mother about Susan's treatment fell on deaf ears. "Can't you see I'm watching this program? Try to get along, for Pete's sake."

The baby was sweet but took up so much time. The twins had to be watched constantly to keep them from jumping on and off furniture. They'd take things apart. She put clocks and small radios and bric-a-brac on high shelves. The boys wore her out, but she felt no personal rancor.

Millicent was a different case altogether. She'd take several shirts and pants out of the closet and try them on before dressing for school. She never refolded anything or returned it to its place. She called Susan, "Maid," and tried to order her around.

After several months, Mr. Klimpton complained that she hadn't cashed her checks and was throwing his bank balance off. She had to go open a bank account, and Mrs. Klimpton must take her. The woman moved the car seat way back to accommodate her fat stomach and legs. Then, because she was short, she could barely reach the pedals. Susan strapped the baby into a seat and sat in the back to keep the twins from rolling down the windows and yelling and hanging out.

In the bank she arranged to make mail deposits and thanked her stars when they got back safely and had parked the car in the garage.

Things changed when, one Saturday, she begged to be excused from going to the mall with the family. No, she had nothing to buy this week. No, they needn't bring her anything. As soon as they drove off she rushed inside and looked again at the ad that had kept her awake all night:

Live-in Housekeeper for Guest Residence.
Cooking, cleaning, record keeping, correspondence.
Prefer experienced caterer.

The ad gave a phone number including an extension and the words "Call Fri. or Sat. A.M."

She knew this was a real job because it sounded like hard work. It also seemed like a job she could handle. She'd catered Mrs. Sterne's parties for years with little help.

The first week the ad appeared she'd felt put off by the "experienced caterer" bit, but it had said "prefer." And when it appeared again a second week, she felt encouraged.

She took out the paper on which she'd written down the various lies she planned to tell and rehearsed them—she was twenty (That seemed old to her), had worked for a caterer (now retired) for four years, had catered mostly church affairs. She mentally reviewed the largest of those: the menus, the service. Anything else she'd have to play by ear. She screwed up her courage, dialed the number, and remembered to keep her voice low and firm. A company receptionist rang the extension.

"Yes?" Brusque male.

"I'm calling about your ad," Sue announced in a deepened voice.

"Which ad is this?"

"For a housekeeper-caterer."

"Oh, good. You've had experience?"

"A lot."

"Okay. Let me think. I have to go to the location anyway and check the place over. So let's meet there. I can show you the set-up, find out more about you and then we can decide whether we're mutually interested."

"All right." Sue wrote down the address and the man hung up, sounding rushed. He wanted to see her at noon. Luckily the Klimptons planned to have lunch at the mall. It was ten-thirty. How could she get over there? She phoned for a taxi—needed immediately, she said. Then she flew upstairs to put on her Sunday dress, shoes and a coat.

Since it was December and foggy she took her umbrella. Now she waited outside, hopping in as soon as the cab arrived. They got to the place at eleven. "Could the cab return for her in two hours?"

"Sure, babe." The gum chewing driver seemed to sense her excitement. "Meetin' someone?"

"Business," she snapped.

Having plenty of time to brace herself pleased Susan. She wandered around and examined the area, raising her umbrella when it started to drizzle. The building where, presumably, she'd work was a fairly impressive two-story brick with a balcony across the second-floor front. It faced a park and a divided boulevard. She walked along one side of it to ascertain its width, stood for a time in the back yard and surveyed the deck. Then she went up to the back windows and peered in. Too dark inside to reveal much of anything.

She returned to the front, went up on the porch and peered earnestly through the glass panels beside the entrance. She could make out dim outlines of a foyer in the shadows.

She descended the steps and walked a block in one direction and a block in the other, taking her time and studying the old, but still affluent neighborhood. Absorbed in this occupation she failed to notice the car that pulled into the driveway. So the potential employer's booming voice demanding, "You're not the housekeeper I was to meet here, are you?" startled her.

"Yes, I am." She hurried toward his car.

A large man in a black suit with a black trench coat over it got out of the red sports car. He had a broad face and bushy eyebrows.

"You don't look much like a housekeeper," he said.

"I'm probably the best in Philadelphia," Sue responded, indignant.

"How old did you say you were?"

"I hadn't said, but I'm twenty."

"Awful young."

"I've been doing this type of work for years," she defended, still indignant, and thinking "like ten."

He unlocked the house and they went in. Sue

glanced around with a practiced eye. Enormous well-furnished living room with a fireplace. "Do I have to keep the fire going?" Fires at the Manse had been a drag.

"Guess not if it's too much work."

"Too much work."

He took a pad from a breast pocket. "I'll get some electric logs installed." They proceeded to a large dining room with several small tables and chairs in it. Susan glanced around. "You need a buffet here. There's no place to serve from."

The man smiled, "Yes, ma'am!" The trace of sarcasm in his voice warned Susan to take a more deferential tone.

"If it's possible," she amended.

"It's possible." He was writing again.

The kitchen had a work island and cupboards on every wall. There was a pantry to one side and a huge liquor cabinet, completely stocked. "We're going to put a lock on this, and you'll have the key. Have to ration this stuff." He regarded Sue with bland indifference. "Drink much?"

"Not at all," she said—and asked, perturbed, "What's the ration?"

"Wine with meals—couple glasses. A highball or two in the evening. Frankly, we don't want anyone to get drunk and out-of-control here."

"Suppose they bring their own?"

"That's a possibility. Anyway, there's a number for security that you can call if they start fighting or something. There's a booklet in the office with all the information you'd need."

Susan masked her dismay. "All right," she agreed trying to sound adult and in charge.

Now he opened another door. "Housekeeper's quarters." He watched while Susan went in and looked at the tiny sitting room, bedroom and bath, set-up like a furniture store display. "It's nice," she said, and wondered why he seemed relieved.

Talking, explaining, questioning he led the way upstairs where they looked at the four luxurious bedrooms each with its bath. "We use this place as a tax write-off and also to reward our better salesmen with a trip to historic Philly. Comes under 'Sales incentives.' Most of those are monetary, and there's no one department that manages this house. You'd be on your own, mostly. The guests are supposed to report if the service is bad. Company Maintenance sends a crew by here to keep up the yard and take care of repairs if there are any."

They were descending. Under the stairs in the foyer a cubbyhole contained a small desk and a two-drawer file. "The winning salesmen bring their wives here from all over the U.S. Once they qualify, they're supposed to sign up at least two weeks in advance. You'll be in charge of letting them know if there's a room available. You also have to file the invoices, do a little record keeping, and mail the paperwork to accounting. A wholesale grocer delivers food and also provides the hooch. Number's in here." He lifted an address book. "You let them know a week ahead what you need. Elemental operation, really." He paused and re-examined her, hesitating. "You look awful young and thin, and there's lots of housecleaning besides the cooking. And people expect good meals here. You won't serve lunch but have to come up with breakfast and dinner unless people say they'll eat out."

"I've had harder jobs. I've served a buffet for fifty people with—an assistant or two. This wouldn't be nearly so much work." She had an afterthought. "How about laundry?"

"There's a company listed in that directory who pick up our tablecloths and linens—all that stuff—and oh, let me see." He found a door off the back hall. "Yes, there's a stacked washer and dryer in here for your use."

"Do I have to wash clothes for the guests?"

"Their clothes? Not on your life." He stared at her, curious.

"Then it really is easier than the work I've been doing. I can handle this."

The man pondered and shook his head once or twice, but at last he said, "I guess we'll go ahead then. Frankly, I've had few calls and no takers for this job until you came along." He named the salary and added apologetically that after all she'd be getting free board and room.

Sue accepted the offer gravely. She accepted the application and other papers he took from the desk. She agreed to send the form in to company headquarters.

He filled in a blank or two and scrawled his name on the bottom of the first page. "Jim Thorn," he said belatedly, "And I'm hiring—?"

"Susan Sterne."

"If you have any problems, Susan, or if you find you can't handle this, or if you have to leave for any reason, call the emergency number in the directory. They'll send a temporary caretaker and we'll find someone else. Whatever you do, don't leave the house unattended for more than a few hours.

"I won't have any trouble and I won't leave," Susan spoke sturdily and looked fifty years old for a moment.

The executive nodded. "I'm off to Europe in an hour or two." He dangled the key to the front door. "All the other keys are on a board in the office. You'll start a week from Monday on January 5. I'll check in with you when I get back in June—or maybe July." He herded her out the front door, locked it and handed her the key. Then he stood for a minute looking her over a last time. "Yes, I think you're okay." He glanced at his watch and walked briskly to his car. Before he closed the door he called, "Don't fail to send in that application I signed. Otherwise they won't know to send your paycheck over here."

At breakfast the next morning she announced that she'd be leaving January 5 and they must find a replacement. The news met with stony immobility from all except Millicent who jumped up, ran to her mother's side and with a sob buried her head in her plump shoulder. Mrs. Klimpton looked a little vaguer than usual. Mr. Klimpton looked grim, but had nothing to say. He finished his coffee and went to his office.

That night, however, he sought Susan out in the kitchen where she sat alone at the table with a cup of tea. "Has something upset you, Sue?" The bald little accountant looked nervous and concerned.

"No, I just wanted to do something different."

"Your mother seemed to think you'd be around a good long while. I know things haven't been easy, but I for one have really appreciated all you've done. I wish you'd reconsider."

"I can't. I've signed up for another job." Susan had a sudden vision of that application—full of blank spaces and lies she'd told.

"I could—we could pay you a little more. You've saved me money—less wasted food—all that sort of thing."

"It's not money that I'm after—just a change."

Mr. Klimpton sat down opposite her. "You don't know what it was like before you came," he said. "Having to fix dinner myself, do the laundry."

"I can imagine." For a fleeting moment she felt really sorry for the man but her resolution never wavered. "You'll find someone else. There's no way I could get out of honoring the commitment I made."

Uneasiness about the future inspired Susan to go to her new job at the Guest House on Sunday evening instead of Monday. Declining Mr. Klimpton's help, she summoned a taxi. The driver grumbled about handling her little trunk, but managed to stow it away.

And when they arrived at the appropriate building and Sue unlocked the door with a proprietary air and flipped on lights he became respectful and thanked her deferentially for the tip.

She dragged her trunk into the housekeeper's rooms and then lay down on the bed, with a small lamp for a light, and reflected. Suppose someone found her application inadequate? Would an authority figure appear and dispatch her? She had claimed she could do a job for which she had no exactly comparable experience. How would things work out when guests started arriving? With quickening pulses she leaped up and rushed to the tiny office, groping for switches in the mostly dark building.

Rummaging in the desk she found an official looking, hard covered record book titled: SCHEDULE. Inside she found pages for every day of the year for two years. Nothing on the page for January fifth, but on January sixth names appeared: Mr. and Mrs. Michael Stowe, neatly annotated with addresses and phone numbers. She looked at the previous pages—nobody scheduled for the last two weeks of December. Before that guests had arrived regularly. And in the future who else would be coming? For the next six weeks there were one or two couples listed on each page. She stared at the names as if she could make personalities emerge and declare themselves. And others might still write or call in for reservations. Might already have written, in fact. She sprang up and hurried to the porch. The mailbox was stuffed. She took everything to the office and sorted it. Lots of advertising. Three letters. And an official envelope with the company letterhead addressed to Housekeeper. Inside a typewritten notice from the Maintenance Division listing Installations made last week:

> Lock on liquor cabinet
> Electric logs
> Buffet

A thrill went through her. She'd changed things! She, Susan Sterne, seventeen going on twenty.

Chapter
4

Susan awoke the next morning before daylight, feeling very much in charge. She flipped on lights all over the house and looked first at the electric logs. A dirty footprint smudged the carpet. She'd have to clean that away. Next the buffet: large, heavy, black—out of place with the light tables and cane chairs. Sobered she looked into the kitchen. The liquor cabinet key was stuck in the new lock; underneath lay a tiny pile of sawdust. She put the key in her pocket, mentally listing chores. Clean, dust, order food. She flew back to the office snatched up the directory, and under Grocer/Vinter found the number. As soon as she saw broad daylight she'd call. Guests would be in tomorrow.

When the mail came, she opened three letters, one a cancellation. She crossed out that reservation, found a postcard and wrote, "We have cancelled your reservation as requested," and signed it, Susan Sterne, Housekeeper. The others asked for bookings for February. She entered them under the appropriate dates and neatly penned cards acknowledging them. A small drawer housed a large roll of stamps. Activity restored her natural confidence and she began feeling complacent.

Next afternoon the very first pair of couples arrived and, to her chagrin, they totally ignored her, as if she were a nonentity, giving all their attention to each other. Still, things proceeded normally—much as she'd expected.

The next pair of guests were totally different. They ordered her around, treating her like a combination maid, bellboy, valet, cook and bottle washer. She racked her brains, and decided to avoid exploitation by excusing herself hastily, citing pressing duties. Elsewhere. This worked to her advantage.

Then, in the last week of January, three couples appeared all together. Tired of dancing attendance she put breakfast on the buffet with a sign, "Serve yourself," and hid in her quarters with the door ajar until she heard what sounded like a general exodus, as they went out to start visiting all those places tourists wanted to see. But when she ventured into the kitchen she was startled to find one of the guests still there, staring through the glass windows at the top of the liquor cabinet.

"Who's got the key to this?" the burly, red-faced man demanded.

She didn't answer.

"You have, don't you? Who told you to be so stingy with this? Didn't serve us a whole lot to drink last night, did you?"

"Company policy. It's rationed."

"And what's the ration exactly? Who decides?

You?"

She was dying to say, "What if I do decide?" but maintained a cautious silence.

"Come on, answer me."

"I have to follow orders."

"Where do you keep the key? In that office out there?"

Another silence. From the foyer the man's wife yelled "Get out here, Slim. We're leaving."

"We'll take this subject up again when I get back," Slim Maxwell promised, throwing her a challenging look over his shoulder.

She did indeed keep the clearly labeled key in the office on the key board. Now she found a long cord, tied the key on the middle of it and hung it around her neck under her shirt. Out of sight, out of mind? But a premonition plagued her all day while she changed linens, vacuumed, dusted and began cooking the elaborate four-course meal she had planned. The quality of food delivered by the wholesaler usually satisfied her, though they sent an occasional head of slightly rusty lettuce or some overripe fruit.

A fourth couple, Cleo and Don Skales, arrived late that afternoon: a stout, moon-faced pair—placid and agreeable. Thank you, Lord, Sue thought, unaware of praying.

She set four tables with an array of china and crystal and went to her room to freshen up before starting final arrangements. "I'll take out all the liquor I need and keep the rest locked up," she decided, walking across her little hall into the kitchen, pulling up the key as she went. To her astonishment Slim sounding drunk, loomed up in the doorway. How had he managed to get through the front door without alerting her?

"So that's why it's not in the office. Got the bally thing around your neck, have you?" He lunged at her, thrust his hand down inside her dress and groped for the key.

She fought for possession, but when the cord tightened around her neck and she thought she'd faint, he got it away from her.

"Now listen," he hissed, triumphant. "I want you to understand a few things. Company lets us drink good bit more'n you're handin' out. Silly, unreasonable kid."

"Give back the key. Go in the living room, and I'll bring you a cocktail. Whatever you like."

"I'll mix my own. I know what I want better'n you do," he declared, voice slurred. He turned to the liquor cabinet. While he fumbled, trying to get the key into the lock, Susan thought despairingly that she'd lost control, had fouled up on her instructions, could lose her job. She had to get the key back, and she would.

Slim had inserted it, but before he could turn it, Sue jumped at him, bit down hard on his fingers, and when he pulled his hand away, crying out in pain, she snatched the key. In three bounds she was across the room, into the hall and entering her quarters. She slammed the door in Slim's face and locked it.

He stood in the hall swearing loudly and

threatening to report to the company that she'd assaulted him. She stood in the middle of her sitting room, knees weak, hands clammy. "Oh, man, what an idiot I've been!" She thought of the emergency number. But how could she get to the office?

After an interminable space she heard the voice of Slim's wife—low and soothing. "Sure honey, you can report her tomorrow. Right now let's go back to our room and get ready for dinner."

"Gotta get that key."

"No, let her have it for now. Don't keep arguing and fussing. People can hear you all over the house. Come along, Slim, that's a sweetie." She led him away.

Because she had to, Sue left the sanctuary of her room and finished dinner preparations. She couldn't think of a safe place for the key, so after taking out the appropriate bottles she relocked the cabinet and dropped the key into a cutlery drawer where it blended with bottle openers and small knives.

She detected uneasiness among the guests who refrained from staring at Slim. He ate morosely, grumbling to himself and nursing his injured hand.

By morning he was sober and quite friendly. He joked and chatted with the other guests who seemed to have forgotten his drunken outburst. He was gone all day but came back still rational. And that evening at dinner he was circumspect and full of compliments.

Gratified by the change Susan answered Slim's call to join the group in the living room after she'd finished dinner chores. No one had ever thought to include her before. Slim kept everybody talking and laughing.

Susan sat quietly on the outer edge, satisfied to be there at all. Then, without warning, Slim focused on her. "Tell us about yourself, Susie." She had a well-practiced spiel about being the only child of a pastor. She even made him a poor pastor to explain her menial job. She'd grown up outside of Philadelphia. Her parents, now retired, lived in Virginia. She'd held a couple of housekeeping jobs.

After this recitation she rose to go, not wanting to risk further questions. "Anyone care for anything else? More nuts or candy?"

"Bring us a pitcher of cocktails, Sue. And make them a bit more potent, will you?"

"Okay."

Agitated, she mixed six drinks, increasing the amount of alcohol called for by the recipe and making up her mind to retire to her room as soon as she'd left the container in the living room. If she guessed right, Slim would imbibe most of this and then go to bed.

But he received it as if he were the host at a festive occasion and detained Sue while refreshing a few glasses, all the while telling her that she was doing a great job and had made their stay "so fantastic." "Don't run off," he urged, "Jim's regaling us with a story about a grizzly that climbed on to the top of his car in Yellowstone Park."

Still cautious Sue sat down again and Jim went

on about how the bear's weight had dented the roof. The
next minute a cocktail glass appeared in front of Sue.
She ignored it. Conversation flowed on. Presently Slim
asked, "Why aren't you drinking? Sophisticated young
lady like you must be used to an occasional nip."

Talk ceased and all eyes fixed on her. Nervous,
Susan picked up the glass and sipped it. It was hot
going down but not unpleasant. The others resumed
their chatter and she slowly finished the drink. When
Slim poured her another she thought, "This won't hurt
me. I'll get it down gradually and then go directly to
bed."

But with the second drink she grew animated
and expansive. She entered into the joking and
banter. She tossed off a third drink, feeling flushed but
confident. She answered questions with great frankness
and laughed a lot. The group seemed centered around
her, their eyes regarded her with humorous attention,
their open mouths created round circles in their laughing
faces. After a fourth drink she found everything blurring
into a colorful, noisy circus.

Chapter
5

Susan awoke in her bedroom with a frightful headache and a bitter taste in her mouth. She was, she realized, fully dressed. Her door stood open and she could hear voices and sensed that there was movement in and out of the kitchen. She jerked upright and her head spun. She forced herself out of bed and cautiously crossed the floor to her cubbyhole of a bathroom where she lost the contents of her stomach. She avoided looking in the mirror until after she'd splashed a lot of cold water on her face. Even so one glance told her she looked ghastly.

Breakfast! What on earth time was it? She looked at her watch. Ten! She rushed into the kitchen. General disarray—cupboards open, utensils on the stove. She glanced toward the liquor cabinet. The key was there, stuck into the lock. She peered into the dining room. All four couples were sitting at tables. Boxes of cereal and cartons of milk. Banana peels. Vestiges of bacon and eggs on some plates. Coffee cups and no saucers.

Appalled, Susan took in their faces. Jim and

Pansy wouldn't meet her eyes. The Skales had mildly shamefaced expressions. But Slim was clowning around as usual and hailed her with delight. "Up at last? We got our own breakfasts as you see. You really outdid us last night!"

His wife's giggling protest angered Sue. She perceived that, while seeming to object, Cheri actually urged Slim on.

Tears of rage welled up. She rushed back to her rooms, locked the door and had a cry. They'd ganged up and got her drunk. She had no idea what damaging things she might have said—lies she might have admitted to. She'd failed to do her job and had made an enemy of Slim. None of those people had the slightest respect for her, nor did she deserve respect. After telling Mr. Thorn that she didn't drink she'd disgraced herself. What if the story got back to him? What might Slim say the next time he was inebriated?

A dry misery replaced her sobs. She bathed, dressed in clean clothes and went to work. After thoroughly cleaning and straightening the now empty kitchen and dining room, she forced herself to go up to the guests' bedrooms. All were out, thank heaven. The room that Slim and Cheri had occupied had the empty disheveled look of an abandoned hotel room. Susan sat on the edge of the bed, relief flooding her. Those two had gone back to Detroit, of course. Why hadn't she remembered?

Detroit was far away. The whole stupid affair might blow over and be forgotten. She guessed that no one but Slim was too proud of what had gone on. And surely his wife would counsel discretion?

After lunch she collected mail and did her office chores—the least time-consuming part of her job, but the part she most enjoyed. For an hour she felt like someone more important than a domestic drudge.

The living room reminded her of last night's debacle. Glasses everywhere, ash trays overflowing, stains on carpets and furniture, candy stuck to the couch covers, pillows on the floor, cushions awry. Slim's bad influence. Had four couples ever before congregated here to "party?" If only she hadn't participated! She'd been forced to lie in order to get even this moderately acceptable job. And keeping secrets didn't combine with alcohol. She'd never take another drink. There had to be ways to avoid it. She'd never again risk letting go of the reins. Already she'd found that it took every bit of her sober brain to handle touchy questions.

Going over her treatment of Slim and Cheri she admitted that she'd asked for trouble. Her own off-hand, friendly approach hadn't helped her, and if she couldn't dominate her situation Mr. Thorn would fire her when he got back.

She finished cleaning up and vacuuming, went to the kitchen and began to cut fruit and vegetables. While she chopped a new image of herself formed, and after a spell she began to work with a grin on her face.

Two weeks of unremitting labor ensued while she was run ragged by a succession of people that she treated well but warily, and at last a free day appeared on the schedule.

She set the laundry pick-up bag out on the back porch, carried out trash bags and stacked the last of the dishes in the machine. Then she put on her Sunday best, hurried out and caught a bus to town. At Wanamakers she rode an escalator upward, looking for a department that sold the clothes she had in mind. She passed a jeans and shirts floor and a sequined and slinky area. When she saw a manikin wearing a suit and holding a briefcase she got off and entered a world of business attire that reminded her of Mrs. Sterne's best.

The price tags alarmed her. She had her checkbook with her and since she'd saved most of her salary from the day she started working she thought she would have considerable choice. She soon learned that she'd have to choose carefully to buy much of anything here.

A rack of "separates" seemed less expensive and recombining for a different look appealed to her. Certain things she liked were the wrong size, however, and shopping became a chore. She was about to leave when a Sale rack caught her eye. She tried on a three piece gray suit reduced to half price: jacket, pants and skirt. Transformation. The outfit made her look older, more dignified, more substantial. She turned this way and that. The skirt was slightly loose in the waist, but the jacket fitted her broad shoulders. She went back to the sale rack and found a plaid blazer that she could wear with the tailored trousers.

The outrageous price for these purchases created mild panic, but she took them to the saleswoman. Then she had to wait while the clerk found someone to okay her check. "No credit card and no driver's license?"

"No, ma'am."

She had to wait once more. Were they calling her bank? They wanted to take her money if she really had it. In the end they wrapped her things in yards of tissue, put them in a box and let her walk out with them. Was she crazy to give up all her savings in one wild splurge?

It was 2:00 p.m. and she realized that she hadn't eaten since breakfast. She found a restaurant and sat down, thankful to get off her feet. A hostess, in a formal skirt and a lovely satin blouse approached with a coffee pot. Her professional manner and the extreme care she took not to spill a drop suggested that this was a special service performed outside the realm of her usual occupation. Susan watched fascinated. The woman's perfectly neat hair and manicured nails put her into another class.

After lunch she went to a library where computers and printers were available, and typed up and copied forms that she'd devised.

Back home she wanted to lie down and recover from the strain, but instead had to finish her chores. People would arrive next day. But at least now she was ready for them.

"I'm Sue Sterne, the Manager," she said. She had manicured nails and every hair in place, and with her hair up and wearing the new suit she felt confident and in charge. The arrivals meekly accepted her directions and the sheet of House Rules. It listed hours at which meals would be served, hinted that to insure possession, personal property must be kept in their rooms, and recommended use of ash trays. She told them firmly which rooms to occupy and then excused herself.

"It worked," she crowed, exhilarated for a few minutes until common sense told her to wait and see. The rest of the day went off equally well, however, and she allowed herself a cautious surge of optimism.

Through the weeks that followed she learned not to serve a fixed menu, but to put a tempting variety of foods on the buffet. Guests preferred it. She searched through cupboards and found equipment to keep hot food warm and cold food cold. At breakfast and after dinner she appeared in her business garb and filled coffee cups. But she held herself aloof. Everyone spoke to her politely.

While she much preferred her managerial image and the deference it brought, she was friendless and alone. She engaged the delivery man in short conversations, offered the mail carrier a cup of coffee when she brought the letters, and went out in the yard and exchanged remarks with the retired diplomat who was clipping the hedge next door.

She rushed through housecleaning during guests' absences. She posted a sign on the kitchen door: EMPLOYEES ONLY so they wouldn't see her in her grubbies slaving over the stove. Once a guest asked her to compliment the cook on the ham and broccoli casserole!

After three months the job became routine, so predictable that she longed for change—any kind. If only she had experience in any other type of employment. If only she'd taken practical courses instead of college prep! All that useless math and science! Why had she trusted so implicitly in Mrs. Sterne's promises?

Knowing typing, shorthand and computers would raise her to the status of secretary. She had to hone her typing skills! She rummaged and searched until she located an old laptop computer in a case, but finding time to practice proved nearly impossible. As soon as she sat down the phone or doorbell rang or a guest knocked at the office door.

In despair she gave it up and in her spare moments read newspapers, magazines, paper backs—whatever she found around the place.

Days when no visitors came punctuated the drudgery of her existence with points of light. She ought by rights to have a day off every week she grumbled, closeted in the tiny space under the stairs with the schedule on her lap. She had five letters at hand. She opened them and made pencil checks on the calendar. If the Browns came Wednesday instead of Tuesday she'd have a free day. She wrote decisively asking them to change their dates. Gradually she came to think of Tuesday as hers and to plan for it.

On these occasions she stayed in and reveled in the sensation of sole proprietorship. And one sunny

Tuesday in April, she carried a tray with her lunch out onto the second-floor balcony where she ate and lounged and read the paper. A large ad attracted her attention: "Become a secretary in six weeks," it proclaimed. "Learn skills and business procedures that will qualify you for your choice of interesting professions." And toward the bottom it promised, "Placement Guaranteed."

She folded the paper carefully, lay back in her chair and gazed across the boulevard and the park with its glorious spring grass and greening trees. Six weeks! She sat up. She could find out about this. She'd already noted that the business school was only a mile away.

She exchanged jeans for nice slacks and within half an hour was walking into the building—disappointingly small and unpretentious—with a straggle of unprepossessing girls coming and going. She located a door marked Office and there encountered a mildly harassed woman who seemed to be doing everything. She motioned Sue to a chair while continuing to talk on the phone and to make notations on a form.

After a few minutes she turned to Susan. "Yes?"

"I saw the ad—about learning to be a secretary in six weeks?"

"Oh, that." The lady—short, gray haired, wrinkled with black rimmed glasses over a pair of dark shrewd eyes—left her desk and sat down next to Susan. "For most people it takes a lot longer than six weeks. I wish they wouldn't run those ads—bit misleading."

"Can anybody do it in six weeks?" Susan's

square chin hardened.

"I suppose if a person did nothing but study and practice sixteen hours a day she might. But who has that kind of time?"

"But if someone did—learned it all, sixteen hours a day—could she really get a job for sure? Like the ad says?"

"I personally take no responsibility for the ad. Most of our girls take at least a year to learn. Of course some of them don't apply themselves and are anything but expert when they leave here. Can't spell, can't punctuate."

The phone rang and the woman went to answer. She talked a while and then returned to Susan. "You can sign up for a six-week course if you want to. It can't hurt." She sounded hard and rather melancholy. "Interested?"

Susan rose. "I don't know. I'd better think about it. But I already know how to spell and punctuate, and I'm good at math and writing."

Chapter
6

On the way home Susan wished she weren't wearing out her good shoes on this pointless trip. Nothing ever turned out the way you wanted it to. She hated advertising. On the other hand, she had some educational advantages. "And I'm smart," she remarked to herself. Given a chance she *could* learn shorthand, advanced computer skills, whatever it took, in six weeks. She was more than willing to study night and day.

Back on her porch she picked up the mail, sorted out the junk and dropped it in the wastebasket. Five more letters had come, representing an endless succession of domestic chores. However skillfully she succeeded in appearing managerial, the dusting and bed-making went on. And on. "All my life in the kitchen and on my knees or pushing a vacuum cleaner." Disgusted, she threw the letters on the desk and returned to her favorite seat on the balcony to brood over the injustice.

Sunlight on the parkway had changed from its brightness at high noon to a mellower glow at three o'clock, but Susan settled in her perch without noticing. Secretaries were through at five, had their evenings free and two days off every week. They wore elegant clothes and acted independent. She saw the newspaper on the floor where she'd dropped it and gave it a kick.

"Oh well, what did I expect?" She had to go down and list those people who'd written for reservations. They were getting more numerous as the weather warmed. She'd already told one or two that they'd have to choose another date because the place was booked solid.

"Choose another date." Suppose she told all of them to choose a date three months off? She giggled. "Clear the calendar." She'd heard Mrs. Sterne say that. For important people or events the pastor always cancelled routine appointments.

Susan sat upright. A look of intense concentration froze the muscles of her face. After a time she gasped, "Why not?" A cloud darkened the sky, but when she gazed upward it seemed that the sun shone as warmly as ever in a clear blue expanse.

From motionless she turned active, nervous. She left the balcony, looked distractedly into every perfectly clean bedroom, descended the stairs and walked unseeing through the first floor from end to end and back and forth. Her mind worked furiously weighing risk against advantage, going over the same ground again and again, rejecting and then reclaiming her conclusion.

At ten p.m. she went into the office and studied every page of the SCHEDULE. May and June of the previous year had been heavily registered. She sighed, opened the current letters and put pencil checks on a calendar. She'd try to squeeze as many people as possible into the last few weeks of April. Then she'd keep all of May and early June open—no guests. After finishing the course, she could start scheduling heavily again after June 15. Let the next poor sucker of a housekeeper worry about how to keep up with things.

She promised herself to make wonderfully good use of the illicit six weeks to hone office skills. She couldn't wait forever to start a different life. And once she'd completed her course she'd disappear as far as the Mellowell Corporation and Mr. Thorn were concerned.

Still, it was midnight before she finally summoned nerve to write the first dozen people to reschedule on the plan she'd worked out.

She left the initial notations in place, however. No sense showing six blank weeks in the official register! Her hands shook and she had to pause often and breathe heavily. "Risky" she muttered from time to time. "Man, is this risky."

Susan had been dedicating herself fiercely to the business course assignments for three weeks before Miss Nichols, the Academic Dean and chief moving force, got around to commending her progress. Besides running the main office where Sue had first met her, the woman taught numerous courses and kept books, assisted by occasional part time helpers.

"If I didn't see you doing it, I wouldn't believe it," Miss Nichols marveled, no trace of a smile on her melancholy face.

"Just so I get a job the first minute I'm through. I have to have a job. It's life and death." Susan's desperation left the stoic dean unperturbed.

"People often call here asking if there's someone I can recommend. Don't worry, I'll recommend you."

"How often do people call? How soon would they want me to start?"

"Someone phoned yesterday and I placed a girl in a dentist's office. Don't get excited, Susan. It will work out."

Miss Nichols had accounts to do, and Susan had to go back to That Place. Once inside, and after she'd dusted up and had eaten and sent those lies through the mail she could relax somewhat and spend the evening in the office typing and practicing on the old laptop. She wrote pages of shorthand and re-read instructions on how to operate the various machines she practiced on at the school. She'd learned quickly and was speeding up every day.

Still, she reacted with terror each time the phone rang. A wrong number, usually. Or a sales person. She'd lie on the sofa afterwards clutching her throat.

In June she grew even more edgy. Hadn't Thorn said he'd be back in June? No, make it July, he'd added. Suppose he turned up early and discovered what she was doing? Could he send her to jail? Suppose he put her out on the street with her trunk. Where could she go?

She passed a graveyard on her way to school

and looked in, calculatingly. Could she hide and sleep there after it closed up at night? If only the tuition and books hadn't taken almost all the rest of her savings. Why had she squandered so much money on expensive clothes? A closer examination of people she met day by day convinced her that most business wear was cheaper by far than the things she'd purchased in her ignorance.

One minute she regretted all those cancellations and postponements and the next stubbornly affirmed her decision. She'd make it. Nothing had happened. She even kept small orders going out to the wholesaler, and occasionally presented gifts of perishables to some of her acquaintances at the school—to their astonishment. She ordered staples and packaged and canned goods in quantity and stood them in the pantry and the now abundantly stocked cupboards.

Busy as she kept herself with her studies the time wore on with painful slowness. The burden of answering letters with lies grew heavier. She comforted herself by remembering that these people were scattered all over the U.S. and wouldn't be comparing notes, would they?

She slept fitfully, rose often and wandered through the big, empty house gazing out the numerous windows into the lamp-lit streets.

The laggard days slogged along without event. And at last there was only a week before the middle of June. She woke early, motivated to stop fretting and take matters in hand. She located the Mellowell

Corporation's headquarters on a map and then took a trip by bus as far as it went in the opposite direction. She reached a run-down residential area with huge, heavily branched trees and rambling old mansions. She wandered around, and finally glimpsed a dilapidated sign in a window: Room for Rent.

After ringing the bell she peered through the glass panels. The foyer looked dusty and antiquated. She heard shuffling and retreated to a discreet distance. Framed in the open door stood a wizened little dried-fig of a woman, older than anyone Sue had ever known. But her sharp gray eyes twinkled and a smile rearranged the mass of wrinkles that was her visage. A halo of snowy hair framed her well-tanned face.

She looked Susan up and down. "All right, my dear. Come in. You're not selling anything, are you?"

"No. I saw the sign in your window." The two walked into a shabby but reasonably clean parlor with damask upholstered chairs and sofas and at least one Tiffany lamp.

"Is that sign still up? I'd forgotten about it."

Disappointed Susan asked whether the room was already taken. "No. I didn't find anyone I liked and wanted to have in the house. My name is Clara— Clara Bowman. People used to say I reminded them of a movie star. But that was long, long ago. Almost more years than I can remember."

Susan didn't know what to say. If the woman knew about her shady doings and why she happened to be in the neighborhood she wouldn't want her either.

"I'm Suzi Sterne."

"Well, Suzi, you've come early and I was about to sit down to breakfast. Come in the dining room and have a cup of coffee with me." Besides coffee there was a pitcher of orange juice and a loaf of whole grain bread. Susan found that she was hungry and the woman handed over several slices hot from the toaster without asking if she wanted more.

She told Susan about working in the yard. "I don't have grass or mow anything. I prune and clip and dig out the flower beds."

"It's beautiful," Sue cried, gazing through the bay windows.

"You're not very old, are you dear?"

"No. I'll be seventeen soon." Susan felt thankful to be able to tell the truth to this woman. Mrs. Bowman accepted a check for the first week and Susan departed with a feeling of thankfulness. She had an address.

As her final week at the Business School drew to a close she reminded Miss Nichols ever more fervently of her promise to find her a job. Yes, she was qualified, had done well, would be recommended. But why the big rush? Miss Nichols wanted to hold out for something desirable.

When Sue heard on Wednesday that someone else had been placed in a stenographer's job in a large company at a good salary, she lost her composure and snarled about it.

"They needed an experienced typist and the

woman I sent had just finished a refresher course on the new computer and was exceptionally suitable. Besides, you wouldn't really like that work."

"I'd like anything I can get to pay my board and room," Sue declared, ready to sob with frustration.

On Thursday Miss Nichols approached with the closest to a smile she'd ever worn in the time Sue had known her. "*The Philadelphia News* called for someone to take classified ads on the phone. I recommended you, and they'll interview you tomorrow at 2:00."

"Will they hire me? Is it a sure thing?"

"As close as you'll get to a sure thing. Just look neat and speak clearly. Of course you always do, anyway."

Sue went home early to make sure that she had something appropriate to wear. Her wool business clothes were too warm, now that the weather had changed. Her last summer's Sunday dress would have to do. She tried it on and discovered to her chagrin that she'd developed. The fitted bodice wouldn't close even when she held her breath and tried to force the buttons into the holes. She had too little money to buy anything new. She tried on various shirt and skirt combinations and even tried wearing a loose shirt over the dress. Hopeless. A dark, boxy shirt was the best choice, but looked inappropriate over a dress with a lace ruffle around the bottom. Reluctantly she snipped off the ruffle. Next she cut the shirt off waist length and hemmed it up. Better. Now she removed the collar from the shirt and then cut away the sleeves. The resulting vest pleased her—tidy and correct. She starched and pressed it.

Knowing her departure to be imminent whether or not she got the job, Susan packed her clothes into her small trunk. Then she went to the office and addressed an envelope to the Mellowell Corporation's Sales Division, Attention Jim Thorn. She took a sheet of paper and tried to think of something to say. Should she complain about the job? How about a family crisis—death or whatever? No. Why tell more lies than necessary?

Finally she wrote, "I'm resigning." Signed and dated this bald statement and indicated the position: Housekeeper at 1202 Parkway Drive. She stamped the letter and put it in her purse to post next day.

At school in the morning she sold her texts to the bookstore for a pitifully small sum. And they'd cost so much! After she'd finished her exams she went to the bank and withdrew all but a few dollars of her savings.

Now she took a bus to the Philadelphia newspaper's headquarters. She really wanted to work there she decided, impressed by its bigness and activity. In the outer office a bored receptionist listened and then handed her an application form. With a constriction in her chest Sue stood by a counter and filled it out. Twenty years old. What year would that make her birthdate? For references she put down Miss Nichols at the school and Rev. Chancellor Sterne. She looked up his Virginia address in her little record book and prayed that they wouldn't notice his name and wouldn't call him long distance. Her hands were damp and she wiped them surreptiously on her skirt before handing in the form.

The woman pressed a button, spoke briefly and rose. She beckoned Sue to follow her to Personnel, an area where women worked in glass-partitioned booths. "This is the girl Nichols sent over for the Classified job."

"Oh, okay."

The new person had dyed red hair, squinty eyes that blinked too much and a bad cold. She glanced at the application. "Suzi Sterne?"

"Yes."

"You'll need to start Monday. The girl you're replacing will leave the following Wednesday. A couple days is all you'll have to learn the work. But Nichols said you learn fast."

"Yes, I do."

The lady pushed other papers toward Sue who signed. Then the woman rattled off information about salary, hours, vacations, benefits and company policy. "You'll forget a lot of things I said, but they're all here in the Company Manual." She handed a copy to Suzi and gave her a bright smile of dismissal. "Welcome aboard."

Suzi sailed out of the Newspaper building on wings of hope. She'd established a new identity, had a job and a place to stay. Now she'd separate from the old life and vanish.

She walked and sat on benches in a series of parks worrying that at the last minute Jim Thorn might turn up over there. She took the letter she'd written him out of her purse and dropped it in a mailbox, snatching at the handle to stop it—but it had gone.

After dark she assured herself that if anyone had come to That House, surely they wouldn't have waited. She caught a taxi and arranged with the driver to put her trunk in the cab and then wait while she took care of one last detail. She went to the office and for the first time dialed the emergency number. "Mellowell," a man's voice said. Slowly and without emotion Susan stated the facts: "The housekeeper, Susan Sterne, has left the premises at 1202 Parkway Drive. She locked up and left the key in the mailbox."

"What was that?" the voice was getting ready to demand more information, but Susan hung up. She walked out, and as she closed the door she heard the phone ring. She dropped the key in the box, got in the cab and gave the address of her new home. Too bad she couldn't have told Mellowell to forward her last paycheck. But that was out of the question.

A few days later she regretted taking the cab all that distance. Too much of her meager cash had gone to pay the driver. By Wednesday she had only a small bill or two and some change, just enough for bus fare. She went for a walk on her lunch hour and drank lots of water. She ate cheese and crackers at home. By the end of the week she had no money and no food at all. She managed to work, but at night grew light-headed, floated off the bed and gave herself up to day and night dreams that blurred reality: herself in a palace looking over wide fields and forest or lounging on the veranda of a vast ocean villa lulled by murmuring waves. And always her faceless Prince hovered nearby ready to fulfill her every whim.

She wondered whether she could wrangle a little cash from Bowman. The old lady had plenty. Every day she chirped and chatted pleasantly when she saw Suzi and asked about her day. She seemed impressed with Sue's job and participated in her excitement.

One Saturday morning, pitifully embarrassed, Sue approached her with the news that they wouldn't start paying her for another week. She'd have to give her the rent later.

Mrs. Bowman seemed mildly put out. "Well, all right. But you could get an advance you know."

"What do you mean?"

"Just tell them you need an advance. Big companies do that for their employees."

Suzi looked up "advance" in her Manual, discovered that indeed she could ask for some cash which would be deducted from later checks. After a long Sunday of fasting she hurried to the Payroll Division on Monday morning where she was given money for food and carfare. "We don't encourage our people to keep asking for advances. You understand that, don't you?"

While standing on a corner after work the next week, waiting, she thought she saw Jim Thorn. Same large face and bushy eyebrows. She walked quickly into a restaurant and looked out. He was getting into a limousine headed for the airport. She imagined that he glanced at her through the windows and over the heads of seated customers. She retreated to the restroom, sat on the commode and trembled.

That night when Suzi thankfully turned over the rent money Clara Bowman, oddly enough, seemed less concerned than she had earlier.

Weeks passed and Sue learned more about her landlady. Saturdays, for instance, were always days of gloom for the old woman. Instead of putting on soft old pants and a baggy shirt Clara donned a dark dress with a white collar and sturdy, well-laced shoes and marched out of the house clutching a large leather pocketbook. Presently Sue would hear loud coughing sounds and explosions and with a roar Mrs. Bowman would back an enormous mustard-colored Cadillac out of the garage and start off. Suzi suspected that it died many times during Mrs. Bowman's absence. But after a few hours she'd be back, triumphantly bringing groceries, parcels and bags into the house.

Suzi knew she could help and offered to clean house, and wash clothes. Mrs. Bowman declined, scandalized. "You're a paying guest, my dear. I have a crew in once every two weeks to clean and launder. You're not responsible for anything but tidying your room and washing your own dishes and clothes."

To Sue's surprise she found herself plagued by a sense of alienation, thus abruptly separated from chores that had for so long given her a sense of competency.

She forced her mind to other pursuits, took long walks in the neighborhood. Summer's fullness adorned the yards of the area with flowers and fragrance. Huge old trees arched green and resplendent over her as she passed along the streets. She decided to fall in love.

Many of the paperbacks left behind by Mellowell guests had been romances. They assured her that love provided the way to rapid fulfillment. She searched aimlessly but continuously for a face, a figure on which to pin her hopes. On several occasions she saw a white faced, black haired boy riding by on his motorcycle. One day their eyes met for a moment, his—dark and fringed with long lashes—lived afterwards in her memory. Through the night as she lay awake in the big old room with its high ceiling and its huge pictures of water lilies and sunlit fields she heard muffled roars and a black jacketed figure moved across the mirror of her mind.

After a few weeks she saw him on one of her interminable walks surrounded by a crowd of junior high girls and heard him talking and bragging. And when she observed that he was taking these girls, one by one, for rides, she derided herself for indulging a silly crush.

Months passed. She felt at home. One Saturday in her landlady's absence she quietly removed the FOR RENT sign and laid it to rest in an empty closet. Although she rattled around alone in the many bedroomed upper story she had no wish to share her good fortune. How much money did Mrs. Bowman have, and when the old lady was gone what would become of it? Once in a while the frugal old woman would make a passing reference to never touching the principal. How much was that? An awkward attempt to find out whether eligible males numbered among potential heirs proved fruitless. Mrs. Bowman only stared at her, obviously intent and curious.

Chapter
8

Three years later, after Mrs. Bowman's funeral, Sue got a jarring reminder of the money question when, from the window of her upstairs room, she saw middle aged grandchildren congregate to "go over the place." Three cars arrived within minutes of each other and parked in the driveway in front. The occupants milled around until, fifteen minutes later, a younger man in a truck pulled up. Single? Eligible? Finding no handy place to leave his vehicle he bumped up over the curb, and to Sue's dismay drove on to the yard, crushing flower beds and tearing bushes.

A stoutish forty-plus lady in a bright red jacket and black pants greeted him and then started up the walk with a decisive, proprietary air that Sue resented. She was glad she'd locked the door. She heard the knob rattle, then a voice called to the others, "That lawyer told me the house would be open, that we could get in to see it."

Suzi descended and opened the door. The five people on the porch suspended conversation and stared at her. "Who are you?" the red jacket demanded.

"I'm Suzi Sterne. Mr. Binton told me to stay on here and keep an eye on the place."

"We'll be selling it real soon," the woman responded, a bit huffy. She led the way inside and peered into the rooms, announcing their use. As if the others couldn't see for themselves. Susan went upstairs, but she could still hear Mrs. Taff (that had to be her name). Mr. Binton had called to say, "Show her around," but apparently hadn't told Taff about her.

Now she could hear Taff's voice talking about the furniture. "Looks to me like worn-out, old timey stuff. We'll get a used furniture man in here to give us a price on the whole lot, I guess."

"This is a cute lamp," a woman's voice said. "But gee, I don't know where I'd put it if I took it."

"No. Don't go hauling this junk halfway across the country."

"The floors are in good shape." That was the younger man, Sue thought. Too bad he had a pug face and muscle-bound body. Still, he'd be inheriting something—

It disgusted her that after failing to show up for the funeral these vultures had descended to claim their grandmother's possessions.

Now she could hear them saying, too bad they wouldn't have time for refinishing and putting "modern cabinets" in the kitchen. Sue loved those old, hand-crafted cupboards, however creaky they might be—even their heavy fronts with the white paint wearing thin.

Hearing them return to the front hall she

descended. Would she be around to let dealers in? Mrs. Taff inquired. And how did they get back to the lawyer's office? Did she know what comparable houses in this area were selling for?

Sue answered their questions as best she could. And when they'd gone she relocked the door and sat in the parlor. She alone truly grieved for Mrs. Bowman.

The almost girlish enthusiasms of that sprightly old lady! "There's a Chekhov play on television. Wouldn't you like to watch it?" And when it was over: "Wasn't that marvelous? It always breaks my heart to hear them chopping down the cherry orchard."

Her birthday celebration during the second year of Sue's stay: "I'm one hundred years old. I don't believe it! If I put a hundred candles on my cake I'd burn the house down!" Clara Bowman: Polite, kind, accepting. Other than old Sally at the orphanage the only true friend Sue had ever had. Tried hard never to give advice, but when Danny proposed—

Susan drifted up to her room, his fair round face before her. Why had she spent so much time with him? For nearly a year she'd seen Danny every Friday evening and every Sunday afternoon. Maybe she liked the notion of having dates and going out. Maybe she thought he was an acceptable escort—tall, lanky, with blond-white hair and eyebrows and in sunlight covered with a pale golden fuzz on cheeks and jowls. Maybe she'd seen him as her one and only chance at marriage. And she had to get married, of course. Dried up little old maids—what were they?

From working in maintenance and on the loading platform of a major retail store, he'd advanced to stocking shelves. She couldn't imagine why he took such pride in just working every day! He even saved a few bucks.

She recalled the evening they'd spent at the Art Museum seeing a black and white version of "Crime and Punishment." The doomed cityscapes of Dostoevsky's mind absorbed her totally. She forgot Danny until she felt a warm, heavy weight on her shoulder. He'd fallen asleep, his full pink mouth open. She didn't wake him, determined to absorb this film of an arresting book she'd read on Mrs. Bowman's advice.

What a contrast that evening had been to the Major League Game Danny had saved up to take her to. So much fervor! Bordering on hysteria! Incredible consumption of hot dogs, popcorn, chips and cola! The game proceeding with methodical deliberation for hours and hours.

She first met Danny in a restaurant after she lost her fear of running into Jim Thorn. For some time the sight of any man with bushy eyebrows threw her into a panic. But she gradually conquered her fear and even tested her assurance by staying downtown twice a week and eating a hamburger before going home. That particular evening, Danny in an adjoining booth had started kidding the waitress in a crude sort of way. The little red head's flustered and flattered response so amazed Sue that she laughed out loud.

His attention diverted, Danny struck up

a conversation with Suzi, followed her out of the restaurant, stood beside her while she waited for her bus. His baby face disarmed her. The next time she stopped into the same restaurant he came unhesitatingly to her booth and sat down.

After they'd been going together for a year he got another promotion. "They're going to teach me to clerk in the parts department," he announced, face lit with joy and anxiety. "I sure hope I can handle it."

"Of course you can. Don't be silly."

He laughed. "You make me feel so good, Suzi. I love you. I'm going to be making more money now. Let's get married."

"Now you really are being silly."

"No, I mean it. I want to get married."

He was old enough—twenty-seven. At first Sue hadn't believed it. He had that infantile face! But he was always honest and unassuming and why should he lie to her?

She told Mrs. Bowman about the proposal. "I can't imagine him asking me."

"Well, you have been going together for a year."

"I mean, I never thought of marrying him. But maybe I should. I'm almost nineteen and I've been working for more than two years and nobody else has even looked at me. And I'm not pretty."

"You could marry him just to get married. Lots of women have found that a sufficient reason. But—" Mrs. Bowman paused and gave her a sly, sidelong look, "there are alternatives."

That's all she'd say, but Suzi gave long serious thought to alternatives. And suddenly it seemed that the risks and possibilities of a future alone attracted her more than a future with Danny. She gave him a definite no and assumed that they'd stop seeing each other.

To her surprise and embarrassment Danny persisted. He called her and even came over to the house uninvited. And when she firmly insisted that it was over, he wrote pathetic letters that she never answered. All about how smart she was and how he needed her. This display of dependency alienated her. If she married, it would be a man she needed. Otherwise, she'd go it alone.

Convinced at last he stopped calling, and one day a few months later she saw him on the street, deep in conversation with the red haired waitress.

Thank God for Mrs. Bowman who'd saved her from a mistake. And who'd given her the car!

A year into Sue's residency Mrs. Bowman got around to confessing that the Cadillac was ailing. She worried all the time, couldn't get it fixed anymore—parts too hard to come by and too expensive. She'd soon save up enough for a new car, Suzi's rent being a help.

"Why don't you buy a car on time?"

"Oh dear no. I'm too old. Installments are for young people."

Sure enough one day Mrs. Bowman turned up with a spanking new Ford compact, purring with satisfaction. "Now, dear girl, you are going to take me to the country for a spin."

"I don't know how to drive."

"I'll pay for lessons, and you'll pay me back by chauffeuring me around."

When the old woman grew weaker and weaker she told her boarder one day that she'd put Susan's name on the title. "I'm giving you the car. You've earned it. And I might go any day now."

"Nothing's really bad wrong with you," Sue protested. "You'll be out and gardening as usual any day now." She fervently believed it, because she wanted to.

She recalled her fright the first day she didn't find Clara Bowman at breakfast in the bay in her dining room. Sue searched and found her lying in bed, her quick bird-like eyes staring out from around the covers.

"Are you okay?"

"Not so swift this morning."

"Do you need a doctor?"

"No, no, please. I hate doctors. They prod and poke. And I'm almost a hundred and two. They don't see any sense in trying to fix the worn-out old equipment."

"Shall I stay home with you?"

"No, indeed! I'll be all right. I'm just tired. Would be nice if I still had spunk like I used to have when I was ninety two."

Next day she was up. Susan joined her for breakfast and flew off to work rejoicing.

Sue now began, however, to insist on doing the shopping and errands on Saturdays. Mrs. Bowman agreed, resigned to her feeble state. "After all," Susan reminded her, "you did give me the driving lessons and I do get to use the car." Employing circumspection, she also took over other household chores.

One Sunday the old woman couldn't take their usual jaunt to the country. "Go without me." Suzi, who enjoyed excursions to places like the Longwood Gardens, felt disappointed, but stayed in and baked breakfast rolls that she knew Clara Bowman liked.

At the last, when her landlady had failed to get up for three days running, Suzi grew alarmed. Without consulting her old friend she arranged to take her vacation and stayed with her. "You're too good to me," Mrs. Bowman said. "You don't owe me anything. We're not even related." Suzi didn't tell her that in arranging for the earlier and longer vacation she'd said that her grandmother was sick and she had to take care of her. "She doesn't have anyone else." That much was true, anyway.

Every morning she assured the lady that she looked better. And every day the fragile form moved around less and less under the covers. Sometimes Sue had to stand close and watch to make sure that Mrs. Bowman was still breathing. Their chief communication was an on-going argument about calling the doctor. "Useless," Mrs. Bowman kept saying. "I forbid you to put me in a hospital and tie me up to machines and pump sap through these withered old veins." She wouldn't tell Sue the name of her doctor, but indicated a card stuck into a mirror. "If anything happens, that's my lawyer's number. Call him. He has all the funeral arrangements on file. I've outlived both of my sons and three husbands and all my good friends. If you weren't here no one would care whether I live or die." Sue imagined a moistness in the bright old eyes.

Gradually she gave up and began to consider Mrs. Bowman's demise inevitable. So one morning when there was no movement in the bed for an hour she ventured to touch the pale skin. When she found it cold, she uncovered the frail body and perceived that it was lifeless. She restored the covers and sat on the edge of the bed feeling disoriented, shaken, and alone. The house belonged to someone else now.

Slowly she took the card, from the mirror, went to the phone and explained the situation to Mr. Binton, the attorney. "Call Dr. Phelps," he said. He gave her a number. "If he pronounces her dead, call me back and I'll come over."

Chapter
9

The lawyer reassured her about a number of things. No, she didn't have to get out at once—had a legal right to thirty day's notice even if her arrangement with Mrs. Bowman was verbal. Anyway, house shouldn't stand empty. Estate could pay expenses while heirs were being notified.

Yes, she had a legal right to the automobile. He recognized Mrs. Bowman's signature. Old girl was clear as a bell to the end and apparently wanted to give Sue the car. "Little old compact," he assessed it. Suzi wanted to protest that it was only a little more than a year old. "Nothing for heirs to sue you over," he added. Neither of the two speakers had the slightest notion that eventually the car would definitively alter the course of Susan's existence.

Only the lawyer and Susan attended the cremation ceremonies next day. She continued to live in the house even after the grandchildren arrived. However, she did propose that since they had to remain in town for several days they might as well stay in the house and save hotel bills. She prepared breakfast for them.   They accepted her help and advice, albeit suspiciously.

After the formal reading of the will, Mrs. Taft inquired whose car that was behind the house. "Mine," Sue replied.

"Grandmother had to have had a car.   Nothing in the will about a car."

"Oh, she does have a car—a Cadillac!"

"Cadillac? Really?"

"It's in the garage."

"House, outbuildings and contents. That would include the Caddy then, right?"

"Certainly." Sue didn't tell her that the dealer had refused to take the car as trade-in.

After ascertaining that the estate was paying expenses, the heirs spent lots of time on the phone. They called their homes and received calls of increasing intensity. Responsibilities summoned them from afar, Sue noted with satisfaction.

One morning while they were out signing papers, she went around the house taking a last yearning look at the valuable antiques that Mrs. Bowman had pointed out when Suzi admired her furniture. "Most of it's shabby old copies—nice enough but not worth much now. But I do have a few genuine pieces."

She took Sue through the house and pointed out the Colonial Secretary, the gateleg table from the Seventeenth Century, a Hitchcock chest of drawers, a French boudoir chair, and the Tiffany lamp, of course.

A person could start to furnish a place with just

these antiques, Sue decided. And it wouldn't be long before she'd have to move. Realization struck her that this very afternoon a second-hand dealer was to arrive to give the heirs an estimate. If he recognized antiques, would he give the heirs their full value? Of course not. If he didn't see their value, these priceless things could wind up battered and unappreciated in lower middle class houses.

Suzi quickly riffled through the yellow pages and contacted a nearby Storage and Moving concern. To a list of items to be stored she added the two pictures in her room which she'd grown attached to. When the mover answered her call she said, "A buyer is coming this afternoon, and I'd like to have a few things out of the way. Could you pick them up immediately?"

"Doubt it. Where you located?" On hearing her address the man held the phone and she could hear him yell, "Has Sam gone out yet?" Silence. Muffled conversation far off. Then the voice came on the phone again. "You're in luck. Man can come by in half an hour if you're sure you'll be there and can have the stuff ready to go."

She could. She flew around, wrapped the antiques in old blankets and tied them down. After the movers had taken them away Sue spent an anxious hour putting other items in empty spaces and sponging the walls to remove evidence of the size and shape of the stolen furniture. If Mrs. Bowman had only seen these ignoramuses, surely she'd be glad that her treasures had been rescued!

To further disguise the changes she brought in huge bouquets of flowers and leaves and set them around.

But really she needn't have worried. The heirs returned in a glow, full of excited talk. Mr. Binton had at last given them a dollars-and-cents calculation of what each could expect to get from property and investments and it had exceeded their most optimistic anticipations. Their hopes rose still more when the last realtor they talked to promised them a higher price for the house.

Then the furniture dealer arrived with a clipboard and began writing down an inventory of every last item including contents of drawers and attic. So exhaustive was he that the heirs grew weary. Only Sue stayed with him. She began to see things she should have taken: silverware, cookware, linens. How many things she'd need to keep house! And where would that be? Rage at being forced out of her home for a third time in her short life distracted her from the second-hand man's doings.

Finished at last, he stood casually visiting with Mrs. Taff, inserting his bid into a lengthy commiseration on the hardships of getting anything repaired these days.

Mrs. Taff glanced at the others. What did everyone think? Though not included, Suzi announced that a friend of hers would give an additional thousand and she advised them not to take this offer.

"Oh, okay," Taff replied. "But we've been here five days and we're leaving tomorrow early. Can you get your friend in here and have him mail me his estimate?"

"Hold on, since you need to get away, I guess I could match that guy's offer." The dealer wrote the larger check on the spot and handed it to Mrs. Taff.

When he'd gone Mrs. Taff asked,, "How come you never before mentioned that friend of yours?"

"Because he's a mythical friend," Sue replied. Everybody laughed and applauded. "So," she told herself, "now I've paid them for the stuff I took."

She persuaded Mrs. Taff that on behalf of the heirs she was obliged to give Sue thirty day's written notice. Instead of paying rent she could be there to open the house to potential buyers and answer calls. She was experienced on the phone and could be helpful. She concealed her anxiety, but the question of where she'd go next gnawed at her.

Back on the job among the welter of dull "for sale" and "for rent" ads that she routinely took down, something arresting turned up. "Will share rent on apartment with employed girl who has furniture. Prefer relaxed person with own car." The well modulated young female voice delivering this ad reported a billing address and phone in what Susan recognized as an elegant suburb. She gave the name H. A. Fairington.

Susan hung up meditating. The ad described her except for that ambivalent word, "relaxed." What did it mean? She was relaxed enough most of the time, but couldn't make up her mind to accept the term as descriptive. She'd looked at apartments, however, and the ones she could afford had little appeal. Sharing rent might be the answer. The voice of the advertiser lingered long in her mind, however. There was something in that voice that suggested—what? Cynicism? Slyness?

Susan accused herself of second guessing everything. Of an unwillingness to risk anything.

So in the end she called, arranged a meeting and drove to the address on a woodsy, winding lane dotted with fine homes, mostly new. A beautiful girl opened the door. Blue eyes, abundant glossy black hair, artfully curled, fair perfect skin, well proportioned figure clothed in black denim. Sue felt self-conscious and wished she'd worn jeans instead of the old gray suit (newly dry cleaned) with an open-necked checkered shirt for a relaxed look.

"Hi. I'm Colleen Fairington."

"Suzi Sterne."

Colleen let her in and yelled, "She's here!" From different directions the refined, well-groomed middle aged parents appeared. They liked Suzi on sight. They sat her down, placed refreshments before her and then found out that she worked for a newspaper and that her parents had retired from the ministry. "How nice!"

Colleen mostly listened. The shock came when Suzi said no, she didn't yet have an apartment. They'd have to look for one.

"That's okay." Colleen put in quickly.

More negotiating about how much rent they could afford and what extra furniture they'd have to buy. "I guess we could spare a bed and dresser," Mrs. Fairington conceded.

While getting back in her car it crossed Suzi's mind that the parents might want to get rid of their daughter? No, no. Ridiculous! They'd shown such concern. This association might open any number of doors. A smashing girl like that could, for example, know a lot of eligible men.

Instead of looking at rental ads Colleen took Suzi to a real estate agency that sent them out to an old court-yard building in Bryn Mawr. Sue admired the old tiled bathroom with its antiquated fixtures, its narrow kitchen full of new cabinets, its dark, shiny wood floors. "It'll do," Colleen decided, acting indifferent.

For Suzi paying the security deposit plus a month's rent and buying a bed strained her slender means, but Colleen wrote a check on the bank account her parents had opened for her without a thought. Within two weeks the girls were in and settled, and Suzi started to learn things about her roommate. Colleen bewailed flunking out of the college her father had "got" her into. College was a blast. Now Dad and Mom had conned Wanamakers into hiring her to sell perfume—a bore except for a few cute guys looking for gifts for women. The main advantage to this apartment was getting away from Mom and Dad and their silly restrictions.

Suzi cautiously told Colleen about Mrs. Bowman. "She sounds like a drag," Colleen said and yawned. Suzi resented that. There were other things she didn't like such as the rude way Colleen rejected Suzi's tastefully presented breakfasts. "Will you stop getting me up so early to eat all this fattening stuff?" Sue stopped.

In the evening when they watched Colleen's portable TV, Colleen stretched out on the sofa they'd purchased with mutual funds, leaving Suzi to sit on the stiff, though artistic, little boudoir chair. She'd succinctly explained her genuine antique furniture to the astounded Mrs. Fairington: "Grandmother's." When lying, the less said the better.

Colleen never assisted with cleaning and one day she even exploded, "Will you stop throwing my stuff in my room?"

"Never threw a thing," Susan remonstrated.

"You know what I mean. I pay half the rent. If I drop something in the living room, just leave it there." But Sue, compulsively tidy, couldn't do that. She picked up and folded piles of opened mail and other odds and ends. She bought plastic trays to hold some of the things. Colleen made no comment on the new arrangement.

She displayed a range of moods. One day she might feel wonderful and chatty. "Oh, Suz'" she'd cry, "you should've seen the old biddy I had at my counter today sniffing the fragrances. Must've been eighty. I tried to sell her Evils-of-The-Night, but she kept wondering if we didn't have a lilac scent or something." Colleen rolled off the sofa and lay howling and kicking on the floor.

After her roommate started calling her Suz'; Sue reciprocated with Col'.

On Col's gloomy days Suzi tried to help her out of the doldrums by luring her out for walks. "Maybe we'll see some interesting guys."

Colleen doubted it. "This neighborhood

and especially this building is full of decrepit senior citizens." Suzi had also noticed that.

"Oh sure, there are retirees here, but all sorts of people live in the area," Susan insisted. "We just need to look around." Firmly she led Colleen along the street, urging her on from block to block. They passed a corner dominated by an enormous mansion. Colleen showed no sign that she'd noticed a pair of young men on the porch steps and a third pushing a lawn mower. But Suzi now knew her well enough to guess that she'd grown watchful.

Sure enough, the lawn mower stopped putting, and its operator addressed a remark to Colleen who replied snippily, but with an engaging air. Presently the three men were clustered around talking almost exclusively to Colleen. To her astonishment Sue heard her roomie invite them to a party Friday night.

As they started back to their apartment, Colleen called out, "Bring friends."

The prospect of a party both excited and worried Suzi. Colleen's indifferent opinion was that they might not turn up.

"In case they do, we have to serve something, provide entertainment," Susan hazarded.

"Oh, they'll bring their own refreshments. And they can always raid the refrigerator."

"Not much in there to raid."

"I've noticed. It's not like home, that's for sure."

Suzi bought chips and dip and prepared trays

of open faced sandwiches. If no one came they could snack on the stuff all week. One of the men had smiled at her. She wasn't beautiful like Colleen, but maybe—

At 8:30 Friday the three men arrived with a bottle. They were polite to Suzi who tried to emulate Mrs. Sterne's hospitable manner. All evening Colleen reigned supreme, however, her enchanting face the focus for every eye. When they left at 11:30 they held her hand by turns and said they'd had a great evening. When invited they promised to come again next week.

After the door closed on the last man, Colleen turned on Sue, rage in her face. "What a party pooper you turned out to be! I should've known."

"What did I do?"

"Gosh, Suz, if you don't even know there's no hope for you. Those guys are gone for good. You at least realize that, don't you?" Colleen stormed into her room and slammed the door.

Sue cleaned up. Was there any pleasing this girl? No, she hadn't known they were gone for good. Were they? Colleen had said they wouldn't turn up in the first place and they had. Why should Sue take the stupid girl seriously?

At work things took a turn that diverted Sue's mind completely. The two older women of her section decided to retire. They'd always lunched together and chatted like buddies, and now they were retiring simultaneously. One of them was known as the "Head." Along with taking her share of calls she trained new people and occupied a larger desk near the entrance to the department where she took the few ads that advertisers handed in personally.

"You'll probably get my job when I'm gone," the Head told Sue.

"Oh, do you think so?" The prospect of a promotion and a rate increase had her keyed up at once.

Sure enough, she got called to the main advertising office. The bald director with a tic in one eye looked up from a table full of papers and illustrations and announced without preliminaries, "I'm giving you Henny Reiter's job. You'll be in charge of training and rating the girls in Classified. It'll be up to you to keep accuracy at the usual high level. Think you can handle it?"

"Yes, indeed."

"I should tell you that there may be more turnover. New policy about starting people on lower, entry-level jobs and moving them up fast."

"Sounds like a great idea!" Moving up fast appealed to Susan.

"Bosses think so. Everything's pretty routine in your area, I guess. But if you should happen to have any questions, let me know."

Suzi wanted to brag about her advancement and rouse Colleen's jealousy, but contented herself with restrained mention.

"Well, aint you the conquering hero!" Colleen laughed, totally unimpressed. Colleen had rich and important parents and no need to earn another identity. Her mother arrived periodically and Colleen indulged her by allowing herself to be taken out to shop. "Sometimes I buy things just because my mother likes them, but I never wear them." The waste outraged Suzi who brooded over every penny she spent.

Friday night the men did return, after all, and brought a friend and two bottles of wine. Susan refused to give any impression of trying to compete with her glamorous roommate, spent time in the kitchen, served another tray of snacks. In her unfulfilled fantasies the man she preferred came to the kitchen and helped with sandwiches, told her she was more his type. She listened wistfully to the talk about money and position and regretted that her new job afforded so little change. At best it provided mild diversion in the form of new employees.

Chapter
10

Colleen grew more talkative as the weeks passed and the guys kept coming over every Friday. She compared their physiques and rated them on "coolness." Suzi tried to get her to express a preference for one or the other, but she had none. Suzi's private yearning went unnoticed. All the men were graduate students, long removed from dormitories. "Too noisy. We have to study." As she gained confidence Sue joined their conversation and felt marginally accepted.

Then one evening one of the men brought his brother along. Kermie. Kermie was different, sported outlandish mismatched clothes two sizes too big for his skinny frame and long bushy hair. He played the guitar and sang shocking ditties that sent Colleen into gales of laughter. He started coming over at all hours and took Colleen out on dates.

When she came in from buying groceries one Saturday, Suzi, from outside heard them moaning and shrieking in Colleen's bedroom. How embarrassing! She hurriedly put things away and went out again. Why didn't they close the window?

Next Friday before guests arrived Colleen asked in her sweetest way whether Suzi wouldn't like to double date Saturday. "I have to pick up my dry cleaning," Suzi objected grabbing the first excuse that occurred.

"That's all right. We could meet you at Rohnee's."

"Do I know this guy?"

"Blind date, Suz'. Friend of Kermie's."

"I'm not sure I want to go out with a friend of his. And his friend probably wouldn't like me."

"Yes, he will. He's great at getting people limbered up. You'll enjoy it. Please?"

"Oh, all right."

All day Saturday she tried to convince herself that Kermie, knowing her, had surely chosen a more serious sort of person. But when she drove into the parking lot she saw Kermie and Colleen at the entrance accompanied by a slouching figure in a garish green jacket. Colleen pointed at this fellow and called out, "Hurry."

Sue parked, stepped out and slammed her car door, seeing as she did so, a green jacket approaching from the side of the building. Kermie and Colleen had disappeared inside.

"I'm Suzi Sterne," she said feeling wary.

"Hi, Suz. Spike. Heard all about you. We're gonna hit it off big—you and me." This friend had spiky orange hair, reflecting his name, pointed high-heeled boots, and obscenely tight jeans. He threw his arm around Susan's shoulder and started leading her in the direction of the entrance. She stiffened.

"Relax, kid!" he yelled, shaking her.

"I'm not deaf." She tried to separate herself.

They'd neared the side wall of the restaurant when she felt herself hurled against the bricks and pinned there while Spike's hands groped her body. Knocked breathless it took her a few seconds to decide what to do. She twisted her fingers in his stiff hair, gave a mighty yank and when he backed off, hurt and grabbing his head, she escaped and ran into the café.

She looked around. Colleen and Kermie sat in a booth half way down one of the aisles in the crowded, smoke filled space. She pushed resolutely through to them. As she sat down she saw them exchange a knowing look and titter. Without saying a word she waited. In another minute she saw Spike enter and to her relief go into the men's room. She was up in a flash, out the door and pulling out of the drive without a second's hesitation.

All the way home she cried with rage and her hands shook on the wheel. "I hate you, Colleen. You dirty slut."

She avoided her roommate for two days, staying downtown or hiding in her room with the door shut.

"Jiminy cricket, Suz, are you going to be mad at me the rest of your life?" Colleen inquired meeting her at the door when she returned home the third day.

"That was a nasty trick. What have I ever done to you?"

"Can't you take a joke? Spike kept holding his head—said you half killed him." Colleen laughed, reminiscing.

Sue made up with Colleen though she found it harder and harder to be civil to Kermie. Kermie brought other friends to the apartment and they all drank heavily, smoked pot and offered it to Suzi who declined. The morning after a party she filled a trash bag with bottles and butts. The regular Friday night gatherings expanded and grew noisier and broke up later and later. Then to Sue's dismay the original guests stopped coming. Colleen didn't seem to notice.

"Gee, Suz, aint it a blast?" she'd ask when her roommate appeared near her in the crowded room.

Neighbors from above and below and beside them knocked often and complained. Sue felt sorry and humiliated and avoided them in the halls.

"We have to quit having parties," she said at last. "People are starting to hate us."

"We're paying rent. We can do whatever we please in our apartment. I'm just starting to have a good time. Why do you want to ruin my life?" After a party, however, Colleen's face had a pale, smudged look that gave her a dramatic air. All her expressions were beautiful: her pout appealing, her sadness wistful, and her smile angelic.

Their rental agency called Sue at work and told her they'd had numerous bad reports and "you girls will have to quiet down." When she reported the call to Colleen, she shrugged. "Just because these old sticks don't enjoy life is no reason I can't." The parties continued and grew frenetic. On the street in front of their building Sue saw a young fellow point at their apartment window. "That's where they party every Friday," he told a friend.

"How do you get invited?"

"Just show up, if you feel like it."

Indignant Sue told Colleen that she refused to be a part of it any longer.

"Then don't. But leave me alone! I'll do what I like."

Suzi tried staying in her room with the door locked. When the police came and sent every one home she felt mortified. She resolved to split up and go her own way.

Colleen cried, said she couldn't pay all the rent. They had signed a lease. Suzi was as responsible as she. "Will you stop these wild parties?"

"Gee, Suz, I can't tell people to go away."

"Yes, you can. If you can't, I will."

"Don't you dare."

The next week they received an eviction notice. "They can't throw us out. We haven't done anything," Colleen cried, so sure of herself that Suzi listened amazed while she called the agency and said that they refused to move. Shortly thereafter they were summoned to court.

The judge asked who was speaking for them and Colleen volunteered. She was at her most attractive in a crisp pink linen dress. With a demure air she explained that the agency had no right to persecute two innocent girls who paid their rent regularly and whose only offense had consisted of entertaining a few friends once a week.

The judge listened impassively as she elaborated on this theme. When she wound up, he inquired, "Have you quite finished, young lady?"

"Yes."

"You took an apartment in a building where the tenants are serious, responsible people who live quietly and respect one another's rights. Into this environment you introduced a disordered mob and created what seems to have become an intolerable disturbance. Even after police intervened, even after you were warned, you refused to modify your behavior." He went on to order Susan and Colleen to vacate their apartment within five days and hinted that they could be thankful not to be fined as well.

She needed more time to resettle, Sue thought, standing tense and chagrined beside her roommate.

Back home Colleen called her parents, sobbed out a garbled version of the persecuting agency and a monstrous judge who'd insulted them. After more than an hour of tempestuous wailing she calmed down. "Yes, Daddy."

She hung up, dull and spent. "He's going to send a van to get my stuff tomorrow. I have to go home for a while."

"What about the sofa?"

"Keep it."

"Your parents won't like that. We'll have to sell it and split the money."

"You sell it."

Mrs. Fairington came the next morning and packed all her daughter's clothes and took her away while Suzi was at work. Searching for a way to save her own future from the shambles. Susan wandered around the place, so peaceful without Colleen. Such a nice apartment. What could she afford by herself? She'd have to hire movers again. Their month wasn't even up. No one would turn up to help her.

On her next lunch hour she went to the agency and disclaimed all responsibility for the noise and undesirable traffic. They said, Oh, all right. She could stay until the thirty-first. But at the first suggestion of trouble she'd have to get out.

That same day she looked at ads and hunted for a place she could afford. Tiny cubbyholes in a decent building. A drafty, dingy room in an old house. At the last place she'd arranged to see she toiled upstairs behind a Latino. Long, blank corridors. They passed a row of one-room apartments, seven on each side and arrived at Number 39. It was large and had three sizeable windows on the outer wall and bright red carpet. Dead bugs lay on the linoleum in front of the refrigerator. "Exterminators have been here. Don't worry," the Latino assured her.

But as soon as Suzi moved in the roaches moved back. Across the hall a strange couple who dressed in rags and colorful scarves were painting murals on their walls. They had small parties in their one room and kept Suzi awake. No one bothered to object.

The Latino was strange also, spoke little English and wanted to be paid in cash. Teresa, the female half of the pair across the hall was pregnant, she said. Her husband was an artist. Currently he only worked on the walls. They invited Suzi to watch TV with them and she accepted out of a desperate need for company. They offered her pot which she declined. It was dark and cozy in their place, all three lined up on the sofa in front of the lighted screen.

One Saturday morning as she left the building to do errands she saw an older woman talking and gesticulating in front of the manager's apartment. "I've called and called and I've been over here three times and knocked at my daughter's door and she never answers," the lady cried, obviously frantic.

Walking out, Sue felt oddly threatened. What sort of place was this? She couldn't keep changing her address and couldn't keep paying movers. The elevator quit and she had to walk up three flights in the dirty, echoing concrete stairwell. After that she double checked the lock on her door and walked swiftly to and from her apartment.

Months passed. Early in December the two young women last hired for Classified announced joyfully that they'd been promoted, at last, and would be going to other departments first of the year. Feeling slapped to the ground, Sue fought to keep a composed face. She'd been there longer and was a kind of supervisor. Didn't she deserve a promotion?

Angry and disturbed she walked miles and pondered. Maybe you had to ask for a promotion. She made an appointment with Mr. Mitchell, the Advertising Manager, and then she could hardly sleep, trying to decide what to say.

Chapter
11

"Having a problem in your area?" Mr. Mitchell inquired, pleasantly enough, after offering Sue coffee. She wished she hadn't accepted it—felt stupid sitting there with a mug in her hand trying to appear dignified.

"A couple women in my department have been promoted?"

"Yes. But we'll send you replacements. They'll be crackerjacks, too. Like the others have been. You won't have any problems."

"I was just wondering—I've been here longer than either of those people and I'm—well, a kind of trainer. I sort of thought if there was an opening I might be considered. You mentioned something about moving people up?"

As she spoke she saw Mitchell start to fidget. "It was my understanding that you came in at the same level as the lady whose place you took. She stayed in the job—gee, can't remember when she wasn't there. It depends on how you're hired."

"So how was I hired?"

"Depending on education, background—people

qualify for different things."

"You're saying I can never qualify for anything except taking classified ads?"

"No. You could move around a little. But always doing comparable things—mail room, maybe."

"Does it pay more?"

"Approximately the same." Suddenly Mr. Mitchell, who clearly didn't enjoy the conversation, decided to end it. "People in personnel are much better at explaining these things than I am. They have your records. If you want to pursue this, talk to them." He stood up rather abruptly and Sue stood and put her mug on the desk.

Too disappointed to make a gracious exit she muttered, "Thanks for seeing me," and left.

She was now twenty. She had a high school diploma and six weeks of secretarial and three years' experience doing the same stupid job. She hated her apartment where she was losing the battle with the cockroaches, she hated the monotony and most of all the sense that life was slipping by and leaving her beached in a blind cove.

She gathered courage once more and went to Personnel. The assistant, a plump, pleasant-faced woman in a blue dress with a large square lace collar, carefully weighed Suzi's complaints and sympathized. "We do hire college graduates to do what you're doing, but with the understanding that they'll move quickly into their field of expertise. One of your people is now a junior accountant, the other an illustrator. You're not qualified for either job, unfortunately."

She pursed her lips while thinking. "Mrs. Retter, your predecessor, never objected to being considered a sort of senior ad taker and that's where you seem to be stuck." Seeing the intense disappointment in Suzi's face she went on. "Your position does require you to do some supervising and training, however. I'll see if I can get them to change your title. You'd get a little more money."

"I wouldn't turn that down, of course. But I'd rather do something else. I learn quickly, I'm good at math. I'm sure I could handle a junior accountant's job."

"I believe you. But I have no choice but to go by the book, and it says you have to be a college math major. Of course, if you were related to one of the top people here—" With a cynical shrug she dismissed that subject. "Off the record I'd advise you to go back to school. You're only twenty three."

Sue remembered the falsified application form and caught herself before she corrected the woman. "College costs so much, and it takes so long to save on what I make."

"I shouldn't say this, but you could get into another line of work. Commission sales, for instance. Right now you could be making twice what we're paying you."

Suzi found it hard to make up her mind to quit, however. She did investigate a few commission sales jobs, but the prospect of giving up a secure income for a gamble frightened her. The change of title came through and her pay shot up by a third. She saved and scrimped. She packed a lunch and ate it on her coffee break so she could relieve the cashier at a neighboring drug store on her lunch hour. Saturdays she handled dry cleaning in a shop at the back of an elegant high rise. None of this work offered challenge or stimulation but her bank balance crept slowly upward.

"To facilitate learning names I seat students alphabetically," Dr. Horton announced. A petite, middleaged woman dressed in a green striped summer suit, she had a pleasantly commanding air, Suzi observed. She lounged against the wall waiting while students shifted about. Presently Susan heard, "Kendrick Shields."

Intrigued she looked to see who that might be. A tall, well-built young man with a lazy, confident air—brown hair, brown eyes, healthy scrubbed looking skin. She was next: Susan Sterne. She moved to the seat beside Kendrick Shields without even the faintest premonition that she was now sitting down beside the man she'd eventually marry.

He sat on the far aisle, and was bending over tucking his shabby back pack under his chair. His clothes suggested a poor student like herself: threadbare jeans and a faded plaid shirt, in keeping with what other students wore and appropriate for this warm night in late August.

Kendrick sat up and smiled engagingly. He had

perfect teeth, a wide mouth. Suzi smiled back. "Have we taken any other class together? Don't recall seeing you around."

"This is my first college class ever. And this is all I'm taking—I'm just a poor working stiff by day."

"You made a good choice. Whatever you decide to take later you can always count English courses."

The professor claimed their attention, handed out syllabi and described her requirements, walking back and forth and moving her hips gracefully under the striped skirt. She let the class out early and Ken fell in with Sue and walked with her across campus.

"What's your major?" Suzi asked.

"I'm like you—just taking this one course. I work days, too."

"At what?"

"Currently on the bottom rung in my office. They have me doing odd jobs and handling routine stuff—pretty boring. But in a year or two things should improve. Oh—there's my bus!" Flashing Sue a smile, he sprinted toward the bus stop.

"Nice," she judged him, but her mind was too crowded to give him much space. She'd quit the classifieds   too suddenly and without preparation, just because doing the same thing endlessly had become intolerable. But now library routine—checking out and shelving books, answering phones, typing labels— bored her equally. No chance to get ahead there either. She had no degree in library science. And her dream that here she'd meet some earnest young scholar with prospects had come to naught. Sunk in gloom she ambled on toward the train station.

Another problem plagued her: she had to move. "What's the matter with me? Why do I drift along like this? Now I'm taking Nineteenth Century English Novel—probably another waste of time." All you could say for it was it took her away from the bugs for three hours one night a week. Then she remembered. To read the assignment she had to buy a text. She turned back to the bookstore.

The following week she arrived early, but Kendrick Shields already occupied his place—reading notes in the back of the text. She greeted him with her habitual slow, shy smile.

He returned her greeting, keeping his book open, however. "How'd you like *Billy Budd*?" he inquired.

"One big metaphor. My father talked a lot about metaphors."

"Your father?"

"Rev. Chancellor Sterne, retired. Anyway, *Billy Budd* was a breeze after those other things."

"Which other things?"

"You know—the suggested readings."

"You did the suggested reading?" Kendrick closed his book and stared. "Which books?"

"*White Jacket, Benito Cereno, Bartleby*."

"*White Jacket*?"

"What a sleeper that turned out to be! Better than pills. If you ever have insomnia, try it."

Ken sat back in his chair. "You read all that stuff this week?"

Sue, uncomfortable with so much astonishment, inquired tartly, "Are you saying I shouldn't have bothered?"

"No, no. I admire your scholarship." And when she continued to regard him with suspicion, "I mean it. If you keep up the good work, you'll get a tremendous education from this one course."

"Costs enough. I should get something out of it."

At first Suzi had nothing to say in class. She listened to the others and pondered ways to contribute. Kendrick seemed to enjoy raising questions. Was that an acceptable approach? After class Kendrick asked whether she took the bus, and learning that she returned home on a train he accompanied her to the station, earnestly soliciting her views on Melville's books. His respect for her opinions encouraged her to join class discussions, and she began to feel accepted and in tune with her fellow students.

She weighed and analyzed Ken's interest in her while guarding her own feelings with rigor. Wouldn't pay to go overboard about someone just starting out on "the lowest rung," as he'd described it. She preferred an image of herself as the bride of a wealthy, established older man who could automatically endow her with position and power.

She read slick magazines and tried (with little success, she thought) to make herself prettier without spending a lot of time and money on the project.

If only she could attend College full time! She was twenty-one now, the age at which she should have finished. She considered taking out loans but didn't know how to go about it and dreaded the idea of owing large sums.

One evening before starting her serious reading she leafed through the latest issue of a magazine. A banner, HOW TO MEET RICH MEN, caught her eye: Join high-brow health clubs, learn to ski, buy groceries at fancy shops and strike up conversations, take a trip and fly first class. There were other even less likely suggestions.

She located a specialty store with the right aura, but while there didn't spot a single prospect. And on second thought, if she had, what on earth could she have said? Back home she wondered what to do with the overpriced jar of pickled mushrooms.

She called health clubs. Phenomenally high fees! She priced ski equipment. Prohibitive. She next toyed with flying first class. She'd never traveled by air, and if nothing else came of it, at least she'd have the experience. She looked with keener interest at the travel section of the Sunday paper.

Boston and New York were too close to Philadelphia. Too little time in the air. She settled on Washington D.C. She'd spend one night there and return the following day. A friend said she couldn't see much of Washington in a day, so she determined to spend most of the time in an aeronautical museum where men might hang out.

She mentioned none of these plans to Kendrick. She knew he'd laugh. He often laughed and followed up with cracks about how refreshing or original she was.

She'd have to look the very picture of glamour and affluence. And that meant a new dress. In Wanamaker's Better Dresses, she brazenly asked for "a sexy outfit," and in a dressing room donned whatever she was brought. In the many paneled mirrors she paraded black sequins, raspberry chiffon cut low to reveal cleavage, green satin with a daring slit skirt.

At last she burst out, "Do people actually buy these clothes?"

The gray-haired, sexless and non-committal saleswoman took offense. "Didn't you say sexy?"

"How about a more reasonable sexy look—something I can travel in?"

"Why didn't you say so?"

A dark green wool dress appeared fitted in a long graceful line over bodice and waist, the tightness eased with a provocatively gathered seam on each side. The color made her gray eyes greenish and accented her thick blonde hair. Because the skirt widened toward the hem, she could walk comfortably. She took it without asking the price and wrote out her check with fortitude.

She'd spent little on makeup heretofore—expensive and far down her list of priorities. Now she took time to sit on a stool in Cosmetics while a salesgirl demonstrated use of mascara, eyeliner and blusher while other clerks observed from a distance with watchful curiosity.

Her good tweed coat with raglan sleeves, once too large, would do nicely.

She arranged to have Monday and Tuesday off. She booked an early flight so she could spend maximum time in D.C. and return the next morning. She could afford only one overnight. On Sunday she experimented with makeup, packed and repacked, nervously took the dress from the closet and re-examined it. She'd have to check her shabby little suitcase, purchased at a Salvation Army thrift store.

Monday morning as she got underway she reminded herself that she could consider the outing a vacation. She took public transportation to the airport and arrived so early that she had an hour and a half to wait. All the passengers she saw except for executive types with briefcases were casually dressed. She took off her coat, slung it over one arm and had a cup of coffee at a stand-up bar, encouraged by covert admiration from a male or two.

Her heart speeded up as she boarded. This was it! With extreme concern and deference the chic stewardess hung up her coat! Coffee appeared by magic. She chose one of the many magazines proffered. The seat next to her remained empty till it looked as if time had run out. She debated whether to ask to have her seat changed, as the magazine had recommended. At the ultimate moment a woman hurtled onto the plane and dropped down beside her.

"Close," she remarked. Then, eyeing Sue with lively interest, "What line are you in?"

"Librarian."   She only assisted the librarians, but who would know?

"What are libraries in the market for nowadays?"

"Better computers, I guess."

"Oh, yes.   Of course."   The woman in a chocolate brown suit and matching coat with a raccoon collar interested Sue so intensely that she temporarily forgot the purpose of the trip.

Her seatmate explained something about her work as a market analyst and while they consumed a roll and coffee she pumped Sue for information on her preferences in computer performance.   At one point she produced a flat pad from a jacket pocket and jotted notes.   Long before the landing the analyst persuaded the stewardess to restore her coat and put her bag near the exit.   And as soon as possible she bolted off.   "Last on, first off," Sue murmured to the attendant who gave her an ingratiating smile and thanked her for flying with them.

Washington D.C.!   The bus drivers told her how to get to her hotel.   She'd wasted half the trip she decided and would have to do better on the return.   But meanwhile—D.C.!   She gazed avidly from the bus windows.   Someday she'd have money and travel the world!

She skipped lunch and went directly to the museums where she brooded over a replica of the Wright brothers' plane and a welter of other aeronautical exhibits.   At closing time they put her out.   Dinner at the hotel was a lonely and costly business and made her realize that she felt exhausted and would be glad to retire.

Early next morning—back to the airport—this time in a hotel limo. When she climbed into the vehicle two men in the back moved apart to make room for her. One had dark bushy eyebrows that startled her for a second until another look convinced her that she'd never seen him before.

The second man claimed her attention. "Hope I'm not crowding you?"

"No, no." But she quickly surmised that there was something deliberate in his proximity.

"Headed—where?" he asked.

"Just to Philadelphia."

"I'm getting off there too." He shifted a bit to get a better view of her, his large dark eyes laughing, challenging. Conviction seized Sue. Here he was! In the limo. Even before they'd boarded the plane!

He urged her to share her impressions of the Capital. She elaborated on the work of the Wright brothers returning his intense gaze, smiling, even giggling at his attempts to appear witty. All at once he stopped and asked to see her ticket. For a second she wanted to say, Mind your business. But finding herself in the safe presence of numerous respectable people she handed it over. He examined it quickly and handed it back without a word.

"Sounds like you spent quite a while with aviation history."

At the airport he introduced himself as Fulton Kling. Before they entered the terminal he took charge of her bag as well as his own and, after ascertaining which gate, sent her on ahead while he went to the ticket counter. She was halfway up the corridor when the conviction seized her that she'd given away her luggage! She stopped dead. Not to worry. Except for the expensive makeup there was little of value in that cheap bag. She went on, checked in, and then bought a pack of cigarettes. She smoked minimally unless out with people who drank. Then she puffed away, keeping her mouth and hands busy. Feeling edgy she lit up and waited. But Fulton Kling appeared within minutes and with warm familiarity resumed their conversation. "Your bag's checked through to Philly" he reported. She thought of television dramas in which drugs or stolen goods were transported by people who didn't know they had them. Then she derided herself for an overheated imagination.

Once on the plane the handsome, stockily built man with high color and hot dark eyes arranged to sit next to her.

He troubled the stewardess for a second glass of orange juice and a third cup of breakfast coffee with such an engaging air that Susan thought she'd like to wait on him herself. Surreptitiously she took note of the expensive material and tailoring of his suit, his expertly cut black hair, his fine leather shoes.

How lucky, lucky, lucky, her heart sang as he devoted himself to her, gently teasing, passing clever compliments on her dress, her eyes, her hair. They absorbed each other. Veering from playful to solemn to sweetly pensive Susan turned on the full power of every charm she could muster.

After they'd eaten he put up their tray tables and the armrest between them and sat close to her. Aroused, Sue let him hold her throbbing hand in the space between seats. In Philly they deplaned together and went to claim their luggage.

"Well, Suzi, are we heading for your place?" he inquired on spotting their suitcases gliding through the flaps. Susan had an instant vision of her crowded room and the wriggling antennae of her unwelcome pests.

"Oh, no. Can't possibly."

Fulton registered displeasure for a moment before saying, "Roommate?"

"Three of them," Susan lied thankfully. They walked away, Kling again carrying the two bags

Outside he set them down and stood looking at her. "What's your suggestion? We can't go to my place, obviously. My mother-in-law's visiting us, for starters."

A wave of humbling disillusion struck Susan with such force that she thought she'd staggered. He noted her look. "What's the matter? We can go to a hotel if you like. I'm not trying to be cheap."

"I—I'm not going anywhere with you. Why didn't you say you were married?"

"You never asked," Kling replied—defensive, bristling. "You gave me a big come-on. Do you think

I'd have switched to first class if I hadn't thought we had something going?"

"You did that?" Outraged, Susan thought she might burst into tears.

"Oh, hell. You're incredible." Abruptly Fulton Kling walked away leaving her standing frozen beside her suitcase.

She brooded over this fiasco, bitterly blaming herself for a romantic idiot. Why hadn't she asked immediately for his marital status? Too blinded by wishful thinking, of course. Successful men were either married or divorced or engaged to one of their own set. She'd have better luck if she looked for a potentially successful man. She mentally appraised the males in her lit class, Ken Shields, in particular. He had possibilities—good looks, an engaging manner, an air of pleasant self-confidence, of authority, even.

He continued to spend time with her after class each week. One evening an engaged couple stopped to chat and invited them to have coffee. This quickly became an expected ritual. And after the others left, Sue and Kendrick tended to sit on, still talking. One night they got on the subject of religion. "I guess you could say I'm a nominal Catholic," Kendrick volunteered at last. "I was confirmed—never doubted the basic doctrines then or since." Sue mulled this over.

"So, I guess you could say I'm a nominal Protestant," she replied. Quite often, as on this occasion, she had no idea why he laughed. Sometimes he also hugged her impulsively. He paid their check and they walked across campus.

He picked up on a subject they'd discussed earlier. "Did your father have any other interesting theories?" They strolled past the School of law buildings, taking a round-about way to the commuter station.

Sue delved into her past and recreated another of Rev. Sterne's "lectures," as Alice had called them. From time to time he'd delivered them with enthusiasm over morning coffee if Alice was in a tolerant mood. "He once told us that he'd written a whole chapter on 'Only God Creates'." Sue recalled.

"Only God?" Kendrick prompted intrigued.

"Neither man nor Satan can create," Susan intoned in Rev. Sterne's voice and even imitated his lofty manner. "But whereas man has the capacity to discover, reassemble and organize elements of creation, Satan can only corrupt."

She stopped until Kendrick prompted, "And so?"

"God gave man dominion over the earth, and if Satan is to achieve his end of total corruption he needs man to devise ways to bring it about."

"Hmmm." While Kendrick digested this, Susan looked about: College of law, college of medicine, college of— Which college produced the most potentially moneyed and prestigious graduates? She could try to look it up in reference books at the library where she worked.

"So do you agree with your father?" Ken

asked.

"On what?"

Ken laughed again. "Oh," she said, "you're still thinking about that theory."

"Forget it." They walked on in silence for a moment or two. "No, don't forget it. Didn't you have a reaction? What's your opinion?" Ken stopped and faced her.

Nonplussed Sue searched for an answer. It was easy to repeat things. She could repeat nearly verbatim almost any serious exposition she heard. But to comment on what she thought about it. "Gee, I don't know. When he talked, I took for granted he was right. He was an author, you know. I told you he had two books published."

"I haven't had any books published. Do you agree with the things I tell you?"

"Of course."

"Why do you? Maybe I'm wrong."

"That's all right. You're nice and a good friend."

Kendrick suppressed what threatened to erupt into hilarity. Then he gave her another wry, judicious smile. "You're not like any girl I've ever known before," he remarked. He pulled her to him and kissed her.

On the train Sue briefly debated whether being unlike any other girl was a plus or a minus, and decided that Ken just didn't know how much she resembled practically all the females she knew. How should she feel about that kiss? It moved their relationship into a different realm. Was this better or worse? He seemed to be just another poor student like herself, and casual friendship had suited her. Oh, well—she liked him and it had been a nice kiss. As long as he didn't get dangerously familiar it didn't matter. She was giving nothing away until the right person committed himself.

Chapter
12

All the way home Susan continued to think about Kendrick Shields. He was too smart for her, too analytical—too contented with himself. If he wasn't keen on getting ahead, how could they hit it off over the long haul? And, as for that his interest in her seemed confined to curiosity. Once he'd figured out what made her tick, he'd get bored.

She knew what motivated her—ambition. Anything else? Wish I knew, she muttered letting herself into her apartment. A scuttling sound announced that insects were taking shelter. Her resolve to vacate this place hardened. In a better building maybe she'd room near a young man going into business—or maybe a rookie broker.

She moved to another one room apartment with a tiny bathroom, this time in the historical district. Many-windowed and furnished with her treasures and a sofa that made into a bed, it took on elegance. The room, more than she could afford, was worth it, because now she could invite men to dinner, starting with Ken Shields.

He arrived, examined her antiques minutely, lay down on the floor and looked up at the undersides. "You've got a fortune here!" He came to the table (daintily set). "I'm impressed. And I'm also eaten with curiosity as usual. Where did you get this furniture, if it's any of my business."

"It isn't, but—but if you want to know, I stole it."

Kendrick predictably burst into laughter. "You're kidding of course."

"No. I'm dead serious." She briefly outlined the acquisition, fully aware that her more outlandish deeds were the ones that entertained Ken.

"Oh, Lord. You've just made me an accessory." He laughed and groaned. "Are these things registered anyplace?"

"Why should they be? I never heard of such a thing." He hesitated as if considering whether to embark on a long explanation, shrugged and dismissed the subject with an ironic smile still playing on his lips.

She resumed her Sunday perusal of the employment classifieds and began toying with the idea of working in a travel agency.

"But all they pay is commissions," she told Kendrick in whom she'd started to confide. "And just suppose I didn't sell enough to pay the rent?"

"Go where they've advertised. If the other agents look busy you can be sure you'll make it."

"I don't have experience. I'd have to begin at a place where they'd take me."

"Do it."

"I'm scared."

"Oh, give it a whirl. If it doesn't pay you can switch to something else, can't you?" Kendrick's untroubled confidence braced her.

"I think I will try it."

Six months later, well established with Travel International, Susan congratulated herself on the move. She also congratulated herself on her continuing relationship with Kendrick Shields. The office he worked at, he'd confessed at last, was a law office, and he a fully qualified lawyer.

"You passed the bar exam and all that?"

"Yes."

"Why didn't you tell me?"

"More fun to have you pitying me for a poor Joe."

On further consideration Sue decided he'd done the right thing. If he'd told her, she'd have become self-conscious—tried to impress him. Fortunately they'd become friends, and now she knew something important about him—he didn't react well to women who made a play for him. If she ever tried to be cute and clever instead of blunt and honest, he'd like her less. There was that platinum blonde student whose artful questions and flirty ways had caused him to disengage himself, politely of course. He still hadn't asked Sue out on what one could call a date, but he dropped by her place a couple times a week. He unabashedly advised her about which courses to take to progress toward a career. And he signed up for ones that met at the same hours, so they could get together afterwards.

One evening she dared presume on their friendship enough to ask him, "Where does a lawyer, starting on the bottom, hope to go?"

He outlined what he called the Process, with easy assurance. Every month they trusted him with more complex matters. In a few years they'd make him a junior partner. After quite a few years, a senior partner. Before he retired he might have his name on the letterhead.

"And you'll make lots of money?"

"Enough. I plan to live well, if that's what you mean."

His prospects excited Sue more than they excited him, she decided. But there were mysteries about him. Every time they started a new course his eye roved through the class, examining and evaluating. Then there were the weekends. She never saw him on a Friday after eight p.m. and not at all on Saturdays or Sundays. For a long time she guessed that he had a steady girl or a number of girls. But gradually she changed her mind—not understanding why. Maybe because golf, racquetball, reading, events at an unspecified Club—all the activities he referred to—seemed to involve men or mobs of people or himself alone.

Kendrick could be difficult too. You couldn't flatter him and couldn't fool him. He forced Susan to expand on statements that she'd uttered without conviction, just to be saying something. She found his combination of off-hand tolerance and punctilious intellectuality irritating at times.

The married women Sue now worked with invited her for an occasional barbecue or pool party. She met young men who talked and flirted, but none had called to ask her out. The visits gave her a window into a plush suburban culture and whetted her already keen appetite for a more affluent life. If only Kendrick— What? What did she want from him? She hardly dared use the M-word even to herself.

He'd call her at the agency. "Shall I bring over a pizza after you get off?" Or he'd arrange to meet her at a coffee shop near her work place. Lately he'd begun to inquire what she did on weekends. Infrequently she'd attended a get-together at her colleagues' houses. Mostly it was the same old routine. Susan caught a hint of uneasiness in him over her answers. Why should he care that her weekends were arid deserts of household chores and visits to the library?

Along in September a change came over him. He seemed to watch her cautiously. Instead of pizza, he'd bring steaks and cook them while she prepared garlic bread and salad. Finally he invited her to dinner on a Friday night! A real date that had her singing and dancing around her room in anticipation. She was earning more money. Should she buy a new dress? No, she was making too big a deal out of this. She appeared in the same pant suit she'd worn all day. And when she saw the nice, but nothing-special café she thanked her stars that she hadn't got all gussied up. After a pleasant meal, Ken inquired with a too-nonchalant air whether she liked dogs.

"Sure. Mutts and breeds of all kinds."

"My mother's exhibiting her prize terrier at a show next weekend, and I wondered if you'd like to see a dog show. Anyway, she wants to meet you."

"Sounds fun." She tossed off this reply, but her heart bounded.

"Mom lives way out—other end of Philly. So maybe you should plan to stay overnight Saturday?"

He was arranging for her to meet his mother! Suddenly she knew where he spent all his weekends. She smiled and nodded at him, scrupulously matching his off-hand manner. So he wasn't promising anything. All right. He needn't imagine that she'd pin her life's hopes on it.

It was hard not to. She examined all her clothes twice—had half of them dry cleaned. Asked him what one wore to a dog show. "Nothing special."

Sue looked up dog shows in a book at the library and assembled the right outfit. She washed and polished her car. It now merited the "little old compact" appellation. And all the time a recurrent phrase ran in her mind: What will his mother think of me? Ken had given her their address. That he wouldn't pick her up and take her there signaled caution. And she was to stay just one night—for convenience sake.

She knew Ken's father had died when he was

twelve.   Now Ken was twenty-six, and, she guessed, warmly bonded with his remaining parent. "If his mother likes me, he'll pop the question." Her heart nearly stopped at the uncertainty. But it was clear to her that everything depended on his mother. He'd never say so, but he went home every weekend. She'd bet all she had on it.

The visit would begin with lunch Saturday. She drove the considerable distance with methodical care, and as she entered their elegant neighborhood began to feel outclassed in her little old car. She plucked a card from behind the sunshield and consulted it again. As if she didn't know the address by heart. On either side magnificent estates stood half hidden in acres of landscaped grounds. So when she located the Shields' house she sighed with relief. A modest brick Georgian on a half acre. It stood at the top of an incline approached by a long concrete walk interspersed with short flights of steps. She rounded a corner and drove up behind the place.

Ken and his mother appeared instantly. Ken carried her suitcase and his mother, a short sturdy, unprepossessing woman with gray hair and straight black eyebrows led the way into the house. "Take her right upstairs," Mrs. Shields directed after greetings and introductions, "in case she wants to hang anything or freshen up."

Ken cleared the long, curved staircase in a few bounds and Susan followed. Through a pounding in her ears she heard the woman say, "Lunch in twenty minutes." Ken came out of her room, took her hand and squeezed it, saying. "Nice to have you here," before he ran lightly down.

She closed the door and stood in the middle of the room they'd assigned her, fighting for control of her feelings. The room was large and sunny, the bedstead white painted iron, the coverlet an elaborate patch work quilt one of those arty things you'd see in an antique dealer's. The recently refinished floorboards gleamed up at her. She forced herself to move around and open doors: closets and a huge private bath with a cavernous porcelain tub, heavy ceramic wall tile, the largest towels she'd ever seen.

She opened her shoddy case and took out the blouse she planned to wear tomorrow. It looked solitary and strange in the big closet. She located a brush and drew it through her long honey-colored hair and retied the silk scarf in which she'd secured it. She was no great beauty, she decided for the hundredth time—that thin prominent nose, the too-square chin. Susan stifled her feelings of inadequacy. Having no choice, she had to descend and face her host and hostess.

At lunch she watched Ken's mother manage things with complete ease. The calm, unpretentious woman talked about her Bedlington terrier, already judged Best-of-Breed. The competition this afternoon for Best-of-Group would be stiffer, and she didn't expect to win. After lunch Susan met the dog and felt startled.

"It looks so much like a—"

"A lamb?"

"Yes."

"Feels like one too." Sue placed her hand on the thick, linty coat. "What a strange dog!"

"Sweet natured and obedient," Mrs. Shields bragged and the dog licked her owner's hand.

Going over to the club Susan was wedged into the front of a large old Buick between Ken and his mother. She tried hard to make appropriate responses while Ken talked about the many breeds of terriers she'd see. "Terrier comes from the Latin—earth, as you can guess."

"Like terra firma, you mean," Sue hazarded.

"Yes. Originally terriers were trained to dig out rats and woodchucks."

"Fascinating!" Her voice sounded too thin and high-pitched to Sue. Would they never reach their destination?

Although it was a crisp day in October the judging would be held outdoors. Mrs. Shields went about her business and Ken took Susan's hand and led her across the grounds to a place in the viewing stands. "My mother gets a big charge out of these shows. For her sake I'm thankful we can still belong to the Club."

"What's to prevent?"

"Actually, the yearly dues are a bit prohibitive. But when my mother couldn't renew, the year after Dad died, they voted us a life membership."

"How nice!" Sue, trying to keep her tone light, had struck a false note she imagined, but Ken went on off-handedly, "Dad was one of the founders and also treasurer for many long years."

"I see." Susan looked around. Indeed, she could have worn anything. Women appeared in silks and furs, in jogging outfits, in designer denim. But commonest and least conspicuous was casual sportswear into which her tweed jacket and dark pants fitted appropriately. She sighed with relief and gained enough confidence to squeeze Kendrick's hand and smile.

As Mrs. Shields had predicted, her dog lost the contest for Best-of-Group. "It's fun to participate, anyway," she remarked on the way home. "And I like to think that Liddy here enjoys it too." She reached into the back and affectionately patted her.

Helping her hostess assemble a simple meal for supper gave Susan more feeling of confidence. At home in any kitchen she deftly arranged the platter of cold cuts and a tray of raw vegetables while Mrs. Shields poked around cutting scones into odd shapes and eliciting comment from Sue on a variety of topics such as her hopes for the future, her ambitions. While not concealing her wish to succeed in business—owning her own agency one day—Susan replied with restraint. Should she be telling these things? What were the right answers? If only she knew the woman a little better! But the worst was yet to come. After supper Mrs. Shields insisted that Kenny, as she called him, entertain their guest. Almost bashfully he first played the piano and sang old ballads in French and English. Susan applauded and laughed, watching Mrs. Shields for the right reaction.

Then he had to play the recorder. "I'm no

musician," Ken apologized.   The thin sounds of
unfamiliar little tunes went on and on. She didn't know
what to do with her face. She'd feel her body tensing
and made an effort to relax. His mother tapped the
carpet with her foot and leaned back in her well worn
leather wing chair, totally at ease. Fortunately her eyes
closed, and Sue took that as a way to escape. "I've been
up since six and I'm sort of tired," she ventured.

"Well, of course you want to get to bed then.
Would you like a snack before you go up? Glass of
milk, perhaps?"

"Thank you, no." Kendrick accompanied her
to the stairs. "I know you saw Mom nodding off. She
turns in early," he said, almost apologetic.   Then he
went on, "Sorry for the Mickey-Mouse concert. Every
time a new person comes into the house Mom makes
me perform."

Sue managed a sly smile. "I'm bedazzled."

"Bet you are."   They parted on this note of
laughter. Ken went back to his mother. The dog wasn't
the only creature put through his paces. And now Susan
had left them alone, and they could dissect her. She
dragged into her room and took a long soak in a hot tub
reflecting and reaching the decision that Mrs. Shields
for all her sweet politeness didn't like her that much.

Chapter
13

In bed Susan tried to read but kept reliving the whole tense, embarrassing day. She'd been "our guest—a friend" never a potential daughter-in-law. She jumped out of bed, exercised for an hour and finally fell asleep. When she woke her sharp ears detected voices far away. She threw on her clothes and ran downstairs. Ken and his mother sat together in the kitchen nook in attitudes of cozy congeniality.

Right after breakfast Sue had to get back to town, she declared. Ken brought her suitcase down and then remembered a book he intended to lend her. "I'll put your bag in the car. Wait one minute." He dashed into the house. She waited. Two minutes elapsed, three—then five. She grew impatient and looked up at the house. There was a back staircase, because she'd seen him flying past the little window on the landing. But no sign of him returning.

What the heck! He could give her the book any old time. And was she too weak to lift her own small suitcase? Decisively she slung it through the open window into the back seat, bounced into the car and was gone.

Ken, delayed by an untimely phone call, paused at the window, arrested by the sight of her precipitate departure.

He burst into laughter, instantly smothered. "That's my Sue," he murmured. Her pragmatic disregard for formalities aroused him. That agile, faintly defiant movement of arms and body—all one piece—inflamed his imagination. He hadn't loved her till that moment, but now resolved to woo her seriously. He was ready to marry and here was the girl who challenged him.

His mother's voice calling from below broke into his reverie. "Who was that on the phone?" He went into the dining room where his mother stood wrapping up the silver that she'd brought out for company. "Bill. Wants to golf this afternoon."

Mrs. Shields inspected her handsome son's radiant face. "You're going to marry that girl, aren't you?"

"Yes."

She nodded. He'd get no opposition from her, though Susan had struck her as rather too cool, too calculating for her warm, accepting boy. But maybe the poor girl was just nervous. If Kenny loved her, she would too.

Resolved to put Kendrick Shields out of her mind forever, Susan went to work more earnestly. She had developed her own set of faithful clients—as had the other two women in the travel agency. All three respected each other and worked to build business. After attending a conference or two and hearing gossip,

Susan understood how fortunate she'd been in her association with mature, self-reliant co-workers.

The senior agent admitted that they'd had doubts about Sue's youth and inexperience. But they'd delighted in the way she developed her skills. Someday, they predicted, she'd have an agency of her own. Pleased to have her secret hopes fanned, Susan worked to make herself indispensable.

When Ken was as friendly as ever at their twice-weekly class, Susan imagined that he wanted to let her down gently. Instead he grew even friendlier. He pulled her into the shadows by dark buildings and kissed her hard.

"I've got to get home, Ken. I don't like to stay out too late."

"I'll take you home."

"No, no. Both of us have to work tomorrow."

He now made dates for weekends and brought flowers and small boxes of frightfully expensive chocolates. She made excuses and avoided him. He'd never marry without his mother's consent, but he wanted to make love. Well, why shouldn't they? She liked him better than any other man she'd known. But she couldn't do it. Because of pride, she admitted. If she wasn't good enough to marry, she preferred the sort of platonic relationship they'd always had. Before they went out on dates she planned ways to keep from inviting him in. His persistence drove her to say, at last, "I don't think your mother liked me."

"Yes, she did," he'd replied. Without thinking,

Sue decided with her usual pessimism.

One evening he escorted her to a dark, formal Italian restaurant with booths set into nooks and corners. After they were seated and had given their orders, he switched to her side of the table. She immediately crowded against the wall to give him plenty of space, knowing perfectly well that she was frustrating his intention.

"What's the matter, Sue? Thought you liked me." He sounded wistful.

"I do like you—a lot." More than she wanted to, she added internally.

"Then why so cool all at once? What's come over you?"

He was so handsome, so educated, such a dear. Mournfully, not looking at him, she picked invisible lint from his coat. "Your mother. You'd never marry someone she didn't approve of." She'd said it and had to swallow hard.

"Don't see why I should have to," he replied.

"She doesn't like me."

"Oh, that again!" He put his arm around her and pulled her close. "My mother isn't choosing my wife. And anyway, she's fond of you."

"You're serious?"

"She tells me how bright and attractive you are. Asks how you're doing."

Sue looked into his eyes, half blinded by his ardor. "And now that you've brought it up, how about it, Sue? Will you marry me? I'm in love with you, Suzi girl."

He waited. Through a constricted throat she breathed a reply. "I love you, too." Did she?

But the fire of his kiss aroused her. "Oh, Ken." She thought she might cry. "Of course I'll marry you. It's what I want most in the world." With a thankful sigh she snuggled into his embrace. Whether or not she really loved this man or even knew what love might mean, at least she'd come at last into a safe harbor.

At their next meeting in her home Gloria Shields embraced her son's bride-to-be with motherly warmth. With a diamond on her finger and Ken kissing her in the hall and sitting familiarly in her room talking, Susan gradually lost all sense of being intimidated by the stately Georgian and its owner. They'd set the date for February 15, but when Gloria asked about wedding plans, Sue confessed helplessness. "Something simple?" she suggested.

Ken instantly backed her up. "Simple. I'd prefer that too."

And Gloria agreed. "We could have the wedding right here, of course. Ken's cousins from New York and Boston would have to be invited. And maybe the two of you have a few cronies you'd like to ask?"

After serious consultation at the dining room table the two women made a short list: Ken's nearest relatives, his best buddies, one or two people from the Club, Susan's co-workers and naturally, her parents.

"Adoptive parents," she corrected.

"Yes, of course. But legally adopted, aren't

you?"

"I am, but—"

"They'll want to know that you're getting married."

"I suppose so.   Can't hurt to send them an invitation."

"How long since you've heard from them?"

"They send holiday cards.   At Christmas my father puts in a check."

After this conversation Gloria grew perceptibly more maternal and protective.   "It's fun to have a daughter—at last!" she confided.   She came into town and took her future daughter-in-law to lunch. Afterwards they walked past a display of wedding apparel and Gloria cried impulsively, "Oh, let's go in and peek at their gowns."

"That's an expensive store," Sue objected.   At twenty-three she could read price tags a block away.

"Don't you want to see what's fashionable?"

Sue succumbed to temptation and called the agency to say she'd be late.   She liked sitting in a posh boutique with Gloria Shields who captivated the saleslady by soliciting her advice.   The woman brought out several gowns.   A silk organdy with dropped shoulders, low-slung puffed sleeves and bouffant skirt attracted Sue.

"We're trying to get ideas today," Gloria announced unapologetically.   "Could she try it on?"

"But of course."

It took a minute for Sue to get accustomed

to the expanse of bare chest and shoulder. Layers of stiffening gave the skirt a romantic fullness. She thought she'd never find anything she liked so well, but she tried on a series of gowns anyway—heavily sequined or embroidered, lacey or filmy, satiny or crepe with trains of all lengths. Mrs. Shield offered the same non-committal approval each time. "You're so lovely, you look wonderful in all of them." The last dress in Susan's size was a plain satin sheath, floor length with long sleeves and no train, its severity relieved by a filmy organza drape. This time Gloria Shields made her walk about a little longer and nodded a trace more emphatically.

Back on the street Susan announced decisively that she couldn't afford any of those gowns. "Parents must help," her mother-in-law-to-be ventured.

"You're already footing too many bills. I'll buy my dress—not one of those."

"But if your parents—"

"I'd die before I'd ask them for anything." Susan couldn't believe that she so confided in this woman.

"I understand completely," Gloria assured her. "They'll volunteer. Trust them."

But Sue didn't trust them. In a way she hoped they wouldn't show up. She still burned with indignation at the way they'd treated her.

A week later Mrs. Shields announced with innocent happiness that the Sternes would arrive a week before the wedding and would stay with her, of course.

"Ken has those two roommates and you don't have lots of extra space," she explained tactfully.

Mildly shocked, Susan had to decide seriously how to treat Rev. and Mrs. Sterne after all these years. They deserved only a cold shoulder. She pictured herself cool and patronizing. Here they'd be outclassed. The Shields were the genuine article—vastly superior in wealth and status to a retired clergyman. And what a contrast to the Sterne's indifference the Shields' honest concern for their new family member provided! But after enjoying a vision of their richly deserved discomfort, she invoked a more realistic attitude and revised her approach. Frigid treatment would get her nowhere. To the *Shields* she'd look mean and unforgiving. And the poor Sternes would lose whatever parental impulses they might have drummed up.

She schooled herself to play the game, and by the time they arrived was able to greet them with respect and filial affection. Did she detect a trace of relief in Alice Sterne? The pair had changed little. The Shields cordially accepted them, and Ken's mother immediately—even ostentatiously—took a back seat. "Whatever you and Susan decide," she kept saying.

Alice found the opportunity to take charge irresistible. She visited caterers, arranged and paid for the reception. She hired a pianist. She examined the inexpensive gown Susan had purchased and made her return it. They revisited the bridal shop and this time, with Alice Sterne looking on with critical attention, Susan paraded the gowns with more seriousness. A second exposure convinced her that her broad shoulders looked too athletic for the organdy gown—her previous first choice. And this time she observed that the gown favored by her future mother-in-law more subtly enhanced the lines of her body. She said nothing to Alice, but waited to hear her verdict. Several gowns now hung about the place but Alice's gaze, moving from one to the other, unerringly settled on the right choice. "They're all lovely, but this one's more becoming." Susan agreed easily, now that Alice was paying.

A high point came when Susan and Kendrick took her parents to see the condominium they'd bought. "We," Ken always said, though he paid for everything. Besides the condo which they'd chosen together after many exhilarating inspections of this place and that, they'd also purchased a huge bed. "With the other furniture Sue and I already own we can furnish the place once we get back from our honeymoon." Chancellor and Alice stood in the large central room with its stone fireplace, visibly impressed.

While Chancellor and Kendrick talked about the former's latest book, Alice lagged behind with Susan. "You've made a fine choice, my dear. Kendrick is so agreeable and seems to have such a splendid background."

"And aren't you surprised that the ugly duckling is swimming away with the prize," Susan thought, but aloud she only murmured, "So glad you like him, Alice."

At the wedding the Rev. Sterne snapped a

hundred pictures. Always in a corner, changing film. They took pictures of the house, of the bridal party (Susan's co-workers made attractive attendants) of the Shields' relatives, of the cake, the buffet table, the minister: ten times the number of pictures they'd taken of their daughter during the four years she'd lived with them.

But Susan—caught up in the almost intolerable excitement of the wedding, the reception and the departure, showered with birdseed as they ran down the long steps and walkway to Ken's decorated car—had no leisure to brood over the Sterne's belated possessiveness.

During the first days of their honeymoon Susan had, in fact, much difficulty coming down from this pinnacle, had to focus hard to respond to all sorts of probing questions posed by her new husband: "Unless you prefer, there's no reason you have to work. What would you like, really?"

Susan, head contentedly pillowed on Ken's chest, arm clasping him, considered gravely. "I have you. That's all I want."

Kendrick hugged her to him, agreeing passionately, "Me too."

But later, walking around the balmy streets of Acapulco whither they'd gone to escape the cold February in Philly, he tried again. "What seems most attractive—work, school, starting a family?"

"Oh, Ken, I've always wanted to finish college. And it's so burdensome puttering along, one course at a time!" The lovers agreed that she should work full time toward her degree in the next two or three years, depending on how long it took. And privately Sue weighed the advantage to Ken of having an educated wife.

Nor did she forget that he'd proposed a number of alternatives. In the long years ahead there'd be plenty of time to pursue all of them. A hunger to have all, to do everything began to consume her. And as for Ken's placid acceptance of the status quo, he could change. She'd spur him on.

PART TWO

Chapter
14

Before their third wedding anniversary Ken and Susan had worked out a routine and a number of goals. They agreed on "nominal Protestant" as a socially acceptable norm and attended a Community Church at least one Sunday a month. Sue had finished college—majoring in business, minor—English. At age twenty-six she turned her attention to producing a family and immediately conceived.

She opted for a son, decorated the nursery in blue, chose the name Theodore—Teddy, Ted. She liked the sound of all the possible variations. When the doctor declared a girl instead she took it in stride. Next time it would be a boy. Kendrick named his daughter Eileen. Susan installed a pink crib across from the blue one in the nursery and fell easily into the role of wife and mother, much supported and entertained by her mother-in-law.

Gloria persuaded Susan to spend long leisurely hours at her house where she relieved her of the baby's care. But Susan liked it best when Gloria entertained her at the Club. She quickly developed a taste for luxurious service and prestigious associations, the latter only faintly marred by a trace of patronage in the attitude of dues-paying members toward her. No one ever patronized Gloria. That was somehow impossible in spite of her unpretentious manner—or perhaps because of it?

Weekdays in summer Susan and Gloria often swam in the Club pool or sunned beside the glittering blue water. While the baby slept in the shade the two women, glistening with tanning oil, lay side by side, eyes closed or occasionally raised heads and smiled at each other. Gloria had become Susan's true mother—loving, reassuring, seconding her every decision.

Susan removed her cap and shook out her long, thick hair. "Sometimes I think I'll cut all this off," she cried, expecting a protest.

Instead Gloria seemed to assent. "Remember Evelyn Simms? She gets hers shaped at Tonio's." When Sue didn't answer she went on, "Of course I love your hair as it is."

Surprised, Susan mentally filed the information about Tonio's. So her mother-in-law thought it possible to improve her looks?

That winter Gloria became ill, refused to discuss her condition, scheduled no surgery and died a year later, a few months after Teddy's birth. The loss stunned both Kendrick and Susan. She stood beside her husband at the graveside stricken with what she imagined to be an even greater sense of deprivation than her husband's. No woman left to talk to. No one to dote on the grandchildren.

But after a period of confused grief the young couple altered their lives. They sold their condo and moved into the old Georgian which required a surprising number of repairs and refurbishings and more outlay in taxes. "We can handle it," said Kendrick who expected to be made a junior partner within the year.

Would he really? Sue wondered, exasperated by his excessively laid-back style. He never showed much competitive spirit.

Now Susan had to drive longer distances to shop, necessitating replacement of the old car her one-time landlady had given her so long ago. What she wanted was a luxury automobile, something to wheel up to the Club in without feeling ashamed. She had to settle for a modest used car, however.

And Gloria's death had raised a question that she decided to consult Kendrick about: "Memberships, Ken. Your mother's was for life and yours too, I guess. Does that cover me as well? And how about your children?"

Kendrick hemmed and hawed. "I don't know—doubt it. As long as we go together, nobody will question."

Sue felt mildly humiliated. True her husband made more money every year, but not enough to pay for the extra memberships. No more afternoons at the pool. No more lunches in the Club dining room. Too expensive, anyhow.

Teddy comforted her. A laughing little bundle of charm from the first, unlike his sister, now a serious infant of two. It was clear that with a baby brother on hand Eileen felt bigger and more in charge, and Susan encouraged her nurturing attitude.

Settling into the big house and mothering two children kept her on the run all the next year while Ken's advancement did materialize. Then they had money to replace limp draperies and dingy carpets. At times Sue gloried in her image: the up and coming young attorney's wife. She preened herself on the fine old house with its carefully chosen furnishings—immaculately kept, her children bright and beautiful, especially Teddy.

By degrees, however, her vision shifted from inside to outside her home. The dignified Georgian shrank by comparison with her neighbors' places. To her right a ten-year-old replica of an historic Elizabethan Manor reared its impressive bulk. Across the street she caught glimpses (through a screen of magnificent old trees) of an English half-timber. Someday they'd have a house like one of those, she vowed without sharing this determination with Ken who, she suspected could happily vegetate forever right where he'd been born.

One day Susan came down from rummaging in the attic with an old portrait of Ken's parents in their youth. Gloria as a young woman was pretty in a composed way. Ken's father wore glasses and his face reminded one of Woodrow Wilson, only with a more hawklike toughness. Ken's father had purchased half a square mile of land when it was cheap, had built the

Georgian, expecting to have a more numerous family and wanting them to grow up in what was then a country setting. Later, realizing that his years were numbered, he'd had the land subdivided and shrewdly sold the lots for astronomical prices to wealthy men seeking a prestigious community. The Club that had followed almost as a matter of course now had a membership of 300. Proceeds from real estate, cautiously invested, had allowed Kendrick and his mother to keep up their rather elegant lifestyle and pay the burgeoning taxes.

Ken held the faded photograph and mused, "I loved Dad, but he kept himself too busy. And he had the old notion that a father's role ended with disciplining or delivering moral lectures. In point of fact, Mom brought me up. I plan to spend more time with our kids." He paused, "Dad died in his fifties with an inherited heart condition. I might have it, but so far the docs haven't found anything."

"They never will," Sue affirmed confidently.

Kendrick sat down on the sofa, summoned his children and sat with one arm around Eileen, the other around Teddy. Watching, Sue reflected that indeed he was his mother's son and a true parent from the first. Why did she want him to change and harden and take on the energetic drive suggested by his father's photo?

Susan veered from self-congratulation to envy—brooded over the society pages, and followed the activities of their wealthier neighbors with avid interest. She reflected long and earnestly while perusing the Club Newsletter delivered to Kendrick alone, and kept track of gala affairs that they could have attended. As his "guest" she was always admitted. Ken cared little for the Club. He'd escorted his mother to many festivities for which he'd had no affinity, starting at an early age, since she'd had no other escort. "I had enough practice playing the little gentleman to last a lifetime," he claimed with a trace of bitterness.

"But now that you're older, I should think you'd enjoy them," Sue protested.

Sometime later Kendrick examined the flyer she put in his hands describing a dinner to honor Senator Krantz. "Do you really want to put all our spare cash into one meal?"

"For the chance to meet a real senator? Yes I would!"

"I can live without it."

Susan wanted to put her hands over her ears. Some of Ken's remarks alienated her. She had to admit his superiority, however, and she let him talk without contradicting. After all, he came home faithfully every day after long, arduous devotion to his cases. He read to the kids and sometimes put them to bed. He enjoyed a late, leisurely dinner with Sue and helped her with dishes. He consulted her about his problems and listened to her ideas.

Kendrick declined to attend the annual Benefit Ball at the Club, firm in his insistence that they had better things to do with their money.

Susan kept track of this splendid event, however, pored over descriptions in the Club Newsletter and yearned to be part of it all. On the night in question, without telling Ken where she was going, she drove her unidentifiable car to the Club and parked outside and up the street where she could surreptitiously observe people making their grand entrances. Among the very first to arrive were the Hendersons. How she envied their relaxed self-assurance as they walked up the steps and into the festive, exotically decorated ballroom!

The children were older now and stayed up later, so after dinner Kendrick sometimes convulsed them with a parody of the pieces he'd once performed at his mother's behest. In the kitchen Sue herself doubled over the sink, laughing as he sang French songs in a hastily improvised translation using a fake French accent. He blew and bellowed into a German bassoon or played his recorder, squeaking and laboring pathetically in the sentimental passages.

As the youngsters grew Susan's ambitions expanded. She wanted them to develop with confidence in their status—looked up to and respected. Kendrick saw nothing to worry about. He loved and played with the children and often brought them special little gifts.

On Eileen's sixth birthday in August he presented her with a kitten—a gray with four white paws. Eileen named him White Socks. Late that month she started first grade and Susan resolutely returned to work in the travel agency part time, leaving Teddy with a sitter for a few hours here and there. To Ken's observation that they "didn't need the money," she replied, "I'll think of a use for it." The use she already had in mind.

That Christmas Susan took a few extra days off work. Her adoptive parents had amazed her by begging for an invitation to spend a few days with "their grandchildren." Before they arrived she rushed about, cleaning shopping, decorating, putting up a tree and fighting off White Socks (now a sizeable cat) who chose to preempt the tree. He sharpened his claws on the trunk, reclined along the branches. Lifted down by the scruff of his neck he awaited his chance to get back his perch. Kendrick laughed heartily to find him curled up among the ornaments.

During the night, Sue, who was often wakeful, heard faint rushing sounds below. Curious as to the cause she listened, then went to the stairs. In the gloom at the bottom she perceived an irregular pattern of white patches hurtling about, and when her eyes grew accustomed to the dark she realized that White Socks had quietly removed his favorite ornament, a ball covered with silky yarn, and was chasing it up and down. A soft sigh startled Sue. Eileen had come down noiselessly and stood there watching beside her. "Such a bad kitty," Eileen murmured, hopeless.

"Oh, well, if he wrecks it, who cares. We'll consider it his Christmas present," Susan replied hugging her daughter.

Perceptibly older and feebler this time, Alice and Chancellor Sterne brought elaborate gifts for the children and made awkward efforts to play with them. Teddy eased the situation with loud, enthusiastic screams and eager demands that Chancellor accompany him to the back yard to push the swing or catch him when he threw himself off the trampoline. Eileen solemnly displayed her stamp collection for Alice's inspection. Altogether the time passed pleasantly enough and Sue felt little need to prove anything to her "parents." She now perceived them as old, aimless and lonely and made up her mind to invite them again next year.

Teddy started kindergarten that fall. And now Susan went back to work full time. She'd accumulated a bank balance and could now add to it more rapidly, reaching the goal she'd set just as the Club Board met and raised the fee for five-year family memberships again! Another four months of working and scrimping. Ken gazed at her, half amused, half incredulous when she finally revealed her intention to pay dues for herself and the children.

After a short inner struggle to find anything commendable in this, he remarked with a trace of irony, "The Club does support a few local charities." He sighed, "If it's worth almost a year's wages to you, go ahead. I don't recommend it, but I won't stop you."

After fighting down an impulse to appear in person at the Club office and write out the enormous check with a flourish, Susan mailed it in, receiving within days four little cards folded in a piece of blank Club stationery. For one minute, sitting in the living room with the cards in her hands, she felt a sense of shame at the amount of work these bits of pasteboard represented. Then her resolution hardened. Though Kendrick already had a card, they'd included another in his name.

The sizeable influx into the Club treasury did not pass unnoticed. Men speculated that young Shields must be doing even better than they'd guessed, had to be a top-notch attorney.

Slowly, following their interests, Sue deliberately involved the members of her family in the Club's doings and noted that the children quickly took belonging for granted and developed friendships in the neighborhood. She herself, in order to cultivate closer association with at least some of the wealthy members, joined an amateur theatrical group and played minor roles in a few performances.

Six months later when the gala event of the year was announced Ken surprised her by agreeing to attend without a struggle.

She'd be on display for the first time as a full dues-paying member and the importance of that so impressed Susan that she thought of little else for two weeks. She shopped and shopped for the right gown, taking her cue from hints her late and sorely-lamented mother-in-law had dropped. At last she chose a pale, silvery satin reminiscent of her wedding gown—simple but superbly elegant. Standing in the fitting room and examining herself in mirrors she perceived that the long thick mane of hair that she'd taken such pride in didn't fit with her image in the new gown. Gloria Shields had recommended a haircut—Tonio's, she recalled.

At the salon she noticed that several hairdressers had the name Tonio. Did it matter which did one's hair? She accepted the operator assigned, a scrawny little fellow, gray haired, wearing a smock, and looked at him in the mirror. "Well, what do you have in mind?" he invited.

"I'm a mother of two children and starting to feel that this long hair is rather juvenile."

"You could put it up." With a firm grip, he twisted, folded and smoothed it and began to jab pins into it—lots of pins.

"No, no. I don't want to deal with a hundred pins."

He let it fall, lifted the honey colored hair and studied her face. "What would you suggest?" she urged.

"You have a great head." He gathered her locks in one hand and held them back. "Wonderful shape, right size. Lucky you."

"So?"

"So show it off, I'd say. The hair should just frame it. But that means cutting all this off."

"Go ahead."

Chapter
15

Kendrick studied the new Susan with intensity. "Makes you look different—sophisticated."

"Like it?"

"You didn't consult me about cutting off all your beautiful hair."

"Was I supposed to?"

Ken laughed. "Of course not. I love to tease you."

"You don't like it?"

"I do. It's becoming—advances you from attractive to glamorous."

Susan gave him a hug and a long grateful kiss.

Driving to the Club on the fateful night Sue examined her husband in his freshly dry-cleaned tux. Men had things so easy—no question about the appropriate wear, the appropriate haircut. Well, maybe some leeway about the latter. She wanted to discuss the Hendersons who were the reigning force at their Club, but had to be careful how she did it. Her democratic husband always said things like, "Let's not equate money with worth," or if she'd described someone as a "lesser light," he'd murmur, "has his own unique contribution."

Bart Henderson had retired three years ago and since then had seized the reins at the Club. Ken claimed it was because Bart couldn't really retire, because he had too much money—a terrible responsibility. Susan wanted to have a responsibility like that, for millions—maybe billions.

"The Hendersons organized this whole affair, didn't they?" she tried.

"Bart's an organizer. Can't help himself—and Nellie's right in there pitching."

"They must be a hundred years old."

Ken grinned. She could see his white teeth in the semi-dark. "Not quite—early eighties, maybe. They're both strong and healthy far as I know. I think Bart was in his late seventies when he retired."

"How did they go about it?"

"About what?"

"Becoming number one? Taking charge?"

"Somebody has to plan and put things together, and they're good at it."

"You're not suggesting that no one else could do those things?"

"Of course not. Why are you on this subject? Are you sensing an undercurrent of resistance to the Hendersons?"

"No. But they won't live forever."

"I think you're exaggerating both their status and their enthusiasm for it. It might well be that they take on these chairmanships because nobody else wants to be bothered."

"Maybe," she said. She didn't believe him.

But when they arrived at the Club and had ascended the long, wide, brilliantly lit steps to the ballroom Susan noted that Bart Henderson stood there greeting people. And Nellie far away in back was inspecting the loaded buffet table and giving instructions. A closer look convinced her that Bart's thick white hair had grown whiter yet since she'd last seen this tall, solidly built gentleman. His wife, equally solid with a shape like a big tree trunk wore—astounding sight—the same gown she'd worn when Susan had observed her from afar on the previous gala occasion—just because Nell liked it, of course, since she could afford ten new outfits a week if she wanted them!

Bart turned his welcoming smile to Susan, shook Ken's hand, even put his arm around Susan's shoulders for a second. "If you happen to run across Nellie, would you tell her I need to see her?"

"Oh, I'll—" Sue, instantly ready, paused when he added, "Any time," and shrugged. At this she relaxed. People who'd known Kendrick all his life now hailed him as the Shields advanced through the crowd. Sue dropped off her wrap, and they moved out on to the floor. Ken had taught her dance steps he'd learned at an early age, had waltzed her through the house, tangoed and two-stepped with their children chasing after them, shrieking and mimicking. They floated about with practiced assurance while Susan kept an avid eye on the

Henderson's doings despite Ken's dismissive attitude. She spotted Nellie Henderson in her massive scalloped lace and murmured, "There she is Ken. Why don't you give Margery Stein a whirl while I talk to her?"

Nellie was conferring with the barkeep when Susan sidled up. "Having a good time, dearie?" Nellie held out a hand and Sue placed her own in it, vaguely flattered.

"Everything's lovely, and yes, I'm enjoying it."

"Where's that handsome man of yours?"

"Sent him to dance with Margery Stein."

"Good for you."

"By the way. Bart says he wants to see you— nothing rush, rush."

"Bet I know why." A smile illuminated Nellie's crinkled face.

Susan had an endless succession of partners and danced until she thought she'd drop. The men complimented her dress, her hair, her dancing. As she spun, dipped and swayed, she noticed that Nellie did get around to conferring with Bart. Later she saw Bart deep in conversation with Kendrick—not once, but three times, and observed when the two of them went off to another room together.

After a particularly breathtaking stomp she fled to the powder room. She'd just banged the door of a stall when a couple of women entered. At first while they primped and gossiped she paid no attention, but presently one said, "That Shield woman's a social climber and a snob. I don't understand what that nice Kendrick ever saw in her."

"Oh, I don't know," the other voiced a feeble protest.

"You didn't notice how they're playing up to the Henderson's?"

"Ken's known Bart all his life."

"But Susan's only now joined the Club. I've been a member for three years, and Nellie never felt obliged to keep the right partners coming *my*_way. I heard Nellie hinting to Mike Button that he should help make this a memorable debut for Susan—that's the word she used, debut—as if this were some kind of coming-out party for that woman."

Susan slipped off her shoes, stepped up on the commode and peered over the top of the stall. Billie Sutton, just as she'd suspected. She got down seething, wanted to barge out and say—what? Accuse the woman of jealousy? of spite? of having a loose tongue? What good would that do? She waited until the gossips had gone and gave the matter serious thought. What she needed in the Club were friends, not enemies. She had to placate Billie and stop the talk, little as she wanted to.

She filled a plate with food and went looking for her. Billie was seated—alone, thank God—on a settee in a corner. The woman's makeup failed to disguise her homely features, her royal blue dress muddied her complexion and her bitter expression made matters worse.

"Oh, there you are, Billie," Sue exclaimed. "I've been looking for you. Since you've belonged here longer than I have maybe you can help me out." She settled down beside the lady and began chomping her food in a rather common fashion. Presently she eased her shoes off. She elicited all sorts of unneeded advice and complimented Billie on her children who, oddly enough, were cheerful and good looking. When they parted she flashed an affectionate look at Billie who returned it with a rueful, half-apologetic smile.

Kendrick appeared. "Have to muscle in here and dance with my wife." The number was slow and dreamy and they held each other close. "Nice to see you befriending Billie," Ken muttered. "I've heard that people haven't tried extra hard to involve her since the Suttons joined and maybe she's felt neglected."

Susan didn't marvel at how he'd misunderstood her motives, but rejoiced that he had. And on the way home she didn't even have to pump him to get him to talk about his discussions with Bart. Ken was preoccupied with the man's finances. At age eighty-three Bart had begun to worry about the whole inheritance thing. "His three children have already taken over the various business ventures he started and are established. Investments he's been handling himself with help from brokerage firms, accountants and foundations. But now he thinks it's time to turn the whole thing over to a law firm."

"Yours."

"He broached that possibility."

"What would he want you to do?"

"It's complicated, but in a nutshell we'd set up and administer trust funds—an ongoing project."

"Sounds like you've pulled off a coup."

"Let's say my future would be assured—if this goes through."

"It will. You deserve this break."

Susan snuggled against Ken in their car, barely starting to warm up on this cold April night. "Once I climb down from this high I'm on, I'll know I'm exhausted," she sighed.

"Quite a shindig, wasn't it?"

"Yes, and we wuz the belles of the ball," she murmured getting sleepy.

Ken reacted predictably by bursting into laughter. "That was the last thing on my mind, but yes we were." There was a period of silence after which Kendrick mumbled, "The Hendersons are up to something." But Sue failed to answer. She was sleeping.

Their elation diminished abruptly when they reached home and found a telegram from Alice Sterne. Chancellor had died that morning. Susan telegraphed regrets and sent a tremendous spray of roses, but didn't take time away from family and Club to attend the funeral.

Chapter
16

Seated in darkness and occupied with prompting, Susan watched director Floretta Francke Griffin (always called Griffie) stride up and down the aisles of the little Club auditorium shouting encouragement and suggestions.

Divorced from a multi-millionaire, Griffie had time to devote herself to whatever caught her attention. For the last year drama had engaged her roaming imagination and she'd developed this core group to which she'd welcomed Susan.

Fair skinned with blue-black eyes and a rosy color—heightened by a tendency to high blood pressure, Griffie attracted admiration in spite of her too thin lips and small stature. Their current production, a little Irish piece, exacerbated Susan's nerves. She privately objected to the constant lamentation that Griffie considered appropriate. She also squirmed to hear the Irish accent employed by only one member of the cast. Griffie should have insisted on all or none, Sue thought, but was too determined to please this woman who'd grown up in the Club to risk offending.

At last rehearsal wound up with final speeches delivered by Tanya Larson in the old mother's role. Tanya never let people forget that she had acted on Broadway and in films. Susan closed the annotated script and rose, thankful to be done until the director stopped by with, "Suzi, I wonder if you'd work with Buddy on the set? He always needs reassurance."

"If you're sure reassurance is all—"

"Yes, that's all. And Sue, could you get Philippe to work on his lines? We're close to performance and he still reads from the book."

"I'll try." Susan pondered whether Griffin gave her these disagreeable tasks because she perceived that Sue would go the second or even third mile in her eagerness to be accepted by long-standing Club members.

Wearily obliging she stopped Buddy at the door and inquired how things were going.

"I wish someone who knows would see if the furniture and props pass muster."

"I don't know much, but I'll take a look tomorrow if you like."

"Gee thanks, Sue. Come earlyish, okay?"

Philippe's problem would require more subtle handling. After a couple days of intermittent consideration, Sue called the fair-haired Philippe, young looking at forty-four, and after she'd shyly mentioned how much she admired his technique inquired if he'd be willing to help her with her part—a few lines in the middle. He readily agreed to get together Saturday morning at his place.

Driving over there she mused that Philippe had tons of money—mostly by accident. His musical and acting talents merited an amateur rating. His current occupations consisted of sorting papers, banking checks and carrying on occasional correspondence with his deceased aunt's debtors or with realtors. Sue wondered if the lady had herself realized before dying that some of the farms she'd purchased would become choice areas of growth in the greater Philadelphia area. Her only heir, Philippe busied himself with appraisals, examining contents of drawers, and separating contracts and deeds from old tax receipts and other miscellany.

Susan parked and walked to the door where Philippe greeted her, a bagel in one hand.

"Want something? I'm just finishing breakfast." While Sue drank coffee she entertained herself by studying her host's flamboyant manners and arty appearance. He was showing off for her, but was he also flirting? She couldn't decide. His thick, stylishly cut hair and long curled mustache had an ash-blond tint so even that she suspected dye. Philippe flung his arms about and twisted his large hands theatrically while he talked.

They practiced together. Philippe encouraged Susan to loosen up and use more body language. She followed his direction. Then she begged him to go through the whole play while she provided clues so that she could watch and learn. They went through his parts again and again and after while Philippe (who had a quick memory) abandoned his script. With both hands freed he could create new effects.

When Susan at length glanced at her watch and exclaimed that she had to get back to her children Philippe seemed disappointed. Nonetheless she dashed off.

She deserved to be commended for her good work, but Griffie seemed not to notice. Her attention flew from one thing to another, and presently she found several other (mercifully less time-consuming) projects for Susan.

In the end, helping worry-wart Buddy proved more complicated than anything else. Once he'd found a sympathetic consultant in Sue he asked her about everything—how to stack the wood next to the fake fireplace, what color to paint the old rocking chair, whether the door frame might need another brace. He'd given Theatrical Supply his home address. Would Sue come to his house and help inventory the costumes when they arrived? Just to be sure they'd sent the right stuff in the right sizes. She tried to excuse herself, but Griffie overheard and seconded the request. Yet another day off work and she'd have to pay someone to sit. No other member of the troupe had her problems with money.

This discrepancy between her own carefully budgeted means and the wealth of other Club members rankled again as she drove up the Dake's long curved roadway. Buddy's uncertainty contrasted ludicrously with the splendor of his parent's estate. The long, low mansion built in Frank Lloyd Wright style stretched out endlessly and encompassed a huge swimming pool, tennis courts, five garages. Dake senior, a manufacturer, produced parts for airplanes and military equipment.

His oldest son, Buddy, led Susan through a maze of rooms and corridors to a place at the very back where deliveries were received and presently a UPS truck pulled up and a couple of minutes later three large boxes stood on a table in the bare little room. Inspection revealed only one mistake: the skirt Susan would wear was two sizes too large.

"That's terrible, Suzi!" Buddy cried, sincerely alarmed.

"Oh sure—it'll bring the theater crashing down all around us!" Susan laughed.

"What'll we do? Shall I get on the phone and make them express-mail another skirt?" In his distress Buddy, six feet of anxiety, strode up and down, covering the little room in two or three strides. "I'll have to find their phone number."

Susan held the shapeless skirt against herself. "It's okay."

"How can you say that?"

"I'll take a couple of tucks in it." When he evinced incredulity she lost patience. "Climb down from the ceiling, will you?" She couldn't believe he was thirty years old!

But he was. At least so Gertrude Joslin, the Club's Director of Recreation, claimed. And Gertrude tended to know everything about everybody. He'd kept going to school, his latest study a Ph.D. in history. Gertrude suspected him of trying to cop out of the family business, although an MBA did figure among his academic degrees.

In the end, the performance, attended by friends and relatives of the actors and a faithful coterie of the Club's theater buffs, went off without a hitch. Standing with other actors to take a bow Susan felt she rightly deserved her share of applause. Griffie came on stage and accepted bouquets from cast and audience.

A few days later Gertrude Joslin in her role as recreation chairperson, called Susan to chat. "That was our first real success," Mrs. Joslin confided. "We've sort of halted and limped along till you joined."

"Oh, Gertrude, it was a team effort. You know that." Toward the end, Gertrude had assisted with props and advertising.

"But teams have to be synchronized. That's what you've done—provided synchronization."

To Sue's embarrassment Gertrude went on and on in the same vein. She knew all about Sue's work with Philippe and Buddy though Susan had never talked about it except to Kendrick who invariably kept his counsel. Gertrude must have pumped the other actors. She hung up feeling uneasy. Was Gertrude developing an animosity toward their director? The poor woman wasn't perfect, but what did it matter? They were only acting for the fun of it, and the degree of success or failure was hardly a life-and-death concern.

She asked Kendrick if he thought Gertrude might want to direct the plays herself. "Doesn't sound like Gert. Sees herself as a kingmaker, not a king." Ken took the last plates out of the dishwasher and stacked them in the cupboard while Susan finished the last pot. She watched him out of the corner of her eyes. How brown, how warm, how wise he was!

Turning, he caught the look of admiration and immediately wanted to "forget about Gert." He untied Sue's apron murmuring, "Suzi, my Suzi!" And she was in his arms, delighted to have so adept a lover, full of laughter because sometimes they didn't bother to mount the stairs, but made love on the sofa.

Gertrude seemed to have no intention of letting Sue forget her, however. After their next casting session she invited Sue to lunch. "My husband might be there or he might not," Gert said. "Anyway, we'll have a chance to talk." A talk with Gertrude was okay. A chance to meet Vergil Joslin, famous for his proliferating schemes, all of which prospered, would be a plum.

The Joslins lived in a genuine Colonial mansion, restored at least twice. The noble white columns, two stories tall stood out against the dark old brick. The cobbled drive that curved around the front had been carefully preserved, but beside the house a new paved lot connected with a brick walk leading to the grand entrance. This was the obvious place to park. Susan left her car and found Gertrude waiting in the foyer. "I thought we might lunch on the patio," she remarked, "but it's too hot." She led the way to an air conditioned dining room which looked out through a tinted glass wall into a pool and garden. Susan suspected that this obviously modern part of the building had been added at a later date.

Vergil, to Sue's carefully concealed delight, was indeed present—looking relaxed and casual. While they consumed artichokes for their first course, Sue idly compared Gertrude and Vergil. Neither would attract a second glance from people who didn't know them. Gertrude—buxom, gray-haired, dim-eyed, middle aged—chattered on and on in uninflected tones until the conversation was preempted by her husband.

Vergil—only slightly taller and heavier had the same gray hair, but his eyes were steely bright and his gaze disconcertingly direct. He concentrated his attention on Susan, using recurrent phrases such as, "tell me," or "what do you know about—?" or "what's your experience with—?"

She found herself expanding on the business of her travel agency, supplying more specific details than was her wont. He listened intently. "You work hard for your money," he concluded.

"People have encouraged me to open my own agency, but I'm not crazy to starve for however long it takes to get established."

"Very wise. Have you ever considered selling houses?" The question came up casually, but Sue thought, "He really cares about my answer to this."

"No. Wouldn't I need a license?"

"Short course—easy exam."

"But my boss where I am is so—considerate! And I more or less set my own hours."

"That's important," Vergil agreed, letting the subject drop.

"Ready for dessert?" Gertrude asked. Sue had consumed chicken salad, broccoli and carrots and an assortment of rolls almost without noticing, she thought guiltily. She glanced at her hostess, but Gert looked preoccupied with her own concerns, thank heaven.

After lunch Vergil disappeared and Gert insisted that Susan sit awhile longer and have another cup of tea. Proffering sugar and lemon she inquired, "Well, Sue—how do you feel about becoming our director?"

"We have a more-than-adequate director already. I haven't the slightest interest in—"

"But the Group has lots of interest in you. Before you joined we had a string of performances varying from semi-prepared to just plain clumsy."

"Oh, not that bad, surely."

"That bad. We've been needing a change."

"Really, Gertrude," Susan fidgeted and squeezed lemon into her tea. "I'm completely loyal to Griffie and will give her my support."

Gertrude nodded in that way she had of knowing the score better than anyone else.

And now Susan began to pick up rumbles of dissatisfaction from Tanya, Philippe and Buddy. She sensed Gertrude's subverting influence. When their director gave Susan jobs she performed them with a will, keeping in the background as much as possible and letting everyone know that she was carrying out Griffie's orders. Was Gertrude angry because Griffie's last chosen play had only three parts with any substance? Buddy as the old servant had his first acting role and Susan became producer in his place. Philippe and, of course Tanya, who couldn't be left out, completed the cast.

Gertrude claimed to be enjoying a rest. She declined to assist until the very end when she consented to handle ticket sales.

At the performance (a success) Gertrude embarrassed Sue by rising in the audience and calling for the production manager to take a bow. Susan declined until Griffie came backstage to get her, whereupon she stood with the director for a roaring ovation.

Not long after that Gertrude waylaid her and announced that things looked good. "You'll be taking over."

"I will not! And Gertrude, if you don't like the way Griffie's doing things, don't you think you should have a talk with her instead of telling the rest of the world?"

Gertrude listened judiciously and at first shook her head. Then she nodded. "Maybe you're right. Maybe it's time for me to talk to her."

Chapter
17

At the next meeting of the Drama Group Griffie resigned. She'd enjoyed her stint as director, but thought it time for someone else to take over. She named no one, but Susan, chagrined when several people gave her knowing looks, felt embarrassed.

Disturbed, she took action, called Griffie and asked if she could drop by. Floretta Francke Griffin lived in a deluxe condominium development near the far edge of the Club golf course. Sue reflected that anyway she'd always wanted to see inside one of these impressive units, rumored to have sold for double the price of a substantial house.

Griffie who'd moved in rather recently wanted to show her around. The curve of the immense living room was emphasized by a similarly curved balcony with a decorative metal railing. The huge bedrooms boasted walk-in dressing-room closets and luxurious baths, the kitchen displayed every known piece of gadgetry.

Griffie, curled up in a white brocade chair, sighed and lamented that she hated to leave all this luxury so soon after moving in. "No, no. I won't be away forever," she responded to Sue's shocked inquiry.

"I'll be wintering in the South of France. An old pal has taken a villa and wants me to share the expenses. So I'm off for a few months."

"Sounds thrilling!" After examining photos of the villa and its setting, Sue ventured to say that she hoped friction in the Drama Group hadn't influenced Griffie's decision.

"Might've speeded things up a bit. But as soon as I heard from Tim I knew I'd have to go."

"Well, I for one will miss you."

"You're a lamb, Suzi, I don't know how I'd have managed without you." Griffie's face puckered and Sue feared that she might cry. But the woman controlled herself. "Gertrude has been critical."

"I know. But I think you've done splendidly, and I hope you'll take over again as soon as you get back."

"Oh, I don't see how I could!"

While Susan lent a sympathetic ear Griffie waxed eloquent about the persecution she'd endured, the long hours she'd put in, the difficulties she'd had to overcome. She talked too long and revealingly and Susan's desire to buttress the lady's position faded. Susan departed at last, her faith shaken, but thankful that Griffie's mercurial attention had shifted to her trip to France.

In the end it was Philippe who approached Susan and requested on behalf of the Group that she become their new director.

"But I have no formal training. And very little experience."

"Oh well, we're all mostly amateurs. And you have such practical good sense about things."

"I wouldn't touch it while Griffie's still here."

"Don't see why you'd have to."

Having given oblique consent, Susan focused her mind on the Group. They should spend their time doing something more substantive, she decided. A month after her thirty-sixth birthday in September she began production of "Hedda Gabler" a full-length play that had always fascinated her. She attracted a few new actors and a set designer and persuaded Buddy that he could indeed play the part of the villainous Judge Brack.

"But I'm not at all like that!" he protested.

"Of course not. That's what acting's all about. You can do it."

"Oh, I don't see how—"

"I'll help you."

Susan entertained herself with visions of the diffident Buddy taking on Brack's aggressive and resolute character.

She showed him how to enter the stage at all times with an air of taking charge and to project an image of self-confidence bordering on smugness. Tentatively at first but with growing enjoyment Buddy gradually assumed the requisite appearance of hardness, spurred on by the admiration of his fellow actors.

Eager but rather unsure of herself, Susan accepted suggestions from the cast, especially Tanya and Philippe. She admired the way that Tanya at fifty-six could appear youthful and impulsive as the brooding, irrational Hedda. They'd had several lengthy discussions before she persuaded Tanya that Hedda was psychotic. But once convinced, Tanya colored her performance with that tinge of mania that Susan considered indispensable for the audience to accept the character's final act of suicide.

Gertrude, competent in the part of Thea, prophesied a sensational hit. And if, in the end, it didn't quite merit that exaggerated term, at least it had been well enough received, Susan determined.

She declared a recess. Everyone, including her long-suffering family, deserved a break before they tackled another production. She spent more time on her job and with the family and read dozens of plays. She hadn't yet settled on a choice for their next production when Gertrude started dropping hints that people were talking about a Gilbert and Sullivan opera.

"Not with me as director," Sue declared. "I don't know music."

"You wouldn't really need to," Gertrude affirmed. And sometime later Gertrude reported that she'd heard rumors that the Club wanted to produce a smashing "Mikado" in place of a Spring Ball. With a reception afterwards to give the children a night of dancing, of course. Gertrude called debutantes and men in their twenties children.

Susan grumbled and again rejected the idea, but her imagination fired at the image of herself in the highly visible role of organizing the venerated Spring Benefit. Should she risk doing it?

The moment of decision came when she was also approached by none other than Henderson, Chairman of the Club Board. "There's so much enthusiasm for the project," he promised, "that you'll have no trouble recruiting help of all kinds. And maybe Kendrick would assist with the music?"

This last suggestion clinched the matter for Sue. Yes, she could organize, and if Ken were involved they might have fun working together. She appealed to him at once, alight with enthusiasm.

Kendrick, always responsive to her moods, struggled between his willingness to oblige her and his reluctance to commit the time. Finally he consented to participate "this once. But never again. Agreed?"

"Of course. I know it's far from a major interest." Susan hugged and kissed him, happily aware that he'd lend an overtone of professional know-how. Sure enough, he located certain members of the Philadelphia Symphony who regularly moonlighted, added Club members who had essential musical talent and hired a music director.

Susan found bit parts for her children and the whole family piled into the car and went to rehearsals for many weeks. She was able to cast Tanya, Gertrude and Buddy in satisfactory roles, thankful to have these faithful and familiar faces around. Buddy, trained in music along with his other numerous attainments, accepted a major part without demur. Philippe coached the singers, and the former set designer shouldered over-all production.

With so much help she should have an easy time of it, Sue thought, but complexities multiplied and arguments erupted. Long before dress rehearsal she began to feel stressed and worn. But the great night came at last and the rollicking performance delighted a packed house. When it ended newspaper photographers appeared and snapped an abundance of pictures.

In the Club ballroom afterwards Kendrick and Susan put in a token appearance. Susan watched Buddy with amazement. Clearly popular he scrupulously divided gallant attentions among a dozen partners. As he danced past her with a remarkably lovely girl Sue heard him say, "Call me Budrow," in his firmest Brackian voice.

Mercifully a peaceful Sunday followed. After a late and hearty brunch prepared as a team effort, the family settled in the living room with sections of the newspaper: Susan with Travel and Business. Presently Eileen with the society news cried, "Mom, here's your picture!"

With both parents bending over her, Eileen read the generally flattering review of the Benefit performance, proceeds to go to the Children's Hospital. The one photo (out of dozens taken) that the newspaper had chosen to reproduce showed Susan with three other people. The caption read: Director, Susan Shields, receives congratulations from cast member, Budrow Dakes and financier Vergil Joslin and wife Gertrude.

"Well, Suzi, you're famous," Kendrick laughed going back to the news. Sue tried to laugh too but a conviction that she'd arrived, that she'd become a recognized member of Philadelphia high society thrilled her more profoundly than she dared to show.

On Monday drab reality set in. She had to find lunch money for the kids and drop them at school. She'd taken so much time off work that her backlog of contacts had dwindled. She had accumulated little in her savings account and two years of the five-year Club membership had sped past her. She couldn't afford all that time with amateur theatricals! On the other hand, it was her chief tie with other members of the Club. On this gray morning, stopped by rush-hour traffic at several busy intersections, she had time to think and to admit that her picture had appeared in the paper only because of her association with members of the influential Dakes and Joslin families. Money was the key to everything. To be somebody in her own right she and Kendrick had to live in a bigger house, drive better cars! She cranked the motor, disgusted when her car stalled at a light.

That evening she asked Kendrick how soon he thought he'd be made a full partner. Nonplussed, he lowered the *Journal of Law* he'd been reading and, not for the first time in their some fifteen years of marriage, favored her with a wary look.

"Need money? I don't have much surplus right now, but in a month I should be getting a fair-sized bonus."

"Oh, Ken—sorry I brought it up. We're perfectly comfortable here. It's just that—well, I guess I miss the money I used to earn before I got so wound up with the Drama Group."

"You could sign off the Drama Group. But not unless that suits you, of course."

"I'm thinking about doing that."

Though he said nothing more at that moment he eventually got around to telling Sue that he guessed it might be another five or ten years before he could hope to reach the top rung in his profession.

Her dilemma was unexpectedly solved when Susan got a call one evening from no less a personage than the Club President. One of the board members had died leaving a vacancy. And since Susan had shown so much initiative and worked so hard this past year they'd decided to offer her a position on the club board. He assured her that the job would require her presence at a meeting only once a month. With something bordering on awe she accepted. New members were elected by the existing board, a self-perpetuating institution, and lasted for life or as long as anyone of them chose to serve.

Now that her status was thus assured, Susan thankfully detached herself from the Drama Group, announcing her resignation with a feeling of relief.

A few weeks later, to her astonishment, Griffie (back from France) took over once again, apparently backed by Gertrude, the Omniscient!

Sue now dedicated herself with sober industry to work in the Travel Agency. And when, a few weeks later, Ken brought her his bonus check with the proposal that she use it however she saw fit, she reproached herself for expressing discontent. She hadn't however totally lost sight of her long-held dream of owning her own agency. If she could start earning more maybe the bigger house wasn't entirely out of the question. Ken would move upward in his own deliberate way, she perceived. So if the family were to make great strides forward, she would have to provide the impetus. One day a board member carelessly alluded to the fact that Ken had first been offered the slot she now filled and had declined in her favor. She felt no surprise.

A year later on her birthday in May, the eleven-year-old Eileen declared that they no longer needed a sitter. "I can look after Teddy."

"Nobody needs to look after me," Teddy objected.

"Oh, shut up. Would you rather have a sitter?" Eileen silenced him with a look.

"We'll think about it," Susan replied.

When consulted, Ken observed that Eileen was unusually responsible for her age, she did have their phone numbers and knew what to do in an emergency. Sue reflected that Eileen had been helping out around the house since age nine and for the past six months had completed most of the preparations for dinner before Sue got home.

She had a serious talk with the children, and then without regret dispensed with the glum retired lady who'd come in afternoons to watch television and yell at the kids to stop fighting. Another saving to add her slow accumulation of money for club memberships and the other signs of affluence that she so coveted.

Chapter
18

On the first day of a new term when she stopped to let her children out at their school and Eileen stayed in the car Susan turned inquiringly to look at her daughter in the back seat and felt startled at how grown up she looked. "I'm in Middle School now! You have to take me up the street," Eileen declared. "I can't believe you didn't remember."

"Of course I remember. It only slipped my mind for a split second. I'm so used to letting you two out together."

At the next stop Sue said cheerfully, "You're looking great, Eileen. Have a wonderful first day."

"Thanks, Mom." Mollified, Eileen flashed a replica of her father's affectionate smile and started up the walk as Susan made a fast getaway. "I'm late for work," she reflected. "It's incredible that Eileen's in Middle School and that I'll soon be forty." She felt particularly bitter today because at the end of last week she'd had to withdraw a huge chunk from her savings. As a Board member she'd had to vote (along with everyone else) for a substantial increase in fees.

Without it the Club couldn't meet their budget. She hated being reminded that the Kendrick Shields family really couldn't afford to belong.

Still, the Club! The Club provided her sole link to a world she valued. Examination of logistics and costs had convinced her that she was far from having money enough to start her own travel agency. And even if she did there was no guarantee that it would prove the bonanza she hoped for.

At work she glanced over her calendar. She was lunching with Gertrude Joslin, a bright spot in an otherwise dull day. Gertrude came uptown infrequently, but made a point of meeting Susan once or twice a month. Along with gossiping about the Club Theater she imparted juicy bits of information about her husband's business deals. Susan had a strong impression that Vergil Joslin profited more from buying, selling and renting properties acquired for his own purposes than from representing sellers. Recently, for instance, he'd bought and renovated an office building. Now, Gertrude reported in her usual quiet voice, her faded eyes devoid of feeling, he was in the process of a re-sale that promised a more than satisfactory profit. Without emphasis Joslin's wife still managed to convey her sense of satisfaction in this lucrative exchange.

In lulls between patrons that afternoon Susan mulled this over. Clearly there was more money in real estate than in travel. She began to toy with the notion of making a change—even at close to forty, even though she'd had no experience in real estate. She was getting nowhere in the job she now held.

Next time she saw Gertrude she asked whether Vergil had an opening for a new agent.   Gertrude shrugged. "Maybe."

"Think he'd hire me?"

"That would be up to Vergil. I have no say-so. Did he ever talk to you about it?"

"Mentioned it once—four years ago."

"Oh, well in that case I guess he'd be glad to hear from you."

She approached Vergil himself with her question to which he replied, "Thought you'd never ask."

Kendrick urged her on. "If you're bored try something different. I know you'll do well."

The real estate course intrigued her, the exam posed no problem and within weeks she was ready for the big switch. "But before I start, let's take a long vacation, Ken." She knew that once into her new job there'd be no time for it. Ken, who'd urged time-out for both of them more than once welcomed the idea. He couldn't remember when they'd enjoyed a real family outing! They left for the airport on the first day of school vacation and spent three weeks in London, Paris, and Rome. Everywhere Kendrick wanted to stay longer. He lingered behind in the Louvre and in St. John's Cathedral. "We'll have to come back!" he'd cry at every turn.

Immensely diverted, Sue kept thinking, "I've got to remember this!" Something to talk about when people mentioned Europe.

From the beginning selling houses brought more money even though Vergil had warned that it would take a while to establish herself. He had, however, seen to it that a discreet mention of her new occupation appeared in the "Goings-on" Column in the Club Newsletter. To her relief people actually approached her about selling their houses or asked if she knew of a bargain they might buy.

"Oh, Ken," she crowed privately, "All these years with the Club are paying off!" He laughed and hugged her, shared her enthusiasm, congratulated her on every sale.

Even when, after a few years, her earnings exceeded his, he showed no resentment. Often she spent time on the phone in the kitchen where she'd installed a small desk. Ken sat in his favorite chair in the living room with papers and books around him and worked on his cases. His earnings had increased and he expected to become a full partner "very soon."

The fly in this wonderfully fragrant ointment was the enormous percentage of every commission that Joslin's Agency retained. She also observed to her amazement that many colleagues came and went, failing to make the grade. Few shared her delight in initiating contacts. Most suffered more over deals that fell through. Susan kept busy. Inevitable slip-ups she charged off to inexperience and directed her attention to the next transaction. Gradually she learned that a climate of active enterprise helped everyone, not just herself. In Joslin's frequent absences she began to encourage, advise and even to gently nudge other agents.

Success fostered feelings of independence and her ambitions grew. She toyed with the idea of going it alone—having her own setup. Maybe she could work out of her home to start with. But before she got around to seriously planning a break, Vergil approached her about managing his agency as a franchise. The residential sales office, only one of Vergil's myriad interests, rated low on his scale of priorities. He spent no more than one or two hours a day there and all pressing matters had to be wedged into that short span. On the day of his conference with Susan, however, he appeared totally unhurried—stopped by with a coffee cup in his hand, sat down in her office and with those sharp gray eyes studied her reactions to a series of questions. He agreed with all she said, praised her, claimed she was a "natural born realtor" and at last inquired whether she'd like to "take over and run things here."

Susan knew that he'd received contracts from state and federal governments and that he would soon be overseeing construction of several buildings. Still, she protested, "I thought that was your job."

"Don't have time for it any more."

Cautious, she then asked, "What sort of deal are you considering?"

He'd drawn up papers and would have his secretary bring them over. "You are interested, right?"

"Maybe." No sense appearing too eager,

Sue decided. He gave her a confident smile, rose and squeezed her shoulder before departing. "I wouldn't offer this chance to just anybody. You know that, don't you?"

"Thanks, Vergil."

The Agreement took up little more than a page. Susan studied it in odd moments between clients and phone calls. She jotted figures and arrived at what she considered the probable advantage to herself. Just before five, Vergil reappeared.

"Well, what did you think? Want to proceed?"

"I'm tempted. But since this is a five-year contract—"

"We can half that time if you prefer."

"I'd prefer that."

He nodded, picked up the paper, took a pen from his pocket and altered the contract. Then he signed his name and pushed it across to her with a pleased look.

She drew it to her but stopped, pen in the air. "What am I doing? I always make it a policy to sleep on anything that requires a signature."

"Good idea. Tomorrow, then." Vergil smiled once more and departed, but she could tell that she'd frustrated a clear intention to "wrap it up."

"Basically, I run the office and pay all expenses. He gets a percent," she told Kendrick at dinner that evening.

"His percentage is part of the take after all expenses are paid?"

"No, the contract says gross." She passed the

paper to Ken.

He turned it back and forth—"Where's the financial report? How does he expect you to know what the expenses are—for this year anyway. There has to be an annual report for the last year in his file. You should see that. And monthly reports for the current year."

"You're making me glad I didn't sign," Susan murmured. "I'll ask for those figures tomorrow."

"After all, it's your life, Suzi. You have a right to complete information when you're about to commit your time and considerable expertise."

The next day, when she asked for the financial reports, Joslin said, "Oh, didn't I send those in to you?"

Then she had to insist that she needed at least a week to study things. Vergil dropped his affectionate pose and became businesslike. "Who are you consulting?"

"Kendrick." Sometime she would have to figure out why that surprised him.

The actual expense of operating the office far exceeded the estimates she'd made. She cut Vergil's percentage twice before she felt satisfied. He'd never accept that, she decided. But so what. Even with all its risks and difficulties, leaving Joslin completely and getting out on her own still looked better than the offer he'd first tendered.

She appealed to Ken. "How can I handle this— it's about to become a touchy situation."

"You could present an alternate contract.

Actually, there are a few legalities that weren't addressed that probably should have been. And you could change over to a percent of net. That way the reduction would look less glaring."

"Would you draw it up for me?" Susan felt shy. She'd seldom before asked for legal aid, and never for anything on this scale.

"Glad to," he agreed promptly.

Vergil took the alternate contract home to look it over. When wife Gertrude asked, "Well?" he replied that it boxed him in very neatly. "I can handle Sue by herself or Kendrick by himself, but this team effort put me in a corner."

"So will you accept it"

"I'll take it naturally. I could get a better percentage from Brad Wise. But he's not nearly so greedy. Susan will build up the business, and in the end I'll be better off."

"The alternative, no doubt, would be to have her for a competitor," Gertrude agreed.

Joslin's unerring judgment proved correct. Two years later the office employed twice as many agents and the volume of business had more than doubled.

And besides all that, Susan had learned how to use both the capital she managed to accumulate and her inside information to ferret out sensational deals. She bought low and resold, netting twenty, thirty, or even larger percentages.

Once when she'd boasted at the evening meal that she'd purchased a house at half its value Ken asked in a pleasant way whether she'd outlined the true market conditions to the seller.

"The old duffer just wanted to unload his place in a hurry. He didn't need to hear a lengthy explanation about market conditions," she answered, instantly defensive. "No, Eileen, don't get up. I'll bring the dessert."

The youngsters, now fifteen and thirteen, took turns cleaning up after dinner, but Eileen and her mother shared the chore of getting food on the table. Eileen treasured the time to talk about her school concerns and, infrequently, to report what Teddy was doing that bothered her.

"He's only thirteen and he's riding Bobby's motorcycle up and down the road—really fast."

"Hmmm—sounds like your father should fill him in on the legal implications in case of accident or injury. That should give him food for thought."

Susan had some food for thought herself. That morning she'd looked at the Granville Estate and had instantly wanted to buy it. If they owned that big spread Teddy could channel some of his preoccupation with wheels into operation of a big tractor-type mower.

As soon as she'd heard that the last of the ancient Granville sisters was dying she'd hired a detective to find out what disposition would be made of their property. None of the sisters had married, it seemed, and the house, along with everything else, had been left to Jefferson Powell, pastor of a now-defunct church, the only person, it seemed, who'd taken a consistent interest in the only surviving sister, half blind and in her dotage. Susan visited the pastor, an old man himself, and asked what he planned to do with his inheritance.

Arthritic and feeble, he lived contentedly on his pensions and puttered in his garden. "I wouldn't know what to do with the place. It's simply enormous. I almost wish she hadn't left it to me."

"Don't you have a favorite charity?" Sue asked, telling herself to keep her eagerness under wraps.

"Well, yes. But what would they do with it?"

"Suppose I sell it for you?" Susan won the man's confidence, and after Miss Granville's funeral he relied on her to chart the way through a maze of legalities that developed. The grounds were closed temporarily and a jungle of high grass, weeds, unpruned bushes and wild vines quickly grew up. Things at last reached a point, however, at which it would be possible to get the pastor's signature on a contract to act as his agent.

Instead, Susan wanted to buy the house herself. She liked its look—all glass, granite and marble, open to the pool and to acres of gardens.

She lured Ken into the car and took him to inspect the Estate. "Beautiful," he said, walking around like a tourist, devoid of any sense of possessiveness.

"We can buy it."

"No, Sue. Think what the taxes and insurance alone would cost."

"Now that I'm running the agency, we can swing it."

"Admit that we'd be completely broke for a long time if we did."

"Well, yes.   But if we could sell the Georgian—"

"I don't want to do that."

"You're sentimentally attached, I know. But—"

"I refuse to sell it, Susan. That's my last word on the subject."

In the end they compromised—rented the Georgian to a lovely retired couple and moved onto the Granville Estate. Teddy loved it, ran through the mammoth rooms with their marble floors, shouted to Eileen to come see the swimming pool, ran back to his mother's side. "Show me my room! Which one is my room?"

Eileen walked around uncertain. "It's so big. Not a bit homey, Mom. I like the other house better. Why do we have to move?"

Sue had to be away when the men brought their furniture over. Kendrick and Eileen managed things. By placing Susan's antique secretary and the old buffet on one side and a sideboard on the other they defined an area next to the kitchen about the size and shape of the dining room at the old house. "A place to feel cozy in," Eileen explained. Sue felt more amused than anything else about this clinging to the old ways. Their placement of her other antiques also entertained her. The gate-leg table and the French boudoir chair stood in the foyer where they would garner endless admiration in years to come. The chest of drawers she found in her bedroom along with her favorite old prints from Clara Bowman's house. The Tiffany lamp hovered over the same piece of furniture it had illuminated in their previous home.

Susan's possessive spirit expanded to fill the great spaces in the new residence. The openness, the oneness with the out-of-doors induced by great floor-to-ceiling windows inspired her. Entertaining in the old place had been confined to small dinner parties, but here—eventually—her imagination soared.

Sooner than she'd thought possible after the move they hosted a splendid summer party that included Kendrick's colleagues and boasted a magnificent buffet, swimming and dancing. Within weeks Kendrick advanced to senior status. He might not appreciate certain efforts she made on his behalf, Sue realized, but he said nothing, and she privately commended herself for the clever way she'd cultivated Ken's peers and superiors.

Now she could count on the cash he brought home to handle day-to-day expenses. With her own funds she paid insurance and taxes and made investments, often borrowing to the limit.

Years of unremitting activity passed. One day the clock Susan had installed to help her keep track of time chimed loudly in her neat, rather barren office with its metal file cabinets and narrow table along the wall loaded with papers. She looked up from her desk and forced herself to listen. With her thoughts and her calculator silenced, she could hear the total quiet of the deserted agency. Everyone had gone home an hour

ago. And now she too had to go. She sighed—was so
close to figuring out the balance she had to maintain in
order to remain solvent, and now she had to interrupt
the process and go eat with the family. And afterwards
she'd have to put in all that time planning meals and
discussing domestic affairs with the live-in housekeeper
she'd hired. The phone would keep ringing and she'd
have to answer and juggle invitations that came in ever-
growing numbers.

"I need a girl Friday," she said aloud. And while
she drove home she warmed to the idea. A right-hand
man—woman actually—could pay for her own salary
in deals salvaged, economies instituted, invaluable time
saved for knitting up loose ends. And knitting up loose
ends now preoccupied Sue. She'd begun living close
to the edge, gambling as it were, on her guesses about
probable directions in the real estate market. She turned
her money over rapidly, usually cleared a substantial
profit, and reinvested immediately, But nothing could
be left to chance. She had no margin to fall back on if
anything went wrong.

After dinner and after the housekeeper went
to her quarters, Susan continued to perch on a stool
by the kitchen counter close to the phone. She could
hear Kendrick talking to his children. She ran through
the household accounts. Mrs. Bird hadn't followed all
her instructions. She could detect waste in purchasing
and in handling contracted-for service. She tossed the
bills into their folder and taking a pad from a drawer
began to compose an ad. Maybe "girl Friday" wasn't

a term that would appeal to the person she envisaged. "Administrative Assistant" sounded too high brow. "Assistant Manager" seemed to work. She went on, "needed to organize educational, business and social details. Flexible hours. Salary—" She hung poised for a moment, then wrote, "negotiable. Send resume to—" She put down the office address.

Absorbed, she failed to see Kendrick till he was there in front of her. His appreciative glance took in her shoes, kicked off on the floor, her long silky legs, her silk blouse, unbuttoned halfway, sleeves pushed up to reveal her arms, still smooth and youthful.

She experienced a surge of thankfulness that, in middle age, she was still desirable. When her husband lifted her down from the stool she went into his arms laughing like a girl.

Her ad ran for two weeks and she received printed resumes from highly-paid traveling salesmen, specialized secretaries and from one social worker who wrote at the bottom, "What kind of job is this?"

When she called a few of the prospects and explained her situation, many declined even to be interviewed. A few showed up and spent the time specifying which responsibilities they'd assume. She'd been a fool to imagine she could locate a person willing to act as a surrogate mother, an informed real estate representative and a social secretary, all in one.

Just when she'd given up, a resume that had obviously been prepared to order arrived. It listed experience in office work and teaching. The woman's education, Sue observed with astonishment, included a Bachelor of Music from Harvard!

She called the indicated number immediately and when a deep voice responded she inquired frankly why Miss Powell, a Harvard grad, would be interested in a job with so many facets, none musical.

"That's its whole appeal. I'm interested in a dozen things. I hate a job that ties me to an invariable routine."

Josephine Powell agreed guardedly to come to the house for an interview. "I can't say for sure that I'd want the job. And maybe you won't like me. But we'll see."

After arranging a time, Susan hung up alive with hope. That wonderful voice with its Harvard accent! So professional sounding, so intelligent!

Her disappointment hit all the harder next day when she opened the door at the stipulated hour and confronted a six-foot-four black woman.

"You're not—" she began, hoping for a Jehovah's Witness.

"Yes. I'm Josephine Powell."

She'd come quite a distance and Sue had to let her in and talk to her. It was impossible, of course. Could this woman stoop to overseeing housekeeping, chauffeuring the kids and dealing with real estate clients—or could she?

Josephine, attractive in a pearl gray suit that heightened the lavender sheen of her perfect black skin, regarded Sue with a humorous twinkle in her large dark eyes. Her well-proportioned body and broad handsome face communicated a self-respecting strength.

Susan soon felt that it was Josephine who was conducting the interview: Yes, she'd expect the person she hired to live on the premises. Susan had a husband and two teen-age children. Yes, it was a critical time for them. No, the employee she was looking for wouldn't do housework, but would oversee the workers both inside and on the grounds. She needed someone willing to learn real estate. People persisted in calling the house, and a little intelligent help could go a long way toward cementing the good relationships that led to sales and listings.

The Shields' calendar sat by the phone in the hall. Just letting friends know of pervious engagements would save precious time. Yes, sometimes they invited rather large groups of people for parties and this would involve hiring caterers, et cetera. "Sounds like you've had your hands full," Josephine concluded.

By this time Susan wished that she could hire Josephine. But it looked impossible. Miss Powell rose. "Frankly," Sue admitted, standing, "I don't understand why you don't go back to teaching music."

"I have a naturally big voice," Josephine replied unselfconsciously. "I can't remember a time in my life when I wasn't singing. I was up on the platform while I was still a tot. My mother cleaned houses to pay for music lessons. At thirteen I joined the church choir."

"So young?"

"I was tall for my age. Still am." That ironic smile again.

"How did you happen to go to Harvard?"

"One of my high school teachers started sending me around to music contests. When I won a national contest the judges helped me apply for a full scholarship to Harvard. I put in four great years there, practiced more than the five hours a day they required and earned my degree. But oddly enough, music isn't my first love. I never wanted to tour the country singing, although an agent approached me about doing that. For a while I taught music in the public school. Nobody wanted me to leave, but I felt restless, couldn't help remembering that in high school I'd held a whole bunch of offices and edited the year book."

"And kept up your grades, no doubt."

"Naturally."

Remembering her own struggles to excel, Sue felt a rush of sympathy.

"So what I'm looking for," Josephine continued, "is a job where I'd do six different things. I need to keep learning something—need to organize my own time."

"I understand," Susan murmured. She'd accompanied Miss Powell to the door, then to her little red car before she realized that she was doing it.

"I think I may take this job," Josephine Powell remarked, folding her impressive length into the car seat. "But first, you have to think about it." She smiled really broadly, displaying for the first time a spectacular set of teeth.

After that final remark Susan thought Miss Powell had reversed their roles with a vengeance. She should send her a note saying that she'd made other arrangements. Instead, she thought of all the advantages of hiring her. What was it that so impressed her about the woman? Back at her desk that day a word came to Susan: integrity. "The woman's an angel," she thought and added ruefully, "a giant black angel."

When she called several days later to ascertain whether Josephine wanted the position, Jo (as she wished to be called) first made a solemn pronouncement: "I'm conservative in politics and orthodox in religion. Does that bother you?"

"Not remotely."

Josephine then named a salary higher than the figure Susan had in mind. And after Sue had accepted it Jo said, "We have to sign a contract. As a business person I know you understand the importance of having things spelled out."

Kendrick and the children, intrigued by the idea of having a new face in the house—especially a black one—volunteered to help with the contract. Teddy, fifteen, languidly proposed that her duties should encompass bringing Mitzie over to do homework with him.

"I wonder if she could help me with my recital piece," Eileen mused. She now played her father's recorder and the piano.

"Ken?" Susan interrupted appealing to her husband.

He obliged with an official-looking page. "The main items are salary and period of employment. I left other matters vague since you said she wants to organize her own time."

Although Josephine would stay with the Shields for ten years and receive annual raises, no mention of the contract was ever again made by any of those concerned.

Josephine Powell moved into one of the apartments over the four-car garage. She and the housekeeper were the only live-in employees. Josephine quickly won the other's friendship with her air of casual camaraderie, and together the two planned ways to cut household expenses.

The night course in real estate that Jo attended at Sue's request proved a breeze. "Amusing" was Josephine's word for it. And becoming a licensed agent seemed to provide what Susan perceived as a need for novelty in the black woman's unremittingly active life.

She rapidly gained respect and acceptance wherever she turned. Sue quickly came to trust her to carry on alone, and when tough financial matters kept her riveted to her computer at the office she'd stay on and on, confident that the whole household prospered in competent hands.

Once, when detained until almost midnight she drove into the parking area of her home and simply sat there, too exhausted to move. Her tired eyes moved across the expanse of windows at the rear of the house—

all dark. Then a light snapped on over one of the garages and after a moment another light in the kitchen. She climbed out of the car and entered, surprised to see Jo putting food into the microwave.

"I hope you didn't get up on my account. You never have to do that."

"I know, but I wake easily and go right back to sleep just as easily. You needn't worry about me. I thought I'd get up and compare a few notes while you have a bite."

Smells of the baked chicken, rice and vegetables reminded Susan that she hadn't eaten since lunch. She often skipped meals, her clothes hung loose and her face that was starting to wrinkle anyway had developed gaunt hollows.

"You work too hard," Jo observed.

"Look who's talking."

"I'm not skipping any meals."

"No, but you keep busy. Which reminds me, thanks for getting a new hot water heater into that rental house. By dashing over there you prevented a lot of potential water damage."

"I do enjoy the little crises. Keeps things popping." Josephine smiled broadly and Sue returned her grin, thinking that Jo's ability to solve problems had inspired staff at the agency to call and consult "that woman at your house" about everything and anything when Sue was unavailable.

Half an hour later, warmed and fed, Susan wished her a good night and carrying her shoes crept contentedly up to her bedroom.

A few weeks after that when her car quit unexpectedly on the road during a driving rain she again profited from Jo's resourcefulness. Since the area was elite residential she had to walk half a block to the nearest house. Arriving at the door, her summer dress and hair dripping she declined to enter. "Please just call my house and tell Josephine what the situation is?" she implored. "I'll go back to the car."

While she waited, shivering, she wondered if she shouldn't have requested a tow truck instead. She'd have to get one of those cell phones for emergencies like this. Now she saw the red blur of Jo's car through the wet window. Clad in a hooded slicker and rubbers, Josephine got out and brought an umbrella to Susan's car.

"Were you on your way back to the office?"

"Yes."

"I can take you there and still get back here in time to meet the tow truck I called for. I brought you a change of clothes." A wool blanket to wrap up in lay on the seat.

On the way to the office Susan thought, "She does things like this for the whole family." Aloud she said, "You're an angel, Jo."

"A black angel," Jo replied, displaying all her teeth in a wicked grin.

Chapter
20

For long years Susan found no fault in Josephine, unaware that her elongated shadow stretched across everyone's future. Of course there were hints that through time the lay of the land had shifted. Neither of the children, for example, studied business as their mother had recommended. Eileen attended the University of Pennsylvania and studied elementary education. Two years later Teddy planned to major in religious education at Princeton.

Susan objected strenuously. "What will that do to further his career?" she cried, demanding Ken's intervention, adding "There's no money in religion."

Ken took a hands-off attitude. "The children have to make up their own minds about what they want to do."

During the summer that preceded Ted's entering Princeton Susan updated computerization of accounting at her office and by fall found her work simplified, and herself free again on Sunday mornings. Since Teddy and Eileen regularly came home on weekends she tried to organize a family brunch at a coffee house.

"Make it lunch," Eileen objected. "We're—away all morning." They made it lunch.

In Kendrick's Buick on the way to the restaurant where Eileen and Teddy would meet them Susan had the sensation that something had slipped past her. She looked around at the bare October landscape. Summer had come with flowers and green leaves and autumn had followed with all that blaze of color and she'd scarcely noticed—so taken up with clacking of keys, marshalling of figures on a lighted screen.

She glanced at Ken, serene and secure, unafflicted with the need to get ahead that so obsessed her. They drove past a small park and approached the grounds of one of the suburb's largest churches. People streamed from the doors or stood gossiping in the parking lots or climbed into cars. Among them Sue glimpsed a tall, distinguished figure with one of the few black faces in that prosperous crowd. Recognition struck her dumb for a moment. "Wasn't that Josephine?"

"Probably, I know she does attend a Presbyterian Church around here."

Two things rose to Susan's remembrance: Josephine's claim to "orthodoxy" and remarks she'd heard about the "vitality" of this ultra-conservative church. And something else clung to the fringe of her mind that she checked out once the family had been seated in the restaurant.

"Weren't you two in the parking lot of that church when your father and I passed?"

Eileen replied, "Probably. We invited Jo to join us for lunch, but she has an exam Monday and begged off."

"You attend there often?"

"Almost every Sunday," Teddy put in. Then, grinning, he added. "We're what you call 'active.'"

"What's that supposed to mean?"

"We sing in the choir, Eileen plays her recorder when there's a musical program. I teach in the junior department of the Sunday School."

"Why didn't I know all this?"

"It's never been a secret," Eileen protested. "Dad knows."

Kendrick put an arm around Susan who sat beside him in the booth. "Ted thinks he should get some practical experience along with his studies in religious education," he remarked in his kind way.

These uncomfortable revelations occupied Susan's mind in spare moments sandwiched among closings, conferences and listings for the next several days. So, okay, Sue decided, Josephine's been steering the kids toward "orthodoxy," for years—whatever that meant. Couldn't hurt—practically everyone believed in God. Charity put a bloom on the Club's most ballyhooed events. And in retrospect she could find value in association with a large, active and well-heeled congregation. When the children came into the business they'd find all contacts useful. The Community Church she had occasionally attended with Ken just sort of sat there, barely maintaining its membership.

Toward the end of her junior year at the University Eileen initiated what proved to be an ongoing source of stimulation for her mother. She brought a young man home for a weekend. Susan immediately cleared her calendar of all commitments that might infringe on Saturday or Sunday. Eileen had the right idea: find a promising young man while still in school before the good ones got snapped up.

As it turned out, the rascally young fellow revealed that it was he who'd insisted on visiting Eileen's home. Skippy Hager's father owned a string of second-hand car agencies and Skip laughed and joked about padding noisy motors with "mashed potatoes" or spraying slow ones with gunk for quicker starts. Susan tried to overlook his brashness. Surely discretion could be learned. In vain she watched for her daughter's reaction. Impossible to assess the extent of her interest while she maintained that noncommittal attitude.

After his departure Sunday afternoon she cornered Eileen and discovered to her relief that their impressions coincided. From that day Eileen turned up, at least once a month, with a new young man. "I was never so popular," Susan marveled. Eileen had never dated much in high school, was attractive but no raving beauty, dressed inconspicuously. In fact, her appearance at this time rather resembled her demised grandmother's in her youth. Short like Ken's mother, she had the same straight dark eyebrows, the same delicate features. And the composed sweetness she radiated also reminded Sue of her lamented mother-in-law.

The men Eileen brought to the house inevitably followed her around, many with unconcealed devotion. Susan applauded and urged her daughter on, convinced that a choice from a broad field must necessarily surpass one from a narrow. At twenty Eileen had exceptional insight into character. Her comments were incisive and free of illusion and entertained her mother who felt her bond with her daughter strengthening.

This process continued into Eileen's senior year. Then Cyril Dakes began courting her. Susan swelled with pride as he aggressively monopolized Eileen at Club functions. Unlike his much older brother Budrow (now married) Cy had always enjoyed a quiet consciousness of his family's eminence and already worked as a junior executive in one of his father's enterprises. Susan now brought work home when she saw that he regularly turned up on Saturdays—playing tennis with Eileen in impeccable whites or splashing around with her in the pool.

Sundays he sometimes attended Eileen's church. Then he started coming home with her and staying for lunch. Susan beamed at him approving his custom tailored suit and rich silk tie. The slight imperfections of his broad face—thin eyebrows and too-prominent cheekbones—only emphasized his overall good looks. Susan engaged him in conversation and found him knowledgeable about business. Teddy and Kendrick looked on from the sidelines with tolerant detachment.

Alone with her mother Eileen said, "Too bad you're already married, Mom. You and Cy really hit if off."

"He's the catch of the season."

But Eileen made no visible effort to reel him in. To Susan's dismay, her manner toward Cyril grew more not less reserved as time went on. One day she overheard Eileen telling Teddy that she didn't know how much longer she could keep Cy from proposing.

"Do you want to?" Susan asked, walking in on them without warning.

"I can't marry Cy, Mom."

"Can't?"

"I don't love him."

"Could learn."

"No. I don't want to try."

"What's wrong with Cyril? His family are old, well-established people. Moneyed. Influential."

"It's too hard to explain."

"Try."

"Well, Cyril is— Just too stuffy for me. No doubts, no questions about himself, no—vision."

"What sort of vision are you hoping to find?"

Eileen glanced at Teddy in desperation.

"I think she'd rather have someone more—spiritual." Teddy offered the last word tentatively and Susan pounced on it. "Spiritual? You're joking. What does 'spiritual' mean? Cy attends church, contributes to charity, reveres his parents. What do you want?"

"Don't get excited, Mom," Eileen intervened.

"If Cyril does get around to asking, I hope you'll give serious consideration to what your future with a young heir to the Dakes Enterprises could mean."

"I will.   I promise I'll think seriously about that."

And when she refused Cy she claimed it was for that exact reason: She couldn't face a future with a Dakes heir.

Frustrated and disappointed, Susan wondered whether her daughter would ever marry. For a time she dated no one. Then one Sunday Teddy, now in his second year at Princeton, brought home a graduate seminary student who'd played his violin for their morning service. Likeable, outgoing, intelligent, he had a seriousness that Susan liked. He was shorter and slimmer than Teddy, had sandy hair and undistinguished features, but his face in repose bespoke refinement, and in company lit up with a sensitive animation. Sue thought the older student might be a good influence for Ted and encouraged Ellis Ronberg to come again. From that Sunday he turned up every week. He had agreed, temporarily, to assist the church music director.

Ellis and Teddy kidded around, pushed each other into the pool, sunned and chatted or played tennis. Susan hoped Teddy would learn to emulate the seminarian's faultlessly appropriate behavior.

She carelessly took his on-going presence for granted until one Sunday afternoon when she'd left her desk upstairs and descended to refresh her eyes in the garden. Teddy sat reading in a lawn chair, and Susan allowed herself a little surge of maternal satisfaction over his blond handsomeness, his tall, healthy, well-proportioned physique. She looked around for Ellis and located his back—far off disappearing with Eileen through the woods on a path leading away from the grounds. They leaned toward one another, engrossed in conversation and each heard and saw nothing but the other. "What a fool I've been," Sue muttered under her breath. For Ellis the chief attraction here wasn't Teddy. That much was suddenly clear.

She followed her daughter's retreating figure with alarm. Every movement, every gesture bespoke involvement with the young man at her side. "Good grief! Is it too late?" Her barely audible voice alerted Ted who rose and came toward her. "Hi, Mom. What's up?"

Susan gestured toward the couple, now rounding a bend. "What do you think of that?"

"Well, gee. I'm glad they get along. I'd hate it if my sister was down on one of my very best friends."

"And if she decided to marry him?"

"You're kidding." Teddy stared, mildly shocked and intensely thoughtful. At last he said, "I've been missing the boat, haven't I? Well, it's okay. A person could sure have a worse brother-in-law."

"What a ridiculous thing to say! Eileen has refused two or three vastly superior men. Why should she settle for this—insignificant—"

"Oh, oh. You don't know Eileen. Her idea of insignificant is just about the opposite of yours!"

Susan marshaled a formidable battery of objections to Ellis Ronberg and tried to have a rational and friendly talk with Eileen. Her daughter defended

Ellis at every turn. He was, she said, "the most serious, most compatible, most interesting" person she'd ever met.

"I suppose you think he has that requisite 'vision' that Cy Dakes lacked?"

"Well, yes. But you have nothing to worry about. He hasn't asked me to marry him."

Susan tried to enlist Kendrick's help. He declined to intervene. "Ellis is a decent young fellow. If he's Eileen's choice we have to live with it. Don't try to make this decision for her."

"Oh, Ken! You're always so permissive!"

In her desperation Susan even appealed to Josephine who made an astonishing response. "A great love taps deep and nothing will uproot it."

"Then I hope this attraction is shallow and can be yanked out." Susan replied tartly, not pleased to hear the problem transposed to a metaphor.

She elicited a promise from Eileen to at least meet Ellis's parents before things got any more complicated. "Invite them here."

And when they came they were awful enough to revive Susan's hopes. The physical resemblance between Ellis and his father was unmistakable, but the father's face and manners were not only older but coarser. A farmer, he had a habit of silence he found hard to break except for a few words exchanged privately with Kendrick from time to time.

The mother, plump and perspiring, clutched Susan's arm at every opportunity and trilled her effusive approval of the house, the food, the entertainment. But when she shrieked, "Isn't it wonderful?" nodding toward Ellis and Eileen, "God's ways—past finding out!" Susan disengaged her arm and ear as speedily as possible.

Afterwards when she tried to get Eileen to comment, her daughter only said, "They were sweet."

"Uneducated, tiresome and commonplace. That's what you call 'sweet'?"

"Oh, Mom. They tried so hard."

"Precisely. So much effort, such painful results."

"I thought they were sweet," Eileen reiterated stubbornly and would say nothing else. All summer she and Ellis continued their eternal dialogue.

Ellis had a last year at the seminary, and Eileen who earned a BA after only three years signed up for a year's graduate work at Penn. At Christmas Ellis gave her a modest diamond which she wore with an unfathomable radiance. And the following summer they were married in the garden, a private family ceremony. Susan made a point of inviting almost no one from the Club to meet Ellis's relatives who appallingly outnumbered the Shields. And Susan's adoptive mother, Alice Sterne, ancient and shrunken, simply got lost in the crowd.

Josephine worked tirelessly in the background to make the affair run smoothly and pleasantly. She found places for all the obnoxious Ronbergs to sleep, saw that their taste in food was considered, directed the caterers, the clergy and the florists.

Kendrick lovingly watched his daughter's every move and often asked her, "Now you won't get too busy to come visit, will you?"

"No, Dad."

The service, admittedly, was beautiful, glorified by the evident devotion of bride and bridegroom.

At their church the current music director took a job in Boston and Ellis accepted the vacated position. The happy couple moved into a small apartment and Eileen worked in the Church's day-care center in the morning. A trivial and stupid life, Susan concluded. Well, let them get sick and tired of it. They'd soon be ready for a change. Ellis was smart and personable and could learn to sell.

Then, as if all that weren't disappointment enough, Teddy started the application process to become a missionary, long before he'd even graduated.

"This time you've got to do something, Ken. We can't have Teddy running off on a wild goose chase to Brazil!" Sue was adamant.

"It is far away." Trouble clouded Kendrick's still-handsome face. "I'll talk to him."

But afterwards he reported that Ted was so eager to go, so full of a spirit of—adventure?—that he hadn't had the heart to discourage him. "I did tell him you were unalterably opposed."

"What did he say?"

"That he'd persuade you."

And Teddy at his most persuasive proved overpoweringly compelling. He sat at the foot of the chaise lounge in his mother's room where she liked to stretch out to read, his face alight with confidence and affection.

He asked about her agency and about the last salesman Sue had hired. Then he talked about the papers he had to finish before the end of term. All before getting around to the subject Susan dreaded. "The board will be meeting to approve my application next week, but there's no real question about my acceptance," he said gravely.

"Oh, Teddy, don't go off to Brazil! Hot, steamy, unhealthy place. You could die out there. I don't know what's got into you!"

"Think of it as a calling, Mom. I have to go—I want to. It's not nearly so impossible as you might imagine. You should hear the returned missionaries talking about boating up the Amazon, trekking through the jungle, cutting trees to build houses!"

"And once you're settled out there in the wilds, exactly what do you expect to accomplish?"

"The board calls it 'church planting.'"

"And what's that?"

"Well, first I find a few people willing to listen to scripture. I form a nucleus of believers, and together we reach out to the whole community."

"All that sounds so—unnecessary. Can't you

reach out here?   Aren't there any needy people in Philadelphia?"

"Of course. And yes, I could minister here, but I'm called to Brazil. And Mom, please try to understand. I love you, I need for you to say 'Go in peace.'" Teddy took his mother's hands and looked imploringly into her eyes.

"How can I, Teddy? I don't want you to go. When I think of my only son out there with the snakes and—the savages—it's so entirely the opposite of all the plans I had for you."

"Whatever the danger, at least I'd be following my conscience. Will you promise to give some thought to what I've said?" His wistful, pleading eyes moved his mother to tears.

Reluctantly she agreed to consider his viewpoint. And, inexorably, Teddy assembled gear, spoke in churches, corresponded with his board and finally booked flight for Brazil.

To her amazement a fair-sized crowd assembled at the airport to see him off. In addition to the family, there were people from the church, chums from school and even a missionary or two. Teddy went around to each person, saying goodbye. Family last. Warm hugs for Ellis and Eileen, the latter with wet eyes and a proud look. A choked-up embrace for Kendrick. And last "Mom?" Teddy held out his arms and Susan clung to him. Temporarily heart broken she found herself murmuring in his ear, so close to her lips: "Go in peace, Teddy."

The last she saw of her son was his look of ecstatic gratitude before he disappeared into the ramp.

After that, all summer frequent air-mail letters with foreign stamps arrived—excited descriptions of people he'd met, stations he passed through on his way to his assigned post. "Benjamin and Paco will stay for a while and help me build my house," he wrote at last. "I'm picking up a few phrases of the dialect here, and have found a man who has agreed to work as my translator. Although he speaks only a little English, he's bright and we communicate well."

Susan began to relax and take his absence in stride. Once he'd had his fill of adventure, he'd be back, glad to escape the mosquitoes and other myriad insects that seemed to be his chief trial. So she was totally unprepared when Ken called her at work to say that Teddy was sick with a rare tropical fever. The mission had flown him into Manaos.

"That won't do. We've got to bring him home!"

"I suggested that. They say he's too sick to move."

That evening the apprehensive parents talked and decided that Kendrick should fly to Brazil and stay with Ted until he could be brought home. Although they retired, neither slept. So when the phone shrilled in the darkness well after midnight both responded instantly. Susan lunged at the phone with such force that she knocked it off the bedside table. Picking up the receiver she heard a strange voice on the extension saying, ". . . an hour ago." And after a long pause, tentatively, "Theodore left me with the impression that he preferred cremation, so if you don't object . . ."

"No! No!" Susan heard her own voice: harsh, strangled. Then Kendrick's—reasonable, ineffably sad, arranging to leave next morning on the flight he'd already booked. He would bring the body home for burial.

The rest of the conversation disappeared into a dull roar that buzzed louder and louder in her ears even after the phone clicked and a dial tone hummed somewhere far away.

Kendrick appeared in her doorway, a ghost in pale pajamas. He approached her, removed the receiver from her hand and restored it. He sat down beside her and tried to embrace her. But she sat frozen like a statue till a passing glimmer of light revealed tears on his face, whereupon, sobbing she flung herself into his arms.

Days passed. Eileen and Ellis came to stay with her, but failed to bring comfort. Teddy's body at the mortuary was an affront: stiff, swollen features scarcely resembling the son she remembered. A rigid, empty body, but not Ted. She turned away, tormenting herself with an account of all the hours and days she could have spent with him and hadn't. Instead he'd turned to Josephine who'd done irreparable harm.

Before the funeral Eileen came to Sue's room and shyly, cautiously broached again the subject of Teddy's preference for cremation. "He asked—he wanted to be buried a certain way."

"The funeral has been arranged, and we agreed to hold it at your church. What else do you want?"

"It's not what I want that matters. It's Teddy's—preference."

"What are you getting at? Be frank, Eileen."

"I know we've arranged a service, that you—that we— But—could the interment—? Instead of burying Teddy, could he be cremated?"

"I suppose so."

"Then, Mom—afterwards a few of us will have a little private ceremony—the one Teddy wanted."

"Whatever you like. If it means so much to you."

Eileen drew a visible sigh of thankfulness and kissed her mother's forehead.

So after the packed-out memorial service where church members indulged in an orgy of praise for God's young saint who had sacrificed himself unstintingly, there was no procession to the graveyard. Just a sentence to the effect that the deceased had requested cremation. And since fall was in the air with gusty winds and chilling rain no one much regretted it.

Several days later Eileen and Ellis, still at the house at Kendrick's insistence, announced that they wanted to proceed with Teddy's "ceremony." Sue and Kendrick exchanged a long look. Then Ken agreed. "Today?"

"Yes."

They'd all consented together to start out within the hour when Ken was called to the phone. Emergency situation at his office.

"We can wait, Dad," Eileen volunteered at once.

Ken refused to hear of postponement. "Your mother has arranged a day off. Go without me."

Because it was roomy and comfortable, they set forth in Susan's car, with Eileen driving. Eileen and Ellis took their instruments and Susan sat in the back with Josephine, suddenly resenting the suppressed air of excitement in the other three members of this pilgrimage.

No one had much to say as the car proceeded beyond the outskirts of the city into the open country. Presently Ellis said, "There, isn't that it?" They drove onto a graveled road and pulled off to one side. Susan gazed at the trees to her right and at a bare hill on the left.

"There's nothing here."

"That's the whole idea," Eileen said. Ellis was already opening the trunk and taking out the flute and violin cases. "Before I get out of the car in this wind, would you mind explaining what you have in mind? Why all the mystery?"

Josephine climbed out of the car, stretched and began to walk toward the hill. Eileen climbed into the back seat. "Teddy talked to us several times about funerals. He had some very definite ideas about appropriate music and—and—" Eileen paused before saying, "and his ashes."

"Well, I guess we'd better go and do whatever

must be done." Susan impatiently jumped out and followed Josephine and Ellis upward. The hill was higher than it had looked, and by the time she reached the top she was breathing heavily.

Ellis opened a Bible and began to read. The wind carried his words away and Susan caught snatches only— "trumpet shall sound—dead in Christ—rise— shall ever be with the Lord."

He played his violin with infinite tenderness, his sandy hair blowing, his pale sensitive face tense with concentration. The music had a vague familiarity, but Susan couldn't give it a title.

Next Eileen played her flute. Less of a musician, her contribution was a hymn with embellishments. This one Sue recognized from her days with the Rev. Sterne. "When I survey the wondrous cross on which the Prince of Glory died." She remembered those and a few other words, something like "pour contempt on all my pride." Since the occasion seemed to demand it Susan gave some real thought to this for the first time. There were better things to pour contempt on, she decided. A little pride never hurt anyone.

Next, Josephine began to sing in a powerful voice that soared confidently above the blast. No doubt about it, she could have been a great concert singer, and in all these years this was the first time Susan had heard her. Neither of the others looked at her or at Jo. Their eyes lifted to the gray sky, they listened with rapt attention.

"He shall stand at the latter day upon
the earth, and though worms destroy
this body, yet in my flesh shall I see
God,"

Josephine affirmed, her voice full and effortless, her dark face angelic.

Eileen bent over, took an urn from her case: Teddy's ashes! Eileen unfastened the clasp, removed a handful of ashes and to Susan's horror flung it into the wind.

"No! Stop, what are you doing?" Sue offered to snatch the urn from Eileen, but her daughter resisted with a look of mingled consternation and determination.

Frantic, Susan, tugging at the urn heard Jo's calm voice and saw a large black hand gently loosen Eileen's grip. "Teddy would never want to hurt his mama's feelings."

Susan found herself in possession of the urn. She refastened and held it, trembling with indignation and cold while the other three sang a hundred "Amens" after which they returned to the car and to the house in subdued silence.

Susan couldn't decide where to keep Teddy's ashes and couldn't talk about it. They were not for display. She carried them to her room and, after deliberating, put them in a top drawer of the antique dresser that had been with her for most of her life.

Chapter
22

A year later Eileen and Ellis took a job in Arkansas. That dreadful term "church planting" came up again. "Do you have to move now—while you're pregnant?" Sue inquired, indignant.

"I'm strong and healthy. We'll manage."

They visited often before putting their belongings in a used truck and taking off. Kendrick helped with loading and waved goodbye, but Sue remained in her office. She worked her computer—adding, subtracting, accumulating figures in a secret notebook in her desk. She looked at office buildings for sale. Time for a move she'd contemplated for more than a year.

The percentage she gave Vergil Joslin every month galled more with every payment. She had tripled the business, she alone took all the responsibility, sweated out every crisis. Even though changing location and company name involved critical adjustments, she had to brave it.

Just before she made the first decisive move, however, Vergil appeared and offered to sell her his agency.

"What are you selling me precisely?" she inquired cautiously.

"The building, name, clientele, good will, the works."

"I think the last two are mine already."

"Whatever. What's it worth to you to keep the location?"

While Vergil prepared a seller's contract for examination, she summed up the considerable advantages in remaining where she was and waited eagerly for his offer.

Kendrick had begun coming by her office at least twice a week to take her out to dinner. He missed Teddy and Eileen, of course, even more than she did. And eating alone with Jo possibly reminded him of the woman's meddling in their children's lives, as it did Susan.

While they dined in this or that posh restaurant, Kendrick confided more about his work than he had in years. His firm, for example, currently advised two huge corporations about legal considerations involved in taking over smaller companies.

"Do I detect a note of disapproval?" Sue inquired, amused and intrigued. Personally, she kindled at the idea of the power plays that would necessarily ensue.

"I have mixed feelings. Smaller companies do have a chance to set their own prices, and they have their own lawyers, too, of course."

"Naturally."

Sue then described the course of her negotiations with Vergil Joslin. If she didn't buy his agency he'd keep it going with someone else in charge. Some of the agents would leave with her, but not all. "Vergil's holding some key cards and he knows it. I should have got out years ago, but always hated to give up this going concern."

Kendrick encouraged her to buy the Joslin agency, "if that's what you really want." It would preserve continuity with what she'd already established.

After weeks of delay Vergil sent over the contract. Susan took a look and found it much as she'd expected. She phoned Joslin anyway. "I think we have to talk about price."

"No, dear. I know you. So to save time I gave you my lowest bid and best terms right off the bat."

"Surely you can knock off a couple thousand—I—"

Joslin broke in. "No, Sue. That's it. Take it or leave it."

She hung up and went through the contract item by item. The monthly payments she could handle. The down payment would drain off all her unmortgaged resources, and then some. Could she swing it at all? Only she knew what a tightrope she walked, the debts she'd incurred. She considered selling this or that mortgaged property. Banks actually owned most of her so-called holdings.

At home she explained her dilemma to Kendrick who listened intently. He'd started looking tired and stressed, Sue decided. But not tireder or more stressed than she felt. Maybe she looked even older. Ken confessed to uneasiness about his firm's latest take-over. "This one will be tough, because the smaller company's putting up a fight—a really heroic one."

"You sound as if you're on their side."

"Actually, I am in a way."

That bothered Sue. Surely Kendrick knew how to keep his loyalties in line despite his evident sympathy for the underdog.

Instead of commiserating with him she began to lament over her own frustration. "If I had anything paid for—" she began.

"We could mortgage this house," Ken suggested.

"Already done. When I bought the Glentnor Building," Sue reminded him, shocked that he didn't remember.

"Oh, yes, that's right."

"We could sell the Georgian," she dared to propose. (No mortgage on that house—ever.)

"Please, Sue. The one thing I couldn't tolerate. Don't even think about it." Since she'd thought a lot about it and even had a buyer in mind, his reply left her feeling slapped down. However, you can't reason with unreason, experience had taught her. People's approaches to real estate were riddled with personal eccentricities and sentiment. You had to accept that before you could list anything at all.

With deep reluctance she selected several

properties in which she had at least some equity built up and put them on the market.

A few days later at the Hollinshed Coffee House Ken confessed that he'd been approached "by the other side!"

"What are you talking about?" Susan took several gulps of water. She drank a lot of it when disturbed, and Ken's manner alarmed her. Something awful had shaken his customary placidity.

"President Baglari of the company we're currently helping SA to swallow is no dummy. I sat through our last joint meeting with what I thought was a totally neutral air, but afterwards he followed me into my office, said he could tell I was on his side, insisted on spelling out why he didn't want the admittedly enormous sum of money SA has named in their latest bid."

"And why was that?"

"He said accepting a chunk of money was like exchanging a living body for dead cash. The family concern is functioning, growing, producing. It's all he and his sons know."

"And you let this argument get to you, didn't you?"

"I experienced a severe—intensely severe conflict of interest."

Susan tried to drink from an empty glass and irritably summoned a waiter. "I don't know why you let that fellow into your office—or why you listened to him when you could see where he was coming from."

"That's very astute, Susan. Why didn't I refuse to hear him? Because, I suppose, I didn't want to go on outraging my sense of justice by taking part in an action I detest."

"What else can you do?"

"I could—" Ken looked as if a path of deliverance had opened in front of him. "I could get out."

"Better give that a lot of thought. Positions like yours take half a lifetime to achieve, as you should know better than anyone."

"That's true, of course. I've got to consider our total situation: yours and mine."

Too disturbed to pursue the matter, Susan chattered on about other things. Eileen would deliver any day now. It worried Sue that she wasn't closer to the hospital. "But at least it's Spring, and the roads out there aren't heavily traveled."

Although Ken looked grimmer than she'd ever seen him for the next several weeks he said nothing further and Susan guessed that he'd had to own up to the sad fact that excessive scrupulosity never pays. "He's too intelligent to throw away a job that brings ten times what the average attorney earns," she murmured aloud, trying to convince herself.

The following Sunday she woke to find Kendrick sitting in her room in a path of bright sunlight. "Eileen's had her baby. A boy, eight pounds."

Susan sat up on the instant, wide awake. "She

came through it all right?"

"Right as rain. And they're gloriously happy. She'll go home tomorrow. They named the baby Theodore, but will call him Theo."

"Theo." Susan stretched and smiled. A new little being—their own flesh and blood. Proud and delighted she held out her arms and Ken rolled easily into her bed.

Afterwards he said, "Let's go down in our robes. The housekeeper is preparing a celebration breakfast." They ate it on the terrace—a basketful of miniature assorted muffins, cheese and fresh strawberries, the table glorified with a huge bouquet of flowers from the garden, Jo's contribution.

Susan had several pressing matters to attend to, but she put them off. There was something about Kendrick this morning—an attitude of appeal, a look of eagerness and solemn determination.

"What's got into you?" she inquired, mystified. "It isn't just that you're a grandfather, is it?"

He leaned back and folded his napkin. "No, it isn't. I've made some vital decisions that I want to talk about."

"Such as?" Under the table Susan felt her toes in the cozy slippers turning cold.

"I'm sending in my resignation tomorrow, for one thing."

"Don't do that."

"I must. I've reached a parting of the ways with my firm. Should have left at least a year ago."

"But we can't survive without the cash you bring home. It pays all our daily expenses."

"I know that. But there's a way we could manage."

"You've found another job?"

"No. And I plan to get out altogether. I'm going to strike out on my own—set up private practice. Then I'll volunteer more time for legal aid."

"Start your charity with me. Without your earnings I'll be on skid row myself."

"Be serious, Susan. I'll earn enough money to support us in reasonably comfortable style."

Now her hands turned icy. She withdrew them from the water glass she'd been fumbling with. "If you think I'm going to move—"

"We were happy in Mom's old house. We can go back there. Think of the savings!"

"You've been dying to do that all these years, haven't you? And now that we're on the brink of really making it big once I own the agency—"

"We're in our fifties, Susan. Time to get our priorities straight."

"It sounds to me like the 'priorities' here amount to doing whatever happens to suit you!"

"I'm sorry you're taking it like this." Ken looked distraught and ill. "But I've made up my mind. I am going to quit now. I can't keep putting it off in order to sustain a house that's too big, cars that waste gas, a Club membership we'd do better without, lavish entertaining that costs a fortune and leaves nothing but a bad taste in the mouth."

"You want to destroy everything I've slaved for, don't you? Where do you think I developed the contacts that made me succeed in real estate? At the Club! Who do you think we'd be if we gave up the club and moved back into that crummy little Georgian? You're not thinking!" When he said nothing she debased herself enough to ask, "Can't you wait till after I've bought the agency?"

"Waiting wouldn't help. Don't you know yourself, Susan? With that deal finished, you'd be over your ears in the next." Kendrick turned sideways in his chair, body tense, eyes hard as Susan had never seen them and delivered his ultimatum. "I will resign. When you've figured out where we can live on the smaller but respectable earnings I'll bring home, let me know." He jumped up angry for once in his life, and went inside.

Susan sat on trembling with an answering rage, fighting a sense of panic. Could she get Vergil to postpone their deal until she could regroup? She saw her precariously constructed empire crumbling. How much would she have to sell at how great a loss to keep their estate and pay the upkeep herself? And how could she consummate the purchase of the Joslin Agency?

She ran into the house, showered and dressed and went to her office. Kendrick could not have chosen a worse time to spring this trap. She hated him for his foolish do-good notions.

About two in the morning, still fiercely wide awake, Susan reached a number of painful decisions.

Two of her apartment buildings and one of her office complexes would have to go. She had searched her memory and her files and had some ideas about potential buyers. Ken had forced her into a corner, but she'd fight her way out.

The next morning she approached Josephine, hiding her embarrassment beneath a breezy demeanor. "Ken and I are experiencing a bit of a crunch, temporarily. We need to cut back for the moment."

Jo agreed easily to closing up part of the house, dispensing with the housekeeper, cutting cleaning and garden services and letting certain areas of the grounds revert to nature. "After all, with only two of you here—" Jo shrugged. But when she also offered to take a cut in wages, Susan demurred. "You more than earn your salary. Time after time people who've called and talked to you here have come to the agency ready to sign contracts."

Susan's office building sold first at a mere fraction above the rock bottom figure Susan had set. Closing on it felt like lopping off a finger. Next, the first of the two apartment complexes had to be sacrificed. With each loss her bitterness toward Ken deepened. They saw little of each other. Kendrick was preoccupied, preparing for his move to a private office and briefing his successor on the myriad intricacies of the cases he'd been handling.

But after he'd worked through his six-weeks' notice, he brought Susan a check. "This is my severance pay and the last of the big money, so to speak. Certain loyal clients will follow me, so I won't be starting from the bottom, but don't count on more than a—maybe a fourth of what I've been giving you."

Susan listened in stony silence. "You might at least say you hear me," he reproached, eyes searching hers.

"I hear you," she repeated mechanically. But as soon as he left the room she snatched up the check. "Oh, wonderful, wonderful!" She kissed the bit of paper fervently. They must have given him the equivalent of six month's earnings. Suddenly she saw that with a few lucky breaks she might salvage almost everything that remained.

The Club memberships came due. She reminded the Board of Ken's honorary status and paid dues for one member for one year.

Still, sale of the other block of apartments lagged. Word was out that she was scrambling for cash and people made offers that she considered insulting. She held out. The date for closing on her contract with Vergil approached. She called and proposed a postponement, humiliated to have to beg. "Six weeks," he said, though she'd asked for six months. "Then I sell to somebody who has the money in hand."

She hung up thinking that Vergil's cash flow might have dried up also. It could happen to anyone who regularly invested to the limit of his credit. Sue felt better about having to sell the third building. Her days were loaded with usual concerns, her nights spent in wakeful juggling of figures and anxious searching through her mind for a buyer for that last property. She grew thin and sinewy, the flesh receded from her already bony nose and sagged about her mouth.

Three weeks from the new deadline a buyer appeared that she'd never negotiated with before, in response to an ad that she'd been running in one form or another for two months—a serious buyer who recognized the property for the bargain he made sure it was. With that deal in the works she could make final calculations.

The result oppressed her. She had so close to enough to pay Joslin for his agency! If only he'd wait for the really trivial balance! But she knew he'd been tracking her doings—would find out somehow the amount of equity she had in each property and what would be left after she'd paid off the banks. He had spies and informers. And if he concluded that she couldn't pay, she was out of luck. No mercy from that quarter. Nor did she expect it. People with Ken's charitable attitudes were scarcer than hen's teeth.

The logical solution was to sell off the estate and go back to living in the old Georgian as Ken had suggested. The thought made her gorge rise. If only she owned even a modest house to sell for cash—one with no mortgage! That small increase would put her over the top.

She thrust all that from her mind and went to take care of an odd situation that she didn't know whether anyone else could handle. A man from Arizona would arrive early this morning to talk about listing his parents' house which had burned. Driving to the site, Susan mentally gave the man low scores for both brains and foresight. He'd let the house stand vacant after his folks' death for more than a year. The empty house attracted vagrants, naturally. To make matters worse, he'd failed to renew the insurance policy.

Walking around outside she found it a nice old place—sturdily built with ample windows. She pushed the back door which opened easily. The interior hung black with soot. A hole chopped in the roof by the fire department had admitted rain. Filthy, sagging couches and broken furniture contributed to the squalor. The bathroom plumbing, blackened and full of debris, revolted her. She didn't want to list this burned-out shell.

With the car key she still held in her hand she idly scratched at a blackened wall. To her surprise, a solid white line appeared. She went around poking and scratching. Except for the kitchen the house was basically intact! She remembered two immigrant uncles of one of her agents who could, and probably would, do a wonderful job of renovating this place and for little money.

She stood arrested in thought for a time and then, with a callous smile she made a decision. Outside the sun passed under a cloud and the room darkened.

Before the owner of the house arrived in a taxi Susan stepped outside to wait for him. A worried little fellow, he wore glasses and looked like a banker. She knew he ran a garage, however, and was a skilled mechanic. They went inside but she let him stand dismayed for only a few minutes before saying, "I can't list the house as it is. You might look around, but I don't think you'll find an agency that will handle it."

"Oh dear, oh dear!" The man moaned and moved anxiously about, avoiding festoons of soot that hung from the ceiling, protecting what was undoubtedly his best suit. "This is my family home. I grew up here, never had the heart to sell it."

"I'm sorry you have to see it like this. Such a pity. It's become an eyesore in this rather nice neighborhood. Haven't you received some sort of notice from the city?" A wild guess that worked.

"Actually—yes. I have to do something."

"You could spend a few weeks here and look around for a buyer on your own."

"Oh, I can't do that! I have to fly back to

Phoenix tonight. Even with the kids there, my wife's afraid to stay in the house at night without me."

"I guess I could take the place off your hands for the price of the lot," Sue murmured as if grasping at a straw.

"I'll take anything. I should have kept up with the insurance. What's the lot worth now?"

After brief negotiation Susan made a few phone calls and then sent the man to her agency to finalize the paperwork. Herself, she had to go downtown to meet another client.

To get to her second appointment she'd take a mid-morning train—one that would make its last stop only a block from where she needed to be. The train was fast and she wouldn't have to park the car in that congested part of Philly.

She headed for a place near the station where she'd often left her car before, tormented once again by her straightened finances. A couple carpenters like those immigrants could whip the house into shape in a matter of weeks. But she'd have to furnish cash for supplies and an advance. Just a bit more—the price of a really good car? Like the Cadillac she was driving? No, she wouldn't give Ken the satisfaction of following his suggestion about getting rid of the gas guzzlers. Anyway, what sort of image would she project in a used compact?

She pulled into a shady parking area near the depot where the backs of a row of residences stood, separated from the railroad tracks by a fenced alleyway.

She glanced at her watch, and since she had time to spare she lit a cigarette, though she'd mostly given up smoking. She walked up and down puffing and pondering and striving to focus her mind on the meeting to which she was headed.

When the cigarette threatened to burn her fingers she dropped it and ground it decisively into the gravel. Thus occupied she barely heard the crunch of tires. She glanced sideways. A car had pulled up beside hers. She followed the man's gaze upward to a second floor window where a pink lace and satin blur flashed for a second.

The man leapt from his car, eyes on the window, darted through a gate in the fence and disappeared. Sue grinned, diverted for the moment from her own concerns. Something had been left out in the scene she'd just witnessed. Oh yes, the man's arm pulling back. He hadn't removed his key from the ignition. What sort of car was he leaving in jeopardy? She looked now to see and started back, incredulous. A pale yellow luxury Cadillac identical to hers! Curious, she ascertained that the keys did indeed hang in the lock. The pale, supple upholstery matched hers, same tires, same wheel covers. Here stood—what? A gift? Not from God, assuredly. But the situation cried out for action and she took it.

She all but threw herself into the driver's seat, its interior dark after the bright sunlight, and drove swiftly for what seemed endless miles to her house. She bumped down a footpath out of sight among the trees and jumped out, thankful that their gardening firm had no workers on the grounds today. Using a nail file and inhuman strength she removed the car's license plate, and after a sharp glance in all directions, she secreted it in a hollow tree.

Now she all but ran to the house and from her bedroom called Auto-Rent. Claiming an emergency she persuaded them to bring a car out immediately.

Next she had to call and postpone the meeting to which she'd been headed when thus delayed. She'd had car trouble, she said, and set a new time for the interview. Then she descended and walked up and down in front of the house waiting. Should she have tried to borrow Jo's car? No, that woman ferreted out things in an uncanny way. What if that owner emerged before or even while she attempted to drive off in her own car? She'd have to brazen it out. But suppose he'd already reported his loss? Would they accept that she'd taken the wrong Cadillac in error? Unlikely excuse.

The rental car arrived, followed by another agent who would take the driver away. She presented a card, signed a form, cool and smiling, and drove away. Then, observing all speed limits and watching lights and intersections she reached a street within a block of the train station she'd left forty minutes ago where she parked the rental car at a meter, inserted coins and strolled into and out of the waiting room and down the little road to the spot where, to her relief, her own car still stood. Before she reached it she took out her keys, glanced up at the windows of *that* house and down at the gate and then slid into the car seat, and shaking with nerves maneuvered the car out of the lot.

Once she reached the street and had merged into a flow of traffic she heard herself almost gasping for breath. Her heart raced. She drove to her office and immediately sent a clerk to return the rental car to the agency. She couldn't risk having it associated, even remotely, with the theft.

To compose herself she deliberately filled a cup of coffee in the kitchenette, took it and a roll to her office and drank and munched in as leisurely a fashion as she could, determinedly steadying her trembling hands, keeping her voice even while she answered questions in an unnaturally deep voice.

The time for her postponed trip to the city arrived. She drove swiftly to a neighboring town. Of course she couldn't return to the location of the theft. She parked, mounted a local train and jolted along from stop to stop forcing her mind to concentrate on the upcoming sale she was to arrange for a client: one of three beautiful new flats in the historic district, sandwiched between two lovely old landmarks—a relatively easy deal—the builder guaranteed quality.

With her business concluded, she employed the return trip to review all that had been said and promised in the negotiations. She made notes and anticipated terms of the contract to be drawn. But the real condition of her nerves revealed itself when she found that she'd unwittingly dismounted at her usual station. She had to sit for an endless hour in the hot waiting room before another train took her on to the town where she'd left her car.

Through all the rest of the late afternoon and evening she experienced flashes of keen regret. Why had she stolen that Cadillac? Foolish, dangerous! If only she could go back and change her decision to set foot in the alien car.

In bed that night waiting for absolute quiet she considered possible ways of undoing the damage: Could she drive back to the scene of the crime and leave the car there? Or suppose she drove a short distance along the road and abandoned the stolen vehicle? She couldn't bring herself to risk appearing on the road even in a dark, deserted place with no license plate nor with the license of a stolen auto for which police would now be on the lookout.

And what would the gardener think when he found a car in the woods of her estate? She crept out of bed, went to the garage and secured a flashlight and a hammer. She started up her car, dismayed at its loud roar in the silence. She eased the Cadillac out of the garage, drove it down the street several blocks and pulled off on a side road that she knew to be isolated and unfrequented. There she left her car, its legitimate license plate visible from the more traveled road. She trudged home, walked softly up the drive and then cut into the woods, carrying the flashlight and her hammer. Once among the trees, she turned on the flash and looked for the stolen car. Its pale bulk appeared sooner than she'd expected. Finding the hollow tree proved harder. She stumbled over roots and twigs in the dark, located the car door, stood beside it and tried to re-enact her previous movements. Presently the right tree emerged from the mass. She groped in the hollow, stricken with fear when at first she felt nothing. Then her fingers touched a metal edge. She withdrew the tell-tale rectangle, laid it on a rock and—cringing at the sound of each blow—she hammered at it until the letters and numbers disappeared.

She laid the mangled tag on the car seat and drove slowly along the path to her garage. The car had a faint but unmistakable male odor. Though afterwards she sprayed it several times with air freshener it seemed to her that it never lost that smell. She locked the pilfered car in the garage and went back to lie awake all the rest of the night, alternately sweating and shivering. At dawn she rose, walked to the deserted road where she'd left her own car and drove it to the office where she locked this one in the Realty's one garage, after removing the license plates and putting them in her briefcase.

The mutilated plate she took to her receptionist along with her registration materials and asked her to get a replacement.

"Wow! What happened to this?"

"Ran into an iron rail."

That afternoon she drove home in another rented car.

In due course the new tag arrived and Susan

attached it to the stolen car. Then she drove her own car with the original tag to a second hand car dealership in Geneva. The proprietor admitted that the car was like new. Top of the line and all that, but gee—"where do you find a Joe with enough moolah to pay for a buggy like this?"

Susan put on her most persuasive and beguiling air, reminded the man that his was one of the most affluent Main-line suburbs, pointed out this feature and the other, subtly flattered and cajoled. He was no match for her and paid her well. She waited and watched, expecting him to verify the identification number, but he flipped through the papers she presented, had her sign a couple of times and gave her a check. She took the train, then a taxi home, feeling deflated. Instead of the joy she usually experienced with success she contemplated her tarnished victory dejectedly.

Paid with her ill-gotten gains, the carpenters went to work on the not-really-burned out house, and by the time it was half done she already had a buyer. She met with Vergil Joslin, laid contracts and bank books before him and convinced him she'd have the rest of the cash in six weeks. He sold her the agency—balance due in sixty days.

Three weeks later a telegram from a lawyer informed Sue that her mother had died. She would need to appear to arrange the funeral and take care of legal matters. Later the pastor of Alice's church called personally to offer condolences and to say that one of his members who habitually looked in on her mother had found her body. He presumed the service would be held in his church? Clearly, she was in charge, Sue realized with a shock.

Kendrick attempted to offer comfort and sympathy but understood her real feelings too well to imagine her deeply grieved. He stood awkwardly in the door to her bedroom while Susan packed. "I spent four years with that woman, treated like a housemaid. She and Chancellor went off to Virginia and left me on my own when I was sixteen. Now I'm her daughter?"

"Well, Sue, someone has to bury the poor old thing. And she did seem fond of the children."

"I hope she left Eileen something, she could use it."

Ken responded with a wry smile. "It's a thought." He carried her bags to his new little car, took her to the airport, and before leaving embraced her for the first time since their terrible quarrel. Susan sat on the plane heartbroken, crying over their ruptured relationship and mourning the chasm that had opened between herself and her husband. She did love him, whatever his faults. He'd let her down when she needed him, had turned weak just when some real muscle could have saved the day. But he was what he was. Dimly and without knowing why she admired his resolution. And in any event, she'd salvaged most of what was really important quite single handedly.

She became aware of a stewardess standing beside her. "Are you in distress? Is there anything I can do?"

"Oh! No, thank you. My mother has died and I'm on the way to her funeral."

"I'm so sorry." The stewardess cast about for something to do "You look cold. Would you like a blanket?"

Susan took a taxi from the airport directly to the lawyer's office. He gave her the name of the Mortuary and the keys to her mother's house. "I presume you'll want to stay there. People will be dropping by. Your mother was quite influential, a real personality."

Typically Alice, Susan reflected. Hundreds of acquaintances. But the only responsible relative anyone could find was myself. At the funeral home she took a detached interest in Alice's remains, laid out in the modest gray casket Mrs. Sterne had chosen for herself. Alice looked peaceful enough, the same shrunken ninety-year-old version of the formerly robust self who had celebrated Christmas with the Shields family only last winter. "You didn't come to Teddy's Memorial Service." Susan reproached her wordlessly. And then Sue provided Alice's reply, "Too depressing."

At the house in an old desk that she remembered she found evidence of Alice's myriad interests: Stacks of chronologically arranged bulletins and brochures from the church, information concerning several charitable organizations with receipts for contributions attached, neatly arranged correspondence from a variety of people across the U.S.A., including relatives—distant both geographically and in spirit. Among the letters she noticed a hastily scrawled note from herself and a fairly substantial missive from Eileen. She read Eileen's letter but found nothing new: the usual ecstasy over the new baby's antics and descriptions of their Mission Church which was growing slowly.

Susan wandered through the house, a well-kept six-room cape cod. One of the rooms that had been Chancellor's study was preserved as a shrine to the departed. All his books and pictures were there exactly as he'd left them. But the old computer and the blizzard of paper he'd always generated had vanished. The huge desk stood bare except for a pile of photo albums.

Susan settled down to spend the evening paging through the three scrapbooks devoted to snapshots of the Shields that started with Susan's wedding. There were pictures of the children at all ages, of the children with Ken, with herself, with both parents and grandparents, inside and outside all of the three places she'd lived with Ken.

She lingered over the snaps of Teddy, so full of life and appeal at every stage. Here he was in his cap and gown on the Princeton campus. The last picture showed him airily blowing grandmother a goodbye kiss. Over that one Sue broke down and wept.

The doorbell rang. Pastor Ives. He mentioned several items Alice had wanted to include in her service. Susan soberly confirmed his desire to do everything "as Mrs. Sterne would have wished." And yes, day after tomorrow would allow ample time for preparation,

Sue agreed. Privately she wished it might be sooner, but the Pastor wanted to announce the day and time at the Wednesday meeting. "A great number of the congregation will wish to pay their respects."

Several church members also came by the house that same evening and the next day. They brought food and sang Alice's praises, frequently commented, "It's so nice to meet her daughter at last. She was always talking about you."

Indeed, Alice did have a genius for making a great ado about nothing, Susan reflected afterwards.

As the pastor had anticipated the church was full for the funeral with a crowd ranging in ages, Sue estimated, from about fifty-five to ninety-five. Alice was properly eulogized, sung over and commended to the Almighty. At the pastor's insistence Susan even had a brief word: "My mother was a woman of strong character—single-minded and determined. I'll never forget her." She sat down. Only she in that crowd could have any notion of what Alice's steely determination had signified in her own life.

The procession to the graveyard, lowering the coffin into place beside Chancellor, and a luncheon at the church exhausted Susan's patience. Yet she still had to see the lawyer and then take an evening flight back home.

To her disgust Attorney Stimson made interminable small talk before getting down to business. His father had handled Mrs. Sterne's legal affairs until his death. "Then I took over. But I think Alice had a hard time taking me seriously."

Confronted with the lawyer's tiny features in his very large face and those enormous dimples, Sue could guess why. But she murmured polite replies and waited.

"Well, I know you're anxious to get to the will." He dimpled roguishly and picked up a file from his desk.

"Make it quick," Sue cried inwardly and made some show of consulting her watch.

"It's basically simple," Stimson remarked withdrawing the will from its long, narrow pocket. He droned through a few preliminaries before coming to the important items—"Give and bequeath." It seemed that Alice Sterne had left everything without exception "to my beloved daughter, Susan Sterne Shields"—a rather large life insurance policy, a few bank certificates and the house.

Susan knew she looked ridiculous sitting there with her mouth open, but she couldn't help herself. Stimson, amazed by her reaction, inquired tactlessly, "Isn't that exactly what you expected?"

Chapter
24

The complication of becoming an heiress obliged Susan to stay an extra day to put Alice's old car and furniture in the hands of brokers and the house in the hands of a realtor. On the way to the airport she sighed over a single regret—she needn't have stolen that car, after all.

Late in December after racking her brain to no avail over how to renew the license on the pilfered Cadillac, she purchased a mid-sized car of conservative style and color and drove it home. "What're you planning to do with the other one?" Ken asked at dinner. They now ate together whenever both happened to be at home and exchanged polite remarks.

"I'll dispose of it," she replied with honest candor. Ken had laughed over her antics with the antiques, but wouldn't find this car theft entertaining.

She took it through a hot-shot car wash and had it cleaned inside and out, removed everything that could in any way connect her with it, and after midnight wearing gloves and heavy wraps drove it from her agency to the Philadelphia area's largest mall in a blinding snow storm.

In a dark spot behind the deserted buildings she took off the tag and put it in her capacious handbag. Then she cautiously moved the car to a regular parking space and left it.

Muffled in a fur coat, heavy cap, gloves, snowboots, and with a scarf wrapped around her face, she slogged half a mile to a pay phone where she called a cab. Inside the warm taxi, voice obscured by the scarf, she instructed the driver to leave her at an all-night café near her home.

She sat at the counter under bright fluorescent lights staring at the cup of inky coffee before her that she had no intention of trying to drink and considered what to do next. She could try to get another taxi, but remembering how long she'd waited for the first one, she chose another solution.

When Ken answered her summons he demanded to know what on earth she was doing out in the middle of the night in this weather.

"Double trouble, fires burn and cauldrons bubble," she muttered.

"I'll never understand you," her husband replied. But of course he appeared promptly, took her into his little car, and drove her home. He helped her up the slippery walk, and once inside the house out of her wrappings. She accepted his offer of hot chocolate and biscuit with dumb gratitude, trembling on the verge of tears from exhaustion and stress.

And that night they might have made love for

the first time since their big quarrel if she hadn't felt so traumatized. When Ken appeared in the doorway of her room after she'd fallen into bed she could only moan, "I can't. I can't."

His abrupt withdrawal alarmed her, but there was no way she could explain.

Their relations waxed ever more distant and formal. Ken grew increasingly selective about invitations he'd accept. "I'm not going to spend three hours with the Dakes, their banker and their insurance broker. They only invite me because I'm their realtor's husband. Go without me." When she could arrange it comfortably she went without him. If she insisted and argued he'd accompany her, grudging the time.

He also absented himself from many Club affairs that she zealously attended and where she could cultivate old and new members and plant those seeds that bore a bountiful harvest of lucrative sales. When Ken was particularly resistive she even enlisted the services of one or another of her agents to act as an escort.

Once its official date was announced Susan approached Ken with trepidation about the Spring Benefit. This year the traditional ball would be held at the plush new Hutton Hotel. "I'll pay for the tickets," she offered with a degree of humility unusual for her. And mercifully, he assented without demur. She'd avoided the embarrassment of turning up at this major event without a husband!

The exclusive shop from which she now

bought most of her clothes sent over an assortment of gowns for her to try on. She arranged the three-paneled mirror in her bedroom to reflect her from all angles, wriggled into a closely fitted green jersey with tiny shoulder straps, then into a black sequined chiffon with a plunging V neckline and no back, and finally into a clinging strapless red velvet. "Beautiful dresses, ugly me," she concluded. Her tall, almost skeletal frame had scarcely an ounce of padding. Her hollow cheeks sagged against her teeth. Her eyes looked enormous in their bony sockets. She should think of food more often.

Her usual garb, casually tailored business suits with long jackets concealed the worst, and she perceived that for the Benefit she'd have to wear something with a flowing cape and a heavily lined skirt. Alas, the six months of unremitting strain she'd undergone had taken their toll. She made a fervent resolve to steer her financial boat into safe waters and keep it there.

By stuffing herself with doughnuts that she didn't particularly want each morning she managed to gain a few pounds before the Ball and in her cleverly draped gown she actually looked statuesque.

Hobnobbing with the elite gave her a sense of exaltation like nothing else. She walked out on the dance floor with Ken, marvelously handsome in his tux, with a relaxed consciousness that she belonged, was accepted—and yes, even esteemed in this upper crust world.

A succession of partners followed, among them

Vergil Joslin who kept turning up. She thought it callous of him to participate so fully in the festivities with his wife in the hospital and made a point of inquiring at length about Gertrude's condition. Instantly solemn, Vergil explained that she had suffered a recurrence of lung cancer, supposedly cured five years ago. Gert hadn't given up smoking, Susan remembered, thankful that she herself had indulged minimally in that vice. The news dampened her spirits and she looked over the crowd for the reassuring sight of her still robust and healthy Kendrick.

He was dancing with an attractive though not exceptional woman, thirty-ish, somewhat stockily built like Ken's mother, unevenly featured with large, steady gray eyes. Those eyes gazed directly into Ken's and he seemed to return their intensity. Since he'd always had that good lawyer's habit of ease and attentiveness Susan didn't understand why—this time—their attitude made her uncomfortable.

At supper she and Ken sat with Vergil, Phillipe and Budrow Dakes and his wife. Budrow, now a successful comptroller and father of two, was on his way to becoming Treasurer of a Dakes conglomerate, Sue happened to know. His beautiful wife had more than compensated for her undistinguished background with a well-developed social consciousness.

While forcing down the last spoonful of her chocolate mousse, Susan ordered the men to go find dancing partners. She wanted to have a chat with Budrow's wife. Ken made a beeline for that woman he'd danced with before, she noted.

"Isn't that a new member?" Sue idly inquired.

Elizabeth Dakes followed her gaze. "Dancing with Ken?"

"Yes."

"That's Budrow's cousin, Dr. Adrienne Jennings, who's just come to town. She's staying with Bud's folks until she finds a suitable apartment. Bud's Dad bought her a years' membership so she could meet a few people." Elizabeth smiled knowingly. "If Adrienne had the least notion of the cost, she'd have refused, I'm sure."

"Single?"

"Yes. Thirty-six and not even looking for a man from what I've heard. Totally dedicated to her work and all that."

"What sort of work?"

"She's a physicist. Researching at Penn— children's medicine, testing new drugs."

"Interesting." Susan deliberately changed the subject, unwilling to appear overly curious.

Going home she remarked off-hand, "You looked pretty intent on your conversation with Adrienne Jennings."

"You wouldn't believe how wrapped up she is in some of the latest break-throughs in the treatment of leukemia."

Not a very romantic topic, Sue determined. She wouldn't waste her time thinking about the austere Dr. Jennings.

She initiated procedures to build capital and reduce debt. This meant that she had to pass up a number of sensational bargains that she anguished over. Still, the abstention enabled her to pay off a number of her oldest acquisitions. And to balance these tedious procedures, she built a modest addition to the Joslin Realty she now owned and recruited more agents. A vastly more exhilarating affair.

Within two years Susan's financial base solidified. Her astutely chosen investments prospered, the Joslin Realty expanded and flourished. Feeling confident she reopened all parts of her mammoth house and afforded elaborate new landscaping.

Kendrick barely noticed. His private practice had done well enough to enable him to take a partner—a young fellow just out of law school. Occasionally Ken talked about his charity cases which seemed to interest him more than the paying clients. Just like Ken, Sue reflected. She'd begun to feel a bit patronizing toward this husband whose contributions to their lifestyle had dwindled to a fraction.

She relied heavily on Josephine for the competent administration of all domestic affairs including lavish parties that she re-instituted now that she could pay for them. Although he'd never admit it, they did expand Ken's contacts and helped him build his private practice.

With no children at home Josephine also increased her services to the Joslin Realty, and Susan began rewarding her with generous bonuses. Josephine looked at the checks, laughed in her deep, throaty voice and protested, "I don't need all this money."

"I thought you were taking night courses."

"Was, yes. But I have my master's in sociology now."

"Why didn't you tell me? I'd have come to your graduation."

"No big deal. I had them send my diploma by mail."

"You're amazing."

"I am—sort of—ain't I?" Jo confessed that she liked to throw out a bit of bad grammar, claimed it was her mother tongue.

"Mine too, I suspect," Sue affirmed wistfully. "One of the few regrets of my life is not being able to remember my parents—except for an emptiness that I tried to fill. First with a poor old sot at the orphanage, then with an ancient but lovely landlady who died on me."

Jo made a motion as if she might put an arm around her employer but thought better of it.

"Well, how are you planning to celebrate my fifty-eighth birthday?" Susan inquired that September and laughed inwardly at the look of mingled guilt and dismay on Kendrick's face. She refrained from mentioning that the year before he'd totally forgotten until Josephine dropped a hint rather late in the day.

"I'm giving it some thought," Ken managed to

say. But later he demonstrated more confidence. "Since you like big parties, Jo and I are planning one." She stifled the urge to remark, "Mostly Jo." This time Jo would be assisted by the recently re-hired housekeeper Mrs. Harris.

To the affair Kendrick invited his colleague, his secretary, and Adrienne Jennings. Adrienne had declined Club membership after that one year. How had she become such a friend to Kendrick? Those three made a separate little group among Susan's employees at the Agency and her closest friends from the Club. After touring the rooms and speaking dutifully to everyone, Ken returned to Adrienne's side and stayed there.

Opening presents provided the entertainment for the evening. All had brought what they considered humorous items—wild bumper stickers, misshapen mugs, a life-size enlargement of a snap of Susan, candy monstrosities and wax oddities of all kinds. Sue chuckled over everything.

The balmy late summer air and the beautiful grounds tempted people out of doors. They drifted into chairs by the pool, on to benches by the grape arbor, into walks and bypaths. But Ken's little coterie never budged from their seats on the marble terrace. "Thick as thieves," occurred to Susan. She watched them surreptitiously. Each person in that group had his input, but the main communicators were Ken and Adrienne. They talked like old buddies—had spent, Sue guessed, a lot of time together since that Benefit Ball two years ago.

At the end of the party Adrienne came to say goodbye and happy birthday again, unselfconscious and with not the least trace of guilt she looked into Susan's face—her eyes luminous and dreamy, her plain face beautiful in its sweetness. The woman was obviously no home wrecker.

Disturbed, nonetheless, Sue sat on the edge of her bed after everyone had departed and thought about Kendrick. Since that night she'd turned him away, he'd made no effort to restore intimacy, but had taken such a formal, polite and detached air with her that, to preserve her dignity, she could only respond in kind.

But the time had come to break out of their separate little shells. Resolute, Susan put on her prettiest gown and stepped out into the hall fully expecting to drift into Ken's room. To her dismay she found his door closed. She stood there, uncertain, for a few minutes that lasted interminably, then with cold, trembling fingers she tried the door. Locked.

She returned to her own room, thoroughly shaken. What had they come to? She fought down her feeling of panic. Ken and I are getting old, she reminded herself. He's sixty. I can't expect him to act like an amorous schoolboy. He's a man of principle. Just because he's found a friend in Adrienne—

But from that hour her suspicions germinated. Finding the situation intolerable she determined to confront Kendrick. In a friendly way, of course. She plotted her approach for weeks, rejecting this or that tactic. Finally one evening, finding him in the immense living room where he'd created a working island with a coffee table and chairs covered with papers, she jerked another chair from its place and set it down nearby. Then she tried to ask him about his day.

He waited patiently with a paper in each hand, giving her brief answers to her questions. She wanted to give up, but pressed on. "We haven't seen much of each other—things aren't the same."

"No. I thought you preferred it that way." He sat back, but retained the papers.

"I don't, Ken. Shouldn't we spend more time together? I know we've had our differences, but—"

"Not just slight differences, Sue. Major differences. And they won't just go away, I'm afraid."

"I'm willing to try to—to throw a bridge across, so to speak."

"We have quite a chasm to span, my dear." He'd never called her "my dear." Susan thought she'd cry, but her ingrained habit of control kept her face rigid.

"At least think about our situation, will you?" She hoped she didn't sound as desperate as she felt.

"I have been thinking about it. And you're right. We should give some serious consideration to the future. I've just been drifting along." He gave her a perfunctory smile. "I'll talk to you in a week or two. How about that? There are some pressing matters that I need to take care of, such as this brief." He waved his papers at her. "Okay?"

She rose wondering if she'd done the right thing. A few days later he announced that he was going to Arkansas to visit Eileen and see his grandchild.

Sue noted that he didn't even ask if she could accompany him and felt hurt. From his trip he returned thoughtful and decided. He spent even less time than usual at home. He was up to something.

Then one morning, as she passed his door on her way to her office, he called, "Sue?"

She paused. "Yes?" A premonition that she didn't want to participate in this conversation seized her.

"Will you come in for a minute?" His voice conveyed tension and worry.

"Well, just for a minute. I have a closing and need to put some papers together." There were suitcases in his room—an empty closet that she refused to see.

"This shouldn't take long." He patted a chair with a shaky hand. She sat down and he perched on the foot of the bed across from her. "I've taken an apartment downtown near my office," he announced, breathing hard.

"Oh, that's good. You can stay overnight then when you have a late schedule," she murmured, being reasonable.

"No, you don't understand. I'm moving out." He took a deep breath. "I think we should start divorce proceedings."

"Divorce?" She repeated the word stupidly. "That's something I never, ever thought I'd hear from you."

"Why should it come as such a shock? For

years you've lived your life, I've lived mine. We haven't made love for more than two years."

"That was your choice."

"I wouldn't say that. But let's not argue about it. Can't we agree on things peaceably? I don't want this house, nor the furniture—nothing. You can have the Georgian, if you like, and sell it if you like. Just divorce me." Every word he said shocked Susan anew. She couldn't bear to hear what he was trying to convey. She wouldn't—she wouldn't stand for anything so awful.

Susan rose. She stood over him menacing and implacable. "Kendrick Shields, if you think you're going to toss me aside like an old pair of shoes, you're mistaken. No, I will not divorce you. And you just try to divorce me! I've given you no grounds. I've never once looked at another man in the thirty-two years of our marriage. I've borne you two children, stood by you faithfully, helped you with your career. Now you want to walk out on me? Because I'm successful? Is that it?"

He flinched, but replied in a mild tone, "I've never begrudged you anything, Susan. Haven't I encouraged *you* in *your* career? Be honest."

"All right then. Since you encouraged me, why do you want to break up at the very point where we could have more leisure, where we could begin to enjoy what we've earned?"

"Sue, please. I don't want this to get ugly."

"Get ugly? The very ugliest thing I ever heard in my life is my husband asking for a divorce." She paused and gulped for air before proceeding. "Well, I'm not going to give in without a fight, Kendrick. We have an obligation to preserve our marriage—an obligation to our daughter, to our grandchild, to the stability of our community.   You're so great on responsibility. How about taking a little responsibility here instead of copping out? Just because we had a stupid fight a few years back."

"It's not just that. My feelings have changed." Ken spoke so softly that Sue who had been shouting could scarcely hear him. His appearance frightened her. He looked deflated, shrunken. She knew she must stop ranting, but couldn't control herself.

"You imagine you're in love with that Adrienne Jennings. Isn't that it? Well, all right, Ken. Have your Adrienne. Enjoy your fling, if you must. But don't ask me for a divorce."

Kendrick straightened with a mighty effort. "Don't talk that way about the most decent person I've ever known. Don't even imagine for a minute that I've tried to seduce a woman so naïve as Adrienne with false promises. She loves me and I want to marry her. And be happy for whatever time I have left. Eileen understands."

"You could talk Eileen into anything. Even something against her religion, like divorce. That's why you sneaked off to Arkansas, wasn't it?"

"I don't know why I thought you'd offer no objections. I've always had trouble understanding you. I can't imagine why you want to hang on to me when we have so little in common anymore—when you hardly respect me." Ken spoke thickly and with difficulty.

Under a towering anger Susan's heart wept for him, but she rushed on, unheeding, "I can't believe you expected me to agree to a divorce, just like that. I'll fight it, Ken. And as a lawyer you have to know that I have a very strong case."

She stormed out of the room, ran down the stairs and flung herself into her car. Half blinded by tears of rage and anguish, caught in rush hour traffic, she had, nonetheless, to get her secretary on her cell phone and instruct her about papers for the closing.

She felt ill and ate nothing all day. Her life lay about her in shards and fragments. She berated herself for handling the situation so badly. She shouldn't have yelled at Ken. After all, he did recognize her rights, she knew, from the feeble way he'd defended himself.

In a lull late in the afternoon she suddenly laid her desperate, disappointed head on the desk murmuring, "Oh Ken—oh—how could you? I'm nothing without you. Nothing."

The admission cleared her mind. She had to tell Kendrick, had to make him see that he lived in the very core of her being— that a divorce would destroy her. Unable to put off seeing him she left the office to its own devices and drove home. En route she kept rehearsing what she had to say, "Before you, I struggled like a fly in a web, getting nowhere. I never became Alice's daughter until I married you. To members of the Club, I'm your wife—just that." Why hadn't she said, "I need you, Ken. I can't live without you"? And especially, "I love you." How much kinder and truer than the ugly accusations she'd made.

She passed a vacant house that she'd observed for long years, assessing the progress of its decay. Today she noticed that it had sagged together. Roof and walls leaned perilously against each other. A strong wind and the structure would collapse.

"That's how Ken looked this morning," she whispered, heart constricting.

Once home she sought him out in the living room, the kitchen, the library. She looked all around the grounds. Why had she imagined that he'd be here and not at work? But there was one last place to look. She hurried up to his bedroom and burst in. Empty and quiet. But, Thank You, Lord, his suitcases stood on the bed, half unpacked. He'd even re-hung some of his clothes before abandoning the task, unfinished.

Laughing and hiccupping with relief she sought the privacy of her own bedroom where she lay down in all her clothes and staring at the ceiling, made a hundred resolves. She'd make Kendrick happy, after all. She'd appreciate him, take an interest in his work—even those ridiculous charity cases. They'd get back together, go places, visit their grandchild. Exhausted, she dozed off.

When she woke it was dark, the house silent. Somewhere a clock chimed three. She tiptoed into Ken's room. He lay asleep, his open-mouthed immobility positively frightening her for a moment until his lips closed, he turned on his side and emitted a faint snore. Reassured she went back to her room, disrobed and lay awake till morning.

Through the wall, after seven, she heard him moving around his room, running water in the bathroom. She could picture his action from the days when they'd shared a bedroom in his mother's house. A crash startled her and sent her leaping out of bed. She stood for a moment in his doorway trying to sort out her impressions. The sound had been too heavy for a can of spray. The furniture stood securely against the walls. He must have fallen!

She raced to his bathroom. He lay sprawled in the doorway not moving. She crept close and looked down at him. His face was livid, distorted and motionless. She ran screaming to the steps, "Ken's sick—get an ambulance! Josephine! Mrs. Harris!"

By the time she reached the bottom, Jo was there. "Ken's passed out," Susan shrieked. "Call the hospit—no, I'll do it."

Josephine caught her in her arms. "Let me call. You're too upset. Put clothes on, so you can ride with him." The tall, competent woman disappeared into the library and Sue obediently remounted the stairs. Breathlessly she hurried into her clothes, resolutely shutting her mind against the probability that he'd died.

On arrival, the paramedics pronounced him "deceased." But Susan refused to believe them. "Idiots, morons! Get him to the hospital emergency—now!

now! Give him oxygen. Do something."

They obeyed. She accompanied Ken in the ambulance while they worked over him, giving each other looks of hopeless dismay.

At the hospital they wheeled him off at once leaving her in the waiting room for an hour by herself. She knew that Kendrick had died, but couldn't accept it. Even when the doctor came to her and confirmed it, a part of her cried out that it was impossible.

"No, no, there's a mistake. What's wrong with you?" The doctor left her. A nurse came with a medication which she refused. Presently she heard Jo's concerned but calm voice, and after a minute saw her. "Poor baby," Jo said. Susan broke down and wept in her black arms.

The next day Eileen arrived and mother and daughter cried and talked. But most of the time Susan felt numb, empty, stunned. Nothing reached her in that sealed off place to which she'd retreated. She had killed her good and kind husband and would have to pay for it for the rest of her life.

She let Eileen choose the plot at the graveyard and the coffin. The minister from her church came twice to talk about the funeral, but Sue listened from a great distance, merely acquiescing when necessary.

The church filled for the service. Susan looked around without curiosity. A hundred people came that she'd never seen. She recognized the usual crowd from the Club, all her own employees, a few business associates, friends of Eileen from the other church. She recalled that Kendrick had attended there himself recently.

Kendrick's colleague arrived with Adrienne, the latter's face ravaged with grief.

Probably imagines that she'll miss him more than I will. Susan remembered her own foolish notion about missing Gloria more than Ken when he'd spent a lifetime with his mother!

After the rites at the graveside people came to squeeze her limp hand or embrace her. A handsome, successful-looking white haired man said, "Your husband saved my business—and my life. I was about to kill myself." And after a pause he added, "Never charged me a penny."

A slim, pale woman holding a child by the hand murmured, "If Mr. Shields hadn't made those partners pay me for my husband's share of the business, I'd be broke today."

There were a dozen other vaguer but equally warm expressions of gratitude from a wide range of personalities. Yet these were a mere sampling of those whom Ken had helped.

Vergil Joslin appeared, pressed her hand till it hurt and said, "Kendrick will be missed." By herself, above all, Sue reflected, riding home beside Eileen.

She looked at her daughter, admiring her steadiness as she managed the car with skill and concentration. Her gray eyes fixed on the road under those straight dark eyebrows. Susan also noted a thickening in her figure, a puffiness in the skin. Why hadn't she noticed before? "You're pregnant?"

"Four months."

"Why didn't Ellis come with you?" Accusingly.

"We decided that he should stay and take care of Theo and the church. I'm all right, Mom. Depend on it."

After while Susan managed to say, "I'm glad you're having another child. I find it comforting."

A few weeks after the baby's arrival Susan visited Eileen in Arkansas for the first time. To her dismay the family picked her up at the airport in a truck. Even with Eileen holding little Elizabeth on her lap there was barely room in the cab for parents, grandmother and Theo—an active boy, now three.

The second shock came when they turned off the road and drove into a garage cut into the hillside. Above the garage their house, a modest log and stone cottage could be reached from below by a stair so steep it was almost ladder-like. Scrambling through a trap door into the main room, Sue tore her stocking and stifled a curse that rose automatically to her lips. The house consisted of three rooms and a bath: a large, all-purpose room and two small bedrooms. The bare wooden floors and complete absence of recreational equipment disturbed Susan. Her suitcase appeared on a rough bench in Theo's room where she would occupy the top bunk. She wanted to protest and look for a motel but refrained. She could survive the one night she planned to stay.

At supper she inquired where the church was located. "We have the service here," Ellis responded taking a large bite of biscuit.

"Here?"

"Yes. We use folding chairs. They're stored in there." Ellis gestured toward a pair of retractable doors in a corner.

"There must be a half dozen vacant church buildings in the area," Sue suggested, trying to hide her irritation.

"Yes, but when the congregation's ready, we think they'll want to build their own church. Some of them helped us build this house."

"And isn't it nice?" Eileen purred with contentment. "We just moved in."

That explained the odor of lumber in the place. "Where did you live before?"

"You don't want to know." Eileen smiled and laid a hand affectionately on her mother's arm. "Actually, we're doing well—making the kind of progress we want to make."

"Slow?"

"Steady. We don't encourage people to join unless they're really committed."

While they washed dishes, Susan inquired whether their Mission Board couldn't provide a little more adequately for them.

"This is how it's done, Mom. We live like other people in the community. Ellis has a part-time job."

"Doing what?"

"Cashiering at a gas station."

"That's absurd! I don't know how you tolerate all this."

"I like it. I'm happy." Her calm, smiling face confirmed her attitude of peaceful acceptance.

"Ellis does a lot of rough work, doesn't he? Isn't he ruining his hands? What about the violin?"

"Don't worry about it. We don't worry. Anyway, it's intermittent."

Before they retired that night Susan lingered with her daughter in the living room. They talked about Eileen's time in the hospital, about Theo and his baby sister. Then Eileen cupped her mother's cold hands in her warm ones and asked, "What's the matter, Mom? I can see that you're troubled."

Sue hesitated but at last confessed in a voice barely above a whisper, "It's your father's death. I was responsible."

"No, Mom." Eileen spoke authoritatively. "You weren't to blame. A doctor warned Dad about his heart condition more than a year ago, told him he was a strong candidate for stroke."

"Why didn't I know that?"

Eileen lifted her shoulders. "Hard to say. But

don't carry a load of guilt about it."

Susan should have felt absolved, but didn't.

On the way back to the airport next day Eileen drove the truck. Ellis had to work his job at the gas station.

After her return Sue shopped long and carefully and purchased an expensive rug in brown tones—durable and rustic-looking to fit into the décor of her daughter's home.   She also purchased the finest compact disk player she could locate and included a set of classical tapes.

Eileen's letter of thanks, full of genuine gratitude, also exuded an aura of guilt. Susan smiled over having successfully introduced a couple of elements that didn't totally fit into the lifestyle of their community.

With nothing to entice her home evenings Susan began to remain for longer and longer periods at the office. She even added a shower and a sofa that unfolded and stayed overnight on occasion. Her real estate investments had more than repaid the care she'd taken.

Gradually she found that the on-going search for suitable employees to help manage things constituted her single most knotty problem. If only her children had come into the business! Again the old grudge against Josephine rankled. That woman with her "orthodoxy" and her "active church."

Still, Josephine did earn her salary at least

twice. She planned and executed the most successful parties and dinners in the city, invitations to which were much coveted. Nor could Susan begin to put a price on Jo's services to the Agency.

So when she received a modest envelope from her employee marked, "Personal" she opened it anxiously. True, she'd seen remarkably little of Jo who worked expertly behind the scenes as a rule. But why couldn't she have phoned or left her a message at home?

Josephine's communication was brief and formal—a type-written note: "This will inform you of my decision to resign, effective July 1. Thank you for a long and stimulating association." She'd given two months' notice. After long, worried reflection Sue determined that with that amount of time she could persuade Jo to stay on.

Changes would have to be made, of course. She tried to put herself in Jo's shoes. She hadn't given the woman either the recognition or the money she deserved. That could be remedied. By late afternoon she'd dictated a new contract and sent it to her attorney for examination. She would make Jo a Vice President, give her an office, relieve her of duties at the house— indispensable as she was there.

When she located Josephine in the kitchen after dinner conferring with the housekeeper, she remarked cheerfully. "Got your note, Jo. In a day or two I'll be offering you an alternative."

Josephine's look of rejection alarmed her, but

of course her employee didn't yet know what she'd be offered.

The new contract in final form came back to her desk the next afternoon, and feeling uneasy, Susan took it home at once. The lawn service truck stood on the grounds and she could see men at work with mechanized clippers shaping the hedges. Inside the house, immaculately kept, all stood empty and silent. She looked for Jo. Messages by the phone in the library attested to her recent presence, all dated and timed, everything clear and concise. But where was she? She looked in the kitchen. Nothing underway there as could be expected since Sue was dining at Floretta Griffin's.

Josephine must be in her apartment. Sue walked through the house and out to the second set of garages and looked around for the staircase to Jo's quarters—couldn't believe she'd never been up there! In the garage area she smelled gas, spilled oil. Unprepossessing steps led up to Jo's quarters. No wonder she was getting discontented. At the top she looked for a bell to sound. None there. She knocked—no answer. Had Jo gone out? Sue tried the door which opened easily.

"Josephine?" No response. She called more loudly—"Jo?" She stepped inside. "Are you here?" She glanced into the bedroom and bath. No one around. Jo went off and left the door open? Not too dangerous. The outer doors of the garages locked automatically, and from the house Sue had let herself in with a key. Idly she examined Jo's apartment.

On one wall hung an assortment of portraits and

snapshots, presumably of relatives and friends. Over the low bookcases a collection of framed snaps and portraits of the Shields family. Comfortable but simple chairs and sofa in a subdued dark blue check. Contrasting white tables and lamps. Increasingly curious, Sue scanned the titles of the many books: Real Estate Law, a substantial collection, texts on political science, books of history, biography, geography, a dutiful gathering of classic novels and philosophy. Recent issues of a wide range of magazines. Battered volumes that she identified as Bibles in a variety of translations. On the open piano pieces of music. More music stacked on top. On the white enameled coffee table an assortment of brochures and an application blank. After a quick look at the door Sue went closer and looked down at the form, meticulously filled out. "Not the Peace Corps!" Susan startled herself with the sound of her own voice. All the brochures came from the same source.

She experienced a sense of defeat so overwhelming that she sat down on the sofa. Jo's apartment had told her things she didn't know how to interpret, but the accumulation convinced her that she'd lost the best worker on her staff and a friend. She went out, laid the envelope containing Jo's new contract in front of the door and slowly descended the stairs.

Next day Jo brought it back, gentle but resolute. "I'm flattered—the position, the salary—such an honor!"

Susan, dining alone, looked up from her shortcake. "Sit down with me, Jo. Please. Have some coffee."

Josephine served herself and took a chair. "I can't accept, of course," she went on, laying the envelope beside Susan's plate.

"What will you do?"

"I'm joining the Peace Corps. I'll serve one or two terms and then try to get into administration."

With a deep sigh Sue breathed, "You won't make money in the Corps."

"No, but money's never been important to me."

"Then why did you name such a high figure when I first hired you?"

"Oh! That was to make you value me. I knew that if you thought I'd work for peanuts, you'd lose respect."

Susan admitted the truth of that. Then she asked with a direct look into Jo's eyes, "I'm curious to know why you're doing this to me."

Josephine laughed. "You'll manage splendidly."

"Yes, but not as splendidly as I manage with you. I may have to hire three people."

"Yes, perhaps."

"Are you bored with things here?"

"No." Jo looked uncomfortable. "I just feel that no one really needs me any more."

"How can you say that when you've just admitted that you're as good as three average Joes?"

Josephine sighed and answered slowly, "Teddy

and Eileen and Mr. Shields—they needed me in ways I can't explain to you. But you—" Jo's dark eyes dropped for a moment before she looked back. "You don't know how to need—people. And for the business you can hire someone else. Besides," now she toyed with her coffee cup, "for a long time you've been angry with me about Teddy." She met Susan's gaze, "Haven't you?"

"I provided the opportunity to influence my children. I'm responsible. Not you. If I had it to do over, I guess I would do things differently. But I never second-guess what's behind. And I do know how to need people. It's the essence of my life. I didn't offer you that contract light-heartedly. It represents my—my need."

"Yes, I wish I wanted to meet that need. But—business, though admittedly intriguing, is not my prime concern. Let me go. I'll be happier in the Corps."

What alternative had she, Susan asked herself. All she'd done for years was let people go—all those she'd cared about—only Eileen left, and she was far away.

Chapter
27

Twice a week Susan went to the hospital to visit Vergil's wife Gertrude Joslin. She told herself that she deserved the punishment of seeing the woman's steady decline and took it stoically. She'd only encountered one other person in the four weeks she'd visited, except for a Chaplain who looked in hurriedly.

She could only recognize Gertrude because this was Gert's room number and Gertrude greeted Sue by name. The skeleton, over which a thin, wrinkled parchment of skin stretched, still housed Gertrude's confident spirit, however. The once faded gray eyes glittered with unnatural light. She spoke in metallic squeaks from a device in her throat. From week to week she kept Susan up-to-date on the treatment she received.

Propped up in bed on one cloudy November afternoon, her bony wrist connected to a feeding tube that dripped a solution into her, Gertrude announced that her medication no longer worked. "I'll die sometime between Thanksgiving and Christmas."

Sue, in a low chair beside the elevated bed,

dropped her face in her hand, not to conceal tears, but to mask the horror she felt. To come to the end of life like this! She was saved from replying by Gert's husband, Vergil, who came hustling in, all business.

His vigor, his muscular body, the vibrant color in his face offended Susan. She wanted him to partake of his wife's illness. His firm red lips planted a dutiful kiss on the emaciated forehead, "Will you stay holed up here for Thanksgiving or come home?"

"Too weak for the trip this time." Gertrude produced a grotesque smile. Susan recalled that for her birthday two months earlier Gert had gone home temporarily in an ambulance.

Vergil sat down on the end of the bed and began to discuss business deals. Gertrude managed to gasp out bits of information about the men he'd be meeting, but she tired rapidly. Distressed Susan rose and began to excuse herself.

"Don't go yet," Vergil said. "I want to take you to dinner."

Sue darted a look at Gertrude and saw her nodding approval. "Keep him company," she clacked. Unable to bear it any longer, Susan went to the ladies' room and then waited in the lounge. She wanted Vergil to suffer, and resolved to induce a little remorse.

Over dessert, therefore, she broke into her companion's jovial gossip about the latest escapade of the Club's most derelict husband. "Be serious, Vergil. How can you joke around at a time like this? Surely Gertrude must have told you that she expects to die soon."

Vergil turned watchful and grave. "Of course she did."

"She's been a true wife to you for most of a lifetime."

"She has indeed! She was a good mother to the boys" (now in business for themselves) "but mostly she lived for me."

"You'll miss her."

"More than anyone can imagine! She worked her butt off for me, always accomplishing things I wanted done. She could really maneuver people into position."

Since Susan, flabbergasted, had nothing to say, he went on, "She has a genius for inviting confidences or ferreting out things people usually hide. I'll never replace her, I know that."

Distressed by the turn the conversation had taken, Sue decided to escape by walking back to where her car was parked at the hospital, but when they got outside it was dark and raining hard, and she had to accept a lift. When he let her out Vergil remarked, "I hope you understand that I do appreciate Gert. Things will be different without her."

Sue waved goodbye and got into her own car. Driving home she considered the painful probability that Gert had maneuvered *her* into prominence in the Club, then whetting her interest in real estate! And to think she'd imagined herself totally in charge!

Disgusted, she pretended to be out when Joslin

called to chat. If he had any business matter to take up, he could communicate in writing. She even made the days and hours of her visits to Gert unpredictable in case he made a point of running into her again at the hospital. On her last two visits, Gertrude lay in a semi-comatose state, opening her eyes briefly and lifting a feeble hand by way of greeting.

Since Joslin was a long standing important figure, the Club members attended Gertrude's funeral in force. The largest church in the area could barely accommodate the throng. Prominent politicians, newsmen and tycoons that Sue recognized but had never spoken to lent an aura of importance great enough to warrant presence of a Media van. The crowd, sporting an ample proportion of Philadelphia's finest black wool and leather, provided somber contrast to a positive wilderness of wreaths, cut flowers and elaborate floral arrangements, banked in front and in the outer aisles.

The ceremony, excessively formal and brief, seemed to contain snippets from a myriad of tributes. Susan decided not to join the long procession to the cemetery. She waited in the Church which grew chilly from the opening of doors, until the congregation had dispersed and then drove to her office. She shivered through the remainder of the day. Unwell, she decided. Needed a checkup, couldn't remember her last one—three? five? years ago?

"Sound as a bell," Dr. Kemper pronounced her. "You should put on a little weight, though. If you should fall ill you've not a spare pound to lose. And try to cut stress."

Susan obeyed, lingering over dinner at a restaurant or at houses of friends. She had a small addition built on to the agency, and installed a tiny sitting room, and, more and more often, slept there feeling little enthusiasm for the wide empty vistas that engulfed her at home. Nor, without Josephine's help, did she like to entertain on a grand scale usually contenting herself with small dinner parties.

Another Spring Ball rolled around with a kind of inevitability that Susan took in stride, with none of the excitement of her previous years at the Club. When Vergil Joslin called and suggested that they "pair off" for the event she assented easily, though she hated his jokes and his graphic descriptions of the improvement in her figure as she added one slow pound after another. His calling the Club Board "Susanna and the Elders" figured among his irritating references. True, she was the only female member, and at sixty, the youngest. The men, in their seventies and eighties, had the gnarled durability of old oaks. But the Board's discussions centered almost exclusively on how to delegate the various tasks that kept the Club operating. "All business," she summarized for Vergil's benefit. His only reply a suggestive leer.

For the Ball she wore a simple forest green jersey with a diamond necklace—Kendrick's gift on the occasion of Teddy's birth. She remembered clawing at the case with weak fingers, her thrill at the sight of the exquisite jewels on the black velvet. Reminiscing she lifted the necklace in her aging hand, dangled and turned it in the light, admiring its delicacy, the graceful setting of the stones. Her initial dazzled, greedy acceptance of this gift in no way resembled her current educated appreciation. The necklace reflected Kendrick: his taste and discernment, his cultured recognition of the truly aesthetic. She thought of pieces she'd seen— expensive and ugly. Some of the jewels Gertrude had worn (Vergil's choice), for instance: those enormous jade earrings, real pearls—too fat for Gertie's neck, a flashy diamond and ruby brooch. The woman had looked better in her every-day ornaments—old cameos and pearl earrings that had been her mother's.

Susan opened jewel cases and tried on a pair of sapphire earrings. No, she'd do with just the necklace and the exotic orchid Vergil had sent.

At the Benefit she and Joslin were soon separated. After two hours of unremitting dance with a rapid succession of eager partners Susan laughingly called time out and sat down at the lounge end of the ballroom where a crowd of solicitous men in tuxedoes clustered around her. A half hour later her ginger-ale had been refreshed so often that a collection of lemon, lime and cherry accumulated in her glass: garbage-on-the-rocks. Younger men, older men and men her age had hinted at a variety of possible liaisons that Susan chose to treat as a joke.

Worn out, finally, and weary of the game, she looked around for Vergil. Across the room, center of his own cluster, her so-called partner caught her eye and made swimming gestures, and with a look of mock despair, of disappearing under waves. Susan laughed but felt frustrated. She made her own gestures signifying departure. He did not break away! Ken would have rescued her at once!

Annoyed, she sent Joslin a note and departed with the Budrow Dakes who were just leaving.

When Vergil called next day it was not to apologize. He started filling her in on information he'd picked up about who was selling what property and what changes in mortgage procedure were to be incorporated in a state government bill now in committee.   In exchange, in all fairness, Sue had to reciprocate with carefully edited gossip and rumors she'd heard, some of which filled gaps in what he'd learned.

"Call me anytime you're bored," Vergil concluded airily and hung up. His brassy confidence, his assumption that she'd get lonely and turn to him exasperated her. She made no move in his direction even while fully utilizing the information he'd shared.

Every week she forced herself to go home at least once. She walked swiftly around the grounds and made notes for the gardeners. The current housekeeper (third since Jo's departure) now had a niece staying with her, she remembered on hearing talk and laughter in the kitchen where a portable TV had appeared on the counter. The house had a slightly dusty, carelessly kept feel. She'd accumulated social obligations and ought to throw another party, but without Jo monitoring the catering, the food in her last effort at entertaining had varied from ordinary to tasteless, and the distraction of having to straighten out glitches in service herself kept her from enjoying the company as she had previously.

Besides, at her last big affair Vergil had arrived early and had re-assessed her house and grounds with a frankly appraising eye. When guests started coming he made his presence felt, welcoming people with a familiar air as if he were a cohost or something. Oh well, she thought, as she continued her tour of the house, all that was past and she could control Vergil.

Upstairs things were even dustier. And in the closets clothes had accumulated. Jo had taken Sue's cast-offs somewhere, promising that they'd be useful. In a brief conference with the housekeeper she gently recommended a higher standard of cleanliness.

"If you'd just let us know when you're coming—" Mrs. Prinz started to protest, but stopped herself hastily when she saw the irony in Susan's face.

At supper she ate a salad alone in the vast dining room and retired early. Why did she sleep better at the office, she wondered putting on plaid pajamas and snuggling under the covers in the huge bed that occupied little space in the oversized bedroom. Maybe because the house haunted her with memories of all she'd lost. She dozed off at last but slept fitfully and woke, feeling a premonition of danger. The illuminated hands of her clock registered 3:32. Why did she imagine that she heard sounds below at this impossible hour? She strained her ears. Yes, away down there someone was moving around!

She slid her feet into soft slippers and padded down the carpeted hall. The rustling sound strengthened almost imperceptibly as she advanced. She shivered and crept more slowly. At the staircase she hesitated before descending breathlessly, keeping close to the railing, her eyes glued to the foyer. Presently she saw a narrow beam from a tiny flashlight. A masked figure had the door of the hall closet open and was stuffing a sable coat into a large bag he carried—one already bulging! A thief! She wanted to scream accusations but stifled the impulse. Suppose he had a gun?

The intruder closed the closet softly, turned, glimpsed her cowering in the stairwell and without hesitating disappeared into the den where she heard him scrambling out through the glass doors.

Suddenly angry, Susan rushed back to her bedroom and summoned the police. Twenty minutes later the house was ablaze with light, officers swarmed over the grounds with dogs baying, and a policewoman was going through the place with Susan to assess the loss. The thief was never found and though reimbursed by the insurance company, Sue suffered a sensation of having been invaded, her privacy violated. She had a sophisticated alarm system installed and ordered an inspection of every door and window before sleeping again in the house. Since the housekeeper's niece was there anyway, she employed the girl to make an exhaustive inventory of her possessions. Too many possessions. A sermon of Rev. Sterne's drifted into her mind. Something about laying up treasures where thieves break in and steal. "Lay up treasures in heaven." Was that how it went? Heaven seemed impossibly vague to Susan.

Susan began systematically to pay off mortgages on certain valuable real estate investments. She had more cash, as a consequence, but found to her dismay that State and Federal income taxes swallowed much of the added intake. Why had she worked so hard only to support criminally wasteful governments?

Her disillusion and diminished enthusiasm combined to leave her with a pervasive discontent. To combat these feelings she ought to do more things that she'd find enjoyable she decided. But where to find that type of entertainment. It wasn't easy. After considerable vacillation she arranged to spend a Saturday evening with Floretta Griffin and that woman's most recent partner. She'd also invite Omar Steyben to join them, she resolved. He was at least acceptably handsome and well mannered. He was also safe. Susan smiled recalling how he'd explained that his elderly wife had left him her fortune in trust with the provision that if he ever married again a certain charity would at once fall heir to all the money. Omar unabashedly broadcast this information to anyone with a willing ear.

Susan's secretary made dinner reservations and purchased theater tickets for the four.

Chapter
28

On Sunday after the Saturday night fiasco she woke with a headache and a foul taste in her mouth. She remembered the two drinks and five cigarettes she'd indulged in, because the atmosphere seemed to demand some minimal participation. Dinner had been a plodding affair through which Omar had talked non-stop about himself in a heavy uninflected voice. It had preceded a so-so performance of "The Three Sisters." Drowsy from too much drink and food Omar kept dozing off during the third act to Susan's disgust. Then they'd adjourned to a Lounge where Susan's companions seemed determined to spend the remaining hours of the night. The thirty minutes she'd sat in the Ladies' room smoking and discussing the play with Floretta Griffin emerged as the only enjoyable part of the entertainment.

Toward morning Omar cast all inhibitions aside and subjected her to the lamentable history of his financial decline. In the hands of indifferent bankers his principal remained constant while the income from it purchased ever fewer of the comforts to which he'd grown accustomed. Inflation, he mourned, had forced him to move twice in the twenty years since his wife's demise: first from a ten-acre estate to one half the size, and more recently to an economical house of a mere fifteen rooms on little more than an acre. "If I have to move again, I'll kill myself." Tears dampened Omar's large dark eyes.

Susan darted glances at people sitting nearby, fearful that some acquaintance might witness this display of self-pity.

How ironic that Omar's alert handsomeness should cloak such an unmitigated bore! Never again, Omar.

Lying in her own bed alone and shifting her vision from ceiling to window, Susan evaluated the quality of light seeping in on this Sunday morning through her bedroom blinds. Ten o'clock, she guessed. She consulted the digital clock and congratulated herself on an accurate surmise.

An hour later, wearing a thick cotton coverall and canvas shoes, she stood in the brilliant sunshine of a mall. The cozy little café where she planned to eat brunch would open in ten minutes. She strolled about the cobbled area with its potted trees and stared into cute little boutique and gift shop windows and then, tired, seated herself on the rim of a tiny fountain and engaged in deep reflection. A recollection of Omar's growing familiarity, of the wet smacks he'd planted at random on her arms and cheek repelled her. She heard a voice, looked up at a pair of handsome young bucks passing by and met the admiring gaze of one who remarked that she made a charming picture. "You could be a model." Susan took it as a measure of her eventless life that she could feel gratified by this passing comment. Inside, consuming a plateful of strawberries and melons before her eggs benedict, she reconsidered her opposition to Vergil Joslin. The man was at least intelligent and never dull or maudlin.

On Monday she called him. His secretary purred sweetly, "I know Mr. Joslin will be pleased to return your call. I'll track him down right away."

"No rush." She hung up, confident that she graced Joslin's priority list and feeling a bit smug. When he called back within the hour she agreed readily to "exchange notes over dinner."

She specified frankly that she abominated being gossiped about and becoming an object for speculation so Vergil cooperated in efforts to keep their ever more frequent meetings private. He located old Inns and picturesque out-of-the-way places to take her. Gradually she allowed herself to enjoy his company and to anticipate seeing him. She tried to picture married life with Vergil, but there her mind balked. It had been gratifying to find that as Kendrick Shields' widow she still commanded the same respect she'd enjoyed as his wife.

In efforts to cut stress, as the doctor had advised, Susan instituted certain patterns that she observed as often as she could manage. She still didn't want to spend too much time at meals so she ate twice a day—the first time on weekdays at a neighborhood café. She liked the old, brightly painted booths with their high wooden backs and checked cushions. They afforded a sense of privacy, and usually enabled her to read *The Wall Street Journal* in peace. But one morning her perusal ended abruptly with the intrusion of a sharp voice, and Susan had a momentary impression of a couple of dark suits disappearing into the booth at her back.

"Oh, come on Vance, don't label every broker a crook just because one man--" A mild voice, trying to stem what appeared to be a tirade on his companion's part concluded, "My brother-in-law's in the business, and he's honest." Wasn't that the voice of a doctor she'd seen a couple of times? The men were probably professionals from a hospital just down the pike.

"Well, okay, maybe there are a few decent peddlers out there, but Vergil Joslin isn't one of them."

Hearing the name Susan put her paper down and tuned in.

"I don't know the man, so I can't agree or disagree. Your mother's experience was deplorable, admittedly."

"He robbed her! After five years she finally admitted that to me this morning, when she confessed that she'd have to sell the house and move into a condo."

"You don't think Joslin could have been mistaken? People do give bad advice if they're misinformed. Maybe Joslin was sincere."

"That weasel knew what he was up to every minute. He started sucking up to Mom even while Dad was lingering on in the hospital. He prepared her for everything—my objections, my sister Kate's objections—and had her signature on a contract to sell him Dad's business two weeks after the funeral. Convinced Mom that she'd never be able to cope with it."

"How do you know she could have?"

"Good grief! The business had already been functioning efficiently for more than a year with just a general manager in charge. What's so complicated about a dry cleaning plant and a string of pick-up stations? I learned the whole operation in high school—just working summers. You can bet Joslin spends a lot less time there than Mom would've. He just picks up the profits."

Susan couldn't control a restrained grimace. She'd had her own experience with Vergil's genius for picking up profits.

"If he'd paid a fair price, I'd feel differently, I guess. Mom never believed the concern was worth twice what Joslin offered. Even after I had it appraised and showed her the figures, she took that SOB's word for it. What a con artist he was!"

"You couldn't stop the deal?"

"No. I hired a lawyer. But in the end he advised me not to go to court. Said that without my mother's cooperation we didn't have a prayer."

Too disturbed by the tenor of that conversation

to listen any longer Susan dropped money on the table and walked out. But the aggrieved voice, the derogatory names applied to Joslin echoed in her mind all day.

Not for a minute did she doubt that Vergil had done every thing the man had accused him of. But after all, in a dog-eat-dog world, it's every man for himself, she defended, marshalling time-honored clichés. So sure—Vergil was shrewd. Weak, sentimental folk did a lot of damage too, in their way—maybe more.

Still, it was an effort to treat him with the same friendly acceptance. Vergil met her increased aloofness with increased aggression. Her refusal to bed with him had been a standing contention, and he now intensified his exactions, urging her to grow up, to consider what she was missing, to drop the blushing-maiden stuff. One evening on returning from the theater, he delivered a half hour's diatribe along these lines, accompanied by the monotonous thwack of windshield wipers in the rain. They drove into the grounds of her estate and Joslin stopped his car and pulled out the key.

"Don't get out," Sue remarked flatly. "If I'd had the least inclination to ask you in it would have died back there, twenty minutes ago." She slammed the car door and walked into the house without a backward look.

Next day, as if to prove his good nature, he called in his usual exuberant way to tell her she'd be getting a call from a prospective agent. "The person asked about you, and I said you're the best in the business."

"Thanks, Verg. What's his name?"

"Her name's Belle Tanner."

Two days later Susan heard her secretary on the phone, sotto voice. "I tried to get rid of her, but this person insists you want to see her."

"Who is it?"

"Mrs. Tanner."

"Send her in." Sue hung up. Something off-key here.

Belle sailed in, a not-too-pleasant smile on her enameled cherry lips. Long fake eyelashes, green-ice eyeshadow, painted cheeks and an abundant wig of platinum blonde hair made it impossible to guess what the woman might really look like. Her portly, well corseted figure strained the seams of her tight sheer green dress.

Susan disliked her on the spot, but schooled herself. She had a policy of discounting first impressions, especially those based on appearances alone. "Please come in."

Belle Tanner threw herself into the nearest chair, huffing a bit. "So hard to find decent help these days. That poor girl out there. Actually tried to turn me away. And after Mr. Joslin told me you'd be glad to talk to me. Such a nice man, Mr. Joslin."

"We do take on a new agent from time to time," Sue murmured. "But only when an opening occurs."

"Vergil—Mr. Joslin, I mean, told me all about the real estate business. Said you'd be the right person to learn the ropes from."

"Really?"

"He thinks I'm a natural. Looks, personality, you name it."

"And did Mr. Joslin define the ropes I'm supposed to teach you?"

"Well, let's see. He said you knew how to turn every trick in the trade. I think those were his words."

"I see. Have you had any sales experience, Mrs. Tanner?"

"Call me Belle." The woman's coy glance implied that they were familiars—or soon to become so. "I've been selling for the past eight years, to answer your question. Mostly lingerie."

"Selling houses would be a rather different experience, I'm afraid. And there's the licensing course you'd have to pass and the examination."

"Oh hell. Vergil didn't say anything about all that. Oh, well, I suppose I could spare a couple weeks. How long does it take?"

"Quite a while. And, as a matter of fact, we aren't taking on new staff at the moment." Susan opened a drawer and took out an application form. "Why don't you take this home, fill it out at your leisure and mail it back to me."

The woman drew back as if stung. "You trying to get rid of me? I got a job here. Isn't this Joslin's Agency?"

"Mr. Vergil Joslin has no interest in this Real Estate Firm, Mrs. Tanner. He sold all rights in it long years ago. I make all the decisions here." She again tendered the application. Mrs. Tanner reached for it, changed her mind and stood up.

"No use sending that back to you," she shrilled. "I can see you don't like me. From what Vergil said I never expected you to be such a stick! Besides I hate to work for a woman!" Belle flung herself from the room, a veritable portrait of indignation.

The phone immediately rang and Susan went on with her day's activities, but in idle moments she attempted to sort out her impressions of this "prospective agent." At best, she could imagine that Vergil had sent the woman over as a joke. At worst it was a form of retaliation for her summary rejection of a few nights ago. She considered persuading Omar to go over and waste Joslin's time on some cheap pretext, but instead treated the affair as it deserved by totally ignoring it. She judged, however, that Joslin by his action had made them adversaries, a circumstance that actually piqued her interest.

She'd been straight with him before, but now she teased him unconscionably, flirted, allowed a few liberties and then broke off, behaved unpredictably. She laughed thinking of the chase she led him. He deserved it. Part of her strategy lay in giving him limitless opportunities to talk about his business. During his long married life he'd used Gertrude as a sounding board and now he'd begun to look to Susan for intelligent feedback. He appreciated her abilities and trusted her, since she'd never betrayed a confidence. She asked astute questions, listened alertly and applauded with subtlety.

As if for the first time Sue observed with keen appreciation when Spring came to Philadelphia. At home she strolled around her grounds, gazing into trees where buds erupted into delicate greenness, where flowering trees showed white or pink or caught sunlight in brilliant sprays of yellow bloom. And when Vergil proposed that they lunch at the Longwood Gardens one Sunday and walk about, she assented eagerly.

She remembered the place from her past—those days she'd spent with Mrs. Bowman. With enthusiasm she identified the slopes, the variegated beds of plants, the charming vistas that opened out everywhere. Vergil paced beside her intent on the deal that occupied him at the moment.

"I used to come here with a landlady I had once--when I was terribly young," Sue murmured, almost shyly. She'd never before shared anything from her past with Vergil.

"Oh, you did?" Susan could tell that the information and her nostalgia meant nothing to him.

"So you're sure they'll widen that street?" she prompted, to encourage him to continue his own line of thought.

"No doubt about it. They've already initiated that whole committee, preliminary survey, opposition-assessment process that they always go through. But it will be a year before the papers get hold of it. So if I unload my building now, I should still get a good price."

"How close to the street is it?"

"By the time the City takes ten or twelve feet off the front, hardly any parking space will be left. And the retail store renting there now won't survive."

"Pity."

"Not too bad for me if I can sell the place this week."

"You have a buyer?"

"Hot prospect—guy who put in my last set of windows. Awfully conservative. He's saved a buck and wants to invest. Trouble is, he blows hot and cold, can't make up his mind."

"Little wonder if it's his total savings. If he takes your building, he stands to lose, doesn't he?"

"Oh, he can rent it—some service concern or something."

"But that isn't a good enough forecast to make you want to hang on to it?" Susan enjoyed using this Kendrick-style approach on Joslin.

Vergil halted on the path and faced her. "Hey, lady, whose side are you on?"

Susan laughed. "Yours, of course. But I can't resist raising questions. It's just my nature to look at all sides of a deal." They ambled onward and presently she asked, "So, if the window-fitter is so uncertain, how do you plan to handle him?"

"I'm taking him out to lunch tomorrow. I'll pour on the pressure, bit by bit until I make him commit himself. Once he's said yes, he'll stick with it."

"And by the same token, if he says no, that will be that?"

"Yes, but I'll persuade him. Don't worry."

"And whereabouts are you planning to lead this lamb to the slaughter?"

"At Maxine's. But I don't really appreciate your description, Sue."

"You'll get used to me. Even when I'm pushing an advantage myself, I tend to call a spade a spade."

Having hit a slump the next day at one o'clock, Susan remembered Joslin and his prospect and took a cab to Maxine's even though she felt certain that by now the objects of her interest would be gone. But as the restaurant began to clear she spotted them at the other end of the place. She'd recognize Vergil's back anywhere: that strong neck and thick, springy black hair only slightly grayed. In front of him his client squirmed and sweated. Vergil had apparently brought the squeeze to its ultimate pressure point, and the man was alternately attending to Joslin as if hypnotized and darting scared glances all around.

But after a minute or two Susan realized that the randomness of his escapes from Vergil's insistence had ceased. When he looked away, it was only to her that his eyes turned with a dumb appeal that she found arresting. She had communicated the intensity of her interest without in the least intending to.

Back and forth the man's eyes went. At last he sat back and spread his hands in a wide gesture of indecision. Joslin would reel him in at this juncture, she surmised. But the client threw a last questioning look in her direction and to her amazement she felt her head make the faintest of negative moves.

Fortunately at the moment a waitress arrived with Sue's order allowing her to begin at once to cut her salad and butter her muffin with concentration so that thus occupied she saw nothing further.

Joslin's voice wishing her a "good afternoon," broke in. "Oh hello." The two men went on, but not before she caught those signals that told her Vergil had been turned down, and that he was darkly angry. She shivered, more from excitement than from fear, wondering if he could have guessed.

Chapter
29

Susan experienced several days of mild uneasiness and was thankful when Joslin called Thursday saying only that he wished to confirm their Friday dinner date. When she hung up she sat for a time analyzing his tone—a touch too amicable? The comfortable familiarity a trifle exaggerated?

But when they met he chattered on in his usual clever fashion and made dinner entertaining. And when, after they'd left the tavern, he started driving without consulting her, she gave little thought to it until she noticed that they were taking an unfamiliar route, leaving the green, leafy road and moving toward a more congested area.

"Where are we headed?"

"Oh, I thought we might stop at my townhouse for a bit. I'm expecting to hear from a stock broker about a new offering coming on the market tomorrow. If he thinks I should buy, I want to get in on the ground floor."

"Oh, Vergil!"

"Indulge me, Susan. I know you don't work the market, but those of us who do like to keep up."

"Oh, all right." Susan remembered that though she'd seen his palatial home often enough, she'd never yet visited his downtown quarters. Curiosity about his bachelor digs erased her reluctance, and when he took her up in the elevator, behaving with decorous restraint, she began to think that maybe she didn't appreciate him enough.

Subject of an evident "decoration" by a designer who favored a dramatic black-white-and-red effect, the very masculine apartment got no more than a perfunctory glance from its owner who went directly to his computer and switched it on. "Look around, if you like," Vergil invited carelessly.

"Thanks, I will." She examined the bedroom where a black velvet spread held a pile of red satin cushions and the kitchen where white floor tile, black counters, and hanging racks full of gleaming copper utensils graced the room.

In her absence Joslin had removed his coat and tie and was sipping a drink while working his computer. She went to snuggle on a softly enveloping couch and by the time Vergil's preoccupation ended, she began to relax and feel sleepy. So when Vergil approached, sat and made a sudden move to possess her with a force just short of violence, she nearly lost her breath.

"Hey, slow down!" She tried to pull away.

His voice, hoarse and loud in her ear alarmed her. "No, Sue. This is the end of the slowdown. You've kept me dangling for nearly two years and enough is enough."

Anger welled up in her. "How dare you suggest that I owe you something? You've voluntarily spent your time with me—not a hint of coercion on my part!"

He released her as suddenly as he'd grabbed her and remarked wistfully, "Forgive me if I imagined that your continuing to see me all these months signaled some sort of interest!" She looked into Vergil's gray eyes, softer than she'd ever seen them—sun on stone. "I'm in dead earnest, you know," he went on, "not trifling—and I think you've understood that from the first." He reached in his pocket and withdrew a small case. He kept his intent eyes on her as he snapped it open. There in its blue satin bed reposed the largest, most brilliant diamond Susan had ever seen, attached to a simple gold band.

Though awed and admiring she made no move to take the ring. "Well? Will you stop wearing that old wedding band and put this on now?"

He took the ring from the box and turned the glittering stone in the light.

"I'm really flattered, Vergil."

"Don't say that. It sounds like letting me down gently. And I won't accept that."

"You're forgetting that I'm a stubborn old woman—set in my ways. Too much of a free spirit to give up my independence."

"I know what you're like. I also know that you're not Gert—never will be. I'm proposing that we team up as we are. Don't worry—you'll have all the latitude in the world to do your own thing."

Susan pondered. "I think you mean that."

"I do." He reached for her hand, but she drew it away. "Don't rush me."

He put the diamond back in its case and set it on the coffee table with an ugly gesture. "I told you—no more stalling. I mean it. Think I don't know there's no one else in your life? I know why, too. You find most men tiresome or contemptible or both. You'd almost outgrown Kendrick when he kicked off, and he was a rare breed. You can't replace me, my lady. And you're not so inhuman that you can go it totally alone."

He waited for some response, but Susan kept silent.

"You're attracted to me, too," he went on. "You want me just as much as I want you, if you'd break down and admit it!" Without warning he snatched her to him and kissed her hard, holding her face with one hand and straining her to him with a powerful arm. She struggled, but her efforts only fueled his ardor. He pinned her under him on the sofa and groped for the buttons on her dress. Unable to release them in such tight proximity he jerked at her bodice. She felt something pop and tear, felt his hot breath on her face and neck and experienced nearly the worst terror of her life.

Keep cool, she cautioned herself. She looked for an appropriate spot and sank her teeth into his shoulder so ferociously that she tasted blood.

With a cry he sat up and Susan jumped to her feet. "You brute!"

Joslin sat gazing for a moment at the spreading blood stain on his shoulder with a dazed look. Then he rose. "If I'm a brute, you're a bitch, you know. Think I couldn't figure out that you blitzed my deal the other day?"

"So we're even. You thought pushing Belle Tanner in my face was some kind of joke?"

To her relief, Joslin laughed. "Tit for tat, eh? What have I been telling you? We're alike, we two. Peas in a pod."

"I don't have to listen to this." Susan grabbed her purse and strode toward the door, but with a bound, Vergil was at her side. He thrust the jewel case into her handbag.

"Try living alone. You won't make it without me. Keep the ring for a while. When you want to see me again, wear it."

"I'll flag a taxi. Don't come down." She opened the door.

"Answer me, Susan. Will you give it some thought while you're brooding and hiding from reality?"

Susan stepped into the hall. "I'll think about it. But don't hold your breath."

On her dresser the jewel case which Susan had dropped there that night with cold detachment became an ever increasing burden as the days and weeks advanced. For a while her mind centered on what a bully Joslin was, how she detested him (let me count the ways!). But time began to ease her resentment and blunt the edge of her resistance. Admissions of her own culpability in what had occurred rose unbidden. She'd mocked and teased and even frustrated him in more ways than one. He'd said "grow up." To her! Well, she'd give him no further cause for complaint.

But even with that decision made, she left the ring there on the dresser where it gradually came to represent a ring in the nose, rather than a gift. Whatever he said at present, after she'd married him he'd soon take a macho-possessive attitude. He'd have lots of instructions—would revert to treating her as he'd treated Gertrude. "And I'm not Gert," she said aloud one day.

Passing from her air-conditioned office to air-conditioned car to air-conditioned house she had only a passing impression that Philadelphia endured an exceptionally hot summer. Fall brought torrential rains and perpetually clouded skies. Evenings she tried watching television, bored and disgusted by eternal obnoxious ads that equated automobiles with love or patriotism with a budget-sized mixer. Then there were glaring one-sided documentaries, gossip shows, and the so-called "news." At last she turned the tube off more or less permanently. On those occasions when she came home, she prowled through her mammoth house—upstairs and down, back and forth.

Most evenings she remained in the office, checked figures and arrived at an approximation of how much she'd made that day. Keeping such close tabs on everything was unnecessary—even ridiculous—but it provided more diversion than anything else she could think to do.

Thanksgiving, a dull thankless day, came and went and now she had to think about Christmas. She sorted through and rejected a dozen invitations--some proffered by people who thought she'd be useful, some out of a sense of duty because poor old Susan shouldn't have to be alone. Now she understood Alice's pathetic eagerness to spend the time with them. She had to call Eileen and did, reassured by the warm, welcoming voice. They talked at length and Susan hung up, oddly comforted.

Business slowed. Susan shopped for gifts, bearing in mind Eileen's restrictions: No clothing (It was ordered from catalogs used by people where she lived). Few toys (limited storage). Keep it small and simple. In an antique shop she found an old hand-carved toy box that would help with the storage problem and had it shipped. For Eileen a necklace of exquisite black pearls that could be passed off as beads. For Ellis, the carving tool Eileen had suggested, obtained after much search and inquiry from an obscure firm that provided precision tools at extremely high prices to a limited clientele.

She bought a plane ticket and waited out her routine problems: plumbing, heating, roofing repairs (how she missed Jo!), questions from her staff posing difficulties that with a little careful consideration they could have overcome themselves.

And at last, off to Eileen's. On Christmas

morning Susan most enjoyed the hour spent opening gifts. After the children had their time in the spotlight the family eagerly awaited Susan's reactions to things they'd made for her: Picture frames, it seemed. "Mine first," both youngsters shrieked. Susan unwrapped the papier-mâché oblong that enclosed Elizabeth's portrait, a bit lop-sided and formed with care by pudgy little fingers. "Thank you, Lizzie," Sue said more touched than she cared to show. The child squealed with delight.

Theo's next. His picture reminded Susan that the handsome boy resembled Kendrick more every day. Very little Romberg in that brown hair, the brown eyes, the friendly smile, so like his granddad's. The frame, consisting of two rows of short pegs tightly fitted and glued together, showed the more sophisticated skill of a seven year old. After solemn thanks to Theo, Sue opened her last gift: Father and mother in a pose Grant-Wood-like in its solemnity, she thought. The intricately carved wooden frame gave evidence of long hours of labor. Eileen claimed that her contribution was arranging for sittings and fitting the photos.

"This is a treasure," Susan assured Ellis, glad that she'd taken trouble with his gift.

But Eileen was now tearing paper, eager as a child herself, delighted with the hand made oddities from her children and the new tapes from Ellis. "More beautiful music!" She sent her husband a fond kiss across the space between them. "And what has Grandma brought?" she asked, opening the cheap little box into which Susan had transferred the pearls. She drew out the necklace. For a time she sat speechless, then a look of amused appreciation crept over her face. "What do you think, Lizzie?" She dangled the jewels from her fingers, awaiting her child's response.

"Pretty beads! Put 'em on!"

Eileen went to a mirror and held the necklace against her white blouse. "Actually, I think I can get away with this." She laughed, and passing her mother's chair dropped a kiss on top of her head. "You're something else."

Susan darted a look at Ellis. He wore the expression of one who knows something's up, but isn't quite sure what. For his children's gifts to him he expressed such gratitude that both ran to him for hugs and kisses. He exchanged a complacent look with Eileen over the white shirt he really needed. He opened Susan's gift, took it out and gave it minute attention. Then he met her eyes. "Amazing. Where did you find this?"

Susan named the company. "Small private concern. They have a few other things you might like."

At this Ellis made a delicate sign of demur. "No, please. I'm sitting here wondering if I'd find courage to lend this out if someone asked." His mother-in-law let the matter drop.

After two and a half fleeting days Sue deposited her bag in the truck which she'd begun to take in stride, and after Eileen had dropped Ellis at his gas station, the rest of the family went on to the airport, a major outing for the children who demanded that their mother park and take them into the terminal.

"I'll contribute the parking fee," Sue offered, seeing Eileen hesitate.

"Well, all right. This once."

Reminded of her return to Philadelphia and to her unresolved option concerning Vergil, Susan fell silent, ignoring her daughter's educational pitter patter about planes and air transport. After a time, Eileen remarked, "You're quiet, Mom. Something on your mind?"

"What would you think if I ever married again?"

"Not a bad idea. You're alone too much." Eileen paused. "Have you met some nice man—somebody like Dad?"

"No, indeed. I don't have anyone in mind. Anyway, I could never replace your father."

Tears started into her daughter's eyes. "No, of course not." But after a few seconds she went on, "If you should happen to meet someone, don't turn back thinking I'd object. I'd be happy for you.

Mail still delivered to Susan's estate house tended to be inconsequential. Personal correspondence, Club notices and bills now came to a P.O. box, and were picked up by a secretary from the agency. Still Susan dutifully sorted through the piles that accumulated in the hall mail basket in her lengthy absences, looking for something like a stray tax notice.

A stiff envelope containing a piece of embossed stationery came to hand and she tore it open wondering: Vergil's scrawled signature and above it a single two-word statement—"Still thinking?"

She mounted stairs to her bedroom, took the jewelry case from the dresser and wandered around opening drawers and looking for a box, wrapping paper or a mailing pouch in which to send it back to him. Having no success, she returned the ring to the bureau and forgot it, her mind distracted by business concerns, especially taxes.

And, for the next six weeks she indulged her preference by just staying on at the office every night, taking an odd pleasure in mundane tasks, preparing simple meals in the employees' lunchroom, dropping off and reclaiming her own laundry and dry-cleaning. She even stopped by a branch library and picked up some of the favorites she'd read in old English classes to read over again: *Great Expectations, Portrait of a Lady, Moby Dick.*

She'd settled into a kind of rut, dull and desensitizing, when a memo from her bookkeeper rudely alerted her to an unpleasant development at home. Expenses for the months of December and January had tripled! Even allowing for winter heating costs, the charges for keeping up the estate were outrageous. Sue collected itemized bills from the files—bills she found revealing. Then she drove out to her house. It was January and little work had to be done on the grounds, she reflected, casting an appraising eye at the trees, lightly dusted with snow.

She parked in the garage and entered from the back. Far off, in the dining area she could hear a low hum of voices. She walked into the kitchen where stacks of dirty dishes had accumulated. Her shoes stuck to the tiled kitchen floor in places. Beside the phone a file Jo had kept stood open at a list of BEST CATERERS. No sign of the housekeeper, Mrs. Prinz. The lady and her niece must be dining, she surmised. She passed up the hall and, hearing sound in the study, entered. No one there. Nonetheless, a manuscript that she identified as an alien term paper clacked methodically out of Kendrick's old printer.

She inspected the living area which looked casually lived-in, textbooks and magazines lying about—some opened. A TV set functioned with the sound off, a pair of snowboots sat just inside the glass patio doors. Susan hung her coat in a closet and stood thinking. Now the sound of voices from the dining room came to her more clearly. She approached without a sound and peered in. At the table sat the young woman Sue identified as the housekeeper's niece. Rather plain and respectable looking. What arrested Susan's startled eyes was the young lady's air of graciously dispensing a brand of hospitality that she took pride in.

The service admittedly was casual since cartons and bottles stood on the table, but it seemed geared nonetheless to providing the best that Huttons (distinguishable by its crest on certain boxes) and other fine hotels and catering firms could supply in the way of food and drink. The young men of approximately college age sat with their hostess. "Mmmm. Now this," said one pointing a fork at a particular carton, "is the tastiest lobster salad I ever ate."

At this moment, loudly declaiming from afar that the exercise equipment had to be tried to be appreciated, a fourth young man came charging in, pausing to exclaim, "Who are--?"

The niece's head snapped up, and on seeing Susan her skin reddened from the roots of her hair to the margin of her blouse. She rose literally gasping. "Mrs. Shields!"

"I'm looking for my housekeeper," Susan announced coldly with a manner that put her resoundingly back in charge.

"Oh, she's—"And with a desperate look around, "I'm sorry, ma'am. Uh, she's in her apartment, I think."

Ignoring the guilt and embarrassment she left behind, Susan walked out to the garage and then upstairs. She rapped and waited. Mrs. Prinz answered the door with one eye still glued to the TV set where a woman in a hospital bed lay sobbing out a tale of woe.

"Oh, Mrs. Shields!"

"How are you, Mrs. Prinz?" The comfortable, competent-looking housekeeper, stout and broad-faced, snapped off the set with only a faint trace of regret and asked, "How have you been? We haven't seen you for a while."

Susan settled herself on the purple sofa without being invited and snapped open her briefcase. "I thought we might run over some of these invoices together." She patted the seat beside her and Mrs. Prinz eased herself down with a wary look.

"Now here," Susan intoned, "we have a caterer's bill for enough gourmet food for a dozen people, don't you think?"

"Oh, Lord!" The housekeeper took the bill, put on her glasses and read the total with horror.

"Ah, but that's just one item," Susan went on bringing bill after bill to the astonished woman's attention.

"I see, I see," the woman cried impatiently after she'd perused a dozen. "Good heavens! Honey asked me if she could order out, and I said yes, thinking she'd get a few pizzas. I never dreamed--!"

"I guess pizzas didn't satisfy the needs of all those growing boys," Susan hazarded. "How long have they been here?"

Mrs. Prinz squirmed. "She asked if a couple fellows from her college could come in at Christmas. They couldn't afford to go home and the school is awful dull over the holidays."

"Apparently they found adequate entertainment here," Susan murmured.

"Honey thought they'd go after a day or two. I suppose she lost track of time. But the boys'll be leaving, right away."

Susan rose. "Get your niece and her crowd of parasites out of here today."

"Not my niece too! I don't see how I can stand it without her! It's so dead and spooky quiet out here all alone. Besides, you hired her yourself."

"The inventory she was assigned was finished months ago."

Susan left the woman grumbling with discontent.

What had occurred was her own fault, Susan conceded. She knew better than to leave workers unsupervised for more than a day or two. Create a vacuum and something or someone will move into it. She'd have to return home almost every evening—a slave to her house.

She descended and peered into the kitchen on her way back to the office. Much of the clutter had been hastily organized into neat stacks and Honey was hard at work loading the dishwasher. No sign of the boys. Susan felt sure the girl sensed her presence in the doorway, but out of shame couldn't make herself look up.

A fleeting sensation of sympathy came and went. Sue had known what it was to feel poor and unattractive and helpless. The kid had enjoyed her ephemeral popularity, no doubt.

Mrs. Prinz resigned, of course, obliging Susan to hire a new housekeeper. She found a dour older woman who liked to see people do things right, and who enjoyed reading and crocheting in her spare time. Most evenings thereafter Susan received a report on the woman's activities, however tedious.

March brought the inevitable announcement of the Club's Spring Ball, greeted by Susan this year with consternation. If she looked to Vergil to accompany her he'd expect her to wear that almost-forgotten diamond, and the affair would turn into a celebration of their engagement.

By inviting someone else she could forestall him. So she reviewed the field of eligible men and experienced revulsion. Of course she could always recruit an agent to act as an escort, but a disagreeable suggestion of doing the boss a favor inevitably hung in the air. Finding the uncertainty and irritation unbearable she determined not to attend. She could make a contribution by purchasing a pair of tickets and then plead a last-minute indisposition. She had no wish to contemplate the spectacle of Vergil enjoying doting attention from a bevy of females. The decision failed to bring her any satisfaction.

During interminable evenings in her enormous house she wandered from room to room after the dinner she felt obliged to eat at home so as to give the housekeeper something to do. Mrs. Trask was clean, methodical and managed things economically. She was also glum and uncommunicative. Susan made a few wistful attempts to befriend her, but when she tried to help out at the sink, cleaning vegetables or rinsing dishes, Trask turned sullen and withdrawn.

Oh, well—you can't have everything.

Susan kept postponing dinner to a later and later hour until she regularly ate at 8:30 instead of 6:00, but the woman offered no complaint.

One dreary Sunday when Sue had forgotten to arrange any sort of outing for herself she toured the house restlessly after an arid church service and a dull but correct lunch. Up and down, she trudged, in and out. In the garden new beds had been dug up and awaited the hundreds of plants that would bloom there: roses, marigolds, petunias, pansies.

She called Floretta Griffen who was away, of course. Then she tried the senior Mrs. Dakes with whom she'd played golf on rare occasions though neither practiced and both were inept at the game. "Oh, sorry, Susan," Edna Dakes said, "I have my grandchildren with me."

To keep demon gloom at bay Susan began tidying dresser drawers. She sat on the floor and started with a deep drawer in the bottom of the antique she'd rescued so long ago from Clara Bowman's house. It held an assortment of gifts she'd received and never found a use for, some still half wrapped in papers of unusual design. Monogrammed pillow cases, a set of heavy linen napkins, a fancy lace chemise too large for her, an assortment of exquisite handkerchiefs from various parts of the world, a silver ash tray, a crystal candy dish. She found a box and loaded everything into it. She dared not give this stuff to her church for their annual bazaar, lest a donor recognize a gift she'd given Sue. No, Mrs. Trask would have to cart it across town to the Salvation Army thrift shop or pawn it.

Other drawers required less attention. In the top drawer Sue came across the urn containing Teddy's ashes. She waited in vain for the tears to start. Instead a dry misery choked her. As she closed the drawer her eye fell on the jewel case. Next Saturday the glittery Annual Ball would proceed without her and Vergil would shine and prance while she sat home, too proud, too stubborn to associate with anyone.

She sat down in the closest chair, pondering her life. Even though taxes now consumed more than half her income she still had money—more than ever before. And what could she do but re-invest? Eileen refused all but a few dollars now and then. The stimulation of acquisition for its own sake had, she decided after surprised contemplation, dissipated with her break with Joslin.

And this house—this estate that she'd defied Kendrick over and hung on to with such tenacity had become an unwelcome anchor. If only she'd moved when he'd asked her, how different things might have been! Too late.

But now, willy nilly, she'd find herself a smaller, more manageable house.

On the night of the ball she took a new agent and his wife out to dinner, then to the premiere of a new play. She put her failure, as she began to regard her life, behind her and devoted herself to business, forgetting other people—especially Joslin. So shock stiffened her when she looked into the mail basket and saw yet another of those stiff white envelopes. She tore it open and deciphered the scrawled message: "Missed you at the Ball. Hope you're close to a decision. Before another six weeks? Love, Vergil."

She went into her coldly ordered living room and sat down, surprised by the sense of panic that hit her. He'd given her a deadline, a generous one, but a deadline. She should have returned his ring long ago. Only—

It was possible that he'd met another woman who would suit him—someone more like Gert, perhaps. That idea deepened her unease. While Vergil had courted her, she'd felt alive, amused, competitive. So he didn't measure up to Kendrick. Who could? Joslin was great company, why not throw in her lot with him? True, his ethics bent a little here and there where the situation required. But who was she to criticize? She'd engineered more than a few borderline transactions herself. Hadn't she once stolen a car?

"I'll say yes to Joslin," she spoke the words aloud. But the decision, instead of bringing relief, sickened her. She mounted the stairs to her bedroom, put the too-colossal diamond on her finger, and standing at a window turned and turned it watching it glitter in the waning light, hypnotized. "You win, Vergil. I need you."

Her eyes lifted, sought the sky outside and caught the last glow of light and color in the west. Then a smothering darkness settled in and stifled her.

She jerked off Joslin's ring and flung it into the open case, snapping it shut. She had to do something to combat the feeling she had of walking into a trap. A trap? No, what was eating at her was of her own devising. Her bleak, meaningless way of life was one she'd constructed herself. And where could she find help to escape a desperation that threatened to overwhelm her? She could think of no one and nothing. She had nowhere to turn.

Still, before she'd show anything but a serene countenance to her elite circle of friends and her employees, she'd kill herself. And wouldn't oblivion be more desirable than this oppressive emptiness?

She threw herself on the bed and lay with an arm over her face contemplating ways and means. But no! Eileen would care! Eileen would be hurt! She had to see her daughter. She rose, pulled a suitcase from a closet and piled clothes and other necessities into it. Then she carried it downstairs where she forced herself to eat the dinner Mrs. Trask had provided. After the meal she informed her housekeeper that she was going to her daughter's house in Arkansas and didn't know when she'd be back. In an emergency she could be reached on her cell phone—but only in an emergency.

She drove until three in the morning, exhilarated by the sensation of flying through the darkness in her large, purring vehicle, concentrating on avoiding every fault in the road. She crossed Pennsylvania and shortly after reaching West Virginia she wheeled into a motel where she spent the rest of the night. Not until she woke up late the following morning did she admit to running away! What a fool. But she was rolling and wouldn't turn back.

Enough common sense reasserted itself, however, to make her call her office and leave instructions with her secretary. Thereafter, she said, she'd call each morning.

All this delayed her departure, and unused to sustained driving, she tired earlier next day and had to get off the road. She perceived that at this rate her trip would occupy five days. Old as she was, she reminded herself, she couldn't expect to have the stamina of a twenty-year-old

At one of the hotels where she stopped a white haired businessman engaged her in conversation and asked to sit at her table while drinking his after-dinner coffee. Sue carefully declined to make the signal he was looking for, and he parted from her in the elevator with a guarded farewell.

Chapter
31

When she knew she'd reach her destination next day, Susan called her daughter and felt cheered by the delighted exclamations coming across the line. Eileen gave directions and it was with a keen sense of anticipation that Susan swerved off the Interstate and began following country roads into a remote part of Southern Arkansas.

Early in the afternoon she found the house, remembering its location on a hill and the look of the stone and log cottage. She drove up the graveled path and sat there uncertainly not wanting to block the way to the garage when Ellis returned with the truck. But in a few minutes Eileen stood beside the car with both children. Hugs and kisses all around. There was plenty of space to leave the car in a sizeable graveled lot down at the foot of the hill.

"I'll hunt up a Motel," Sue offered.

Eileen shook her head. "Stay with us."

There was a third bunk in the children's room over little Elizabeth's bed. The children's room had been partitioned. Under the two windows stood two storage boxes. Susan's gift in Theo's part of the room and a new, almost identical box in Lizzie's, the carving equally intricate but with a different motif. The tool Sue had provided had seen good use, she surmised.

Following her mother's gaze, Eileen explained. "Theo was selfish—took Lizzie's toys out of the chest, wouldn't let her sit on it. So Ellis made her one of her own."

"So your offspring are normal, after all," Susan commented.

"I'm afraid they're not a pair of saints."

Ellis and Eileen had created a snug and charming retreat out of little more than ingenuity and hard labor, Susan began to realize after a day or two. The floors, cabinets and doors glowed with the rich shine that could result only from coats and coats of fine varnish lovingly applied. Curtains, tablecloths and spreads made on an old Singer out of cheap denim, canvas, sacking and muslin, selected and coordinated with care, contributed to the homely coziness of the rooms. Decoration consisted entirely of artfully fashioned pieces taken from the hills or forest surrounding them—stone, wood, dried flowers and leaves. "A hobby," Eileen called it. "We always have a chance to replace things, because anything that a church member admires becomes his or hers."

Susan rested while family and pastoral life flowed and eddied comfortingly around her. On days that Ellis didn't go to his gas station job he occupied himself at a desk in their bedroom, preparing his sermons and writing. Every day he also worked around the house and yard. When church folk stopped by Sue observed that their problems received more earnest attention than her deceased "father" Rev. Sterne had ever found time to provide for his parishioners.

That Ellis was at least as intelligent and more talented than Sue's adoptive father came home to her on Sunday when Ellis played for the congregation. There was ease and virtuosity in those fingers, in the clear, speaking tones elicited by his undulating bow.   His sermon, scaled to his audience, followed an argument so closely reasoned that Susan found herself caught up in it.

Only when one of the hillbillies as she privately named them gave announcements did her mind wander. She gazed around in wonder at the thirty odd people in the congregation all dressed in their bargain-store best, at the rows of folding chairs that had come out of the storage closet (replaced for the moment with her carpet and stereo system she'd provided). She studied the simple lectern behind which Pastor Romberg stood and Eileen, content between her two children in the front row. From time to time her daughter rose to accompany the singing on a portable electric keyboard.

So much ability wasted! Apparently the two were determined to pursue mission work, but there had to be a more appropriate and dignified way to go about it. Sue gave a lot of attention to the problem, and on Monday while walking with Eileen who was gathering wild flowers, she sought a way to bring up the subject. Oblivious to all else her daughter picked a wild rose and held it up. "Can you imagine anything more exquisite? Under a microscope one of these petals would show a perfect, delicate molecular structure—like stones have or grains of sand—anything in nature. Whereas man-made substances such as plastics have crude, simplistic molecular structure. If a person needed a proof that God exists, that alone should convince him!"

Susan broke in, feeling impatient. "Who doesn't believe in God? You'd be a fool not to."

Eileen squeezed her mother's arm and laughed. "You're wonderful. I love the way you quote scripture."

"I wasn't quoting scripture."

"Yes, you were. Psalm 14:1: The fool has said in his heart, there is no God."

"If anyone's wonderful, it's you, Eileen. I could never have cited chapter and verse. I suppose there's a lot of pretty obvious stuff in the Bible."

"Indeed," Eileen agreed with an odd fervor.

"Eileen—" Emboldened by her daughter's acquiescence, Susan decided to expose her ideas, "there's no need for you to go on as you're doing, raising a pitiful sum for the building fund each week. I'm well able to give you a church—rather a fine one, with a lovely manse beside it. Interested?"

Eileen, startled and not at all pleased, stopped in her tracks. "No, no. You'd spoil everything. Can't you see that? This congregation has to build a church they can feel proud of, because they put themselves and their giving into it. It has to be a building they wouldn't feel intimidated in. And they need a pastor who shares their lives and their ways. We've been so careful! Please don't mention what you've just said to another soul!"

"You give your real attitude away when you say you've had to be careful! In point of fact, you and Ellis are totally unlike your congregation. Why don't you admit it?"

"What can I say, Mom? Paul tells us that he became 'all things to all people' in order to win some. Maybe we're not identical in all ways, but we do try."

"And the result is a bit ludicrous, if you ask me. If you honestly want to identify with a congregation, why don't you apply to a Board that will send you to Europe? I've heard of missions there that have a fairly sophisticated following."

Eileen's jaw set. She had that stubborn look that her father could wear. "We're contented here. You couldn't pry us loose or change our purpose. I know it doesn't look like much, but to us it's abundant harvest." Now Eileen grinned. "Heavens. If what we'd wanted was success, a large church building, a wealthy congregation we should have stayed in Philly. The pastor did all he could to keep Ellis—told him he was like a son, that he'd make him an associate pastor, groom him for the top job when he retired.

"He said that! And you turned him down?"

"We felt guilty that we'd stayed there as long as we had."

For a time her mother's only response was a sort of strangled sound. Then she gasped, "All this is so peculiar. I never intended for you to turn out like this."

"No. But you brought Jo to our house, and—we changed."

"True. I blame myself for that."

"Don't. I doubt if you could help it. I think it was meant."

Thoroughly uncomfortable with the turn the conversation had taken, Susan changed the subject rather abruptly.

Occasionally Susan also took walks with her grandchildren, one or the other or both, and began to win their confidence and affection. Elizabeth tagged her around or sat and watched while she put cream on her face at night or makeup in the morning. One day the child asked, "Why do you put that stuff on your face, grandma? Mama doesn't."

"Your mother is beautiful without it. But poor grandma's ugly without makeup. After all, even an old barn looks better with a little paint."

The child continued to watch while Susan brushed her cheeks with blusher. "No," she observed, "You're not ugly without it. Just sad."

But it was Theo who came to sit by Susan while she made her calls to the office early in the morning. Fortunately Philadelphia was in a later time zone.

Theo listened, gravely puzzled, as if entering a foreign world. Most of what she had to say was routine business, but one day her secretary announced that the director of a rival agency had come by and had offered to buy them out.

"Tell the bastard to go to hell!" Sue exclaimed without thinking, disgusted at this brazen assumption.

Little Theo's eyebrows shot up. "Go to hell," he crowed loudly. Eileen appeared at once and led Theo into the other bedroom. Susan finished her calls and put away her cell phone. She could hear a murmur of voices—Theo's childish expostulation and his mother's low, gentle insistence.

Susan took a room in a rickety old hotel in the nearest town and made her calls from there. She offered to stay there, but Eileen wouldn't hear of it. "I know that place. The beds are awful and the place is overrun with cockroaches. Making phone calls there is one thing, but sleeping there is out." So Susan stayed on, thinking every day that she ought to go home.

After she'd spent two weeks with her family she overheard Lizzie one day asking, "Why is grandma staying so long? Why can't she keep things on Theo's side? She puts her suitcase on my chest." Susan recalled guiltily that indeed she'd taken to leaving her bag for long periods on almost the only flat surface in the little space.

After Lizzie's remark an instant silence had ensued. After a time Sue, glancing through the window, saw mother and child in the yard, Eileen dismayed and disappointed, Elizabeth pouting with tears on her cheeks.

Susan made a point of mentioning a number of

problems that had become critical and left the following morning. After one long hard day on the road she deposited her car at an agency in Memphis where they would arrange for a driver to take it to Philadelphia. The next morning she took a flight home and at the airport rented a car which she drove directly to her office where a multitude of questions awaited her.

By afternoon she saw that she'd have to call Mrs. Trask to say she was back, but wouldn't be having dinner until very late. No sense going out to the house yet. Nothing there.

While driving home after she at last detached herself from the agency her trained eye searched for new FOR SALE signs along her route. Who was selling what, she wondered.

As she whirled past her mind registered a fleeting impression of a fine old house that had a Notice in one window and felt inspired anew to move away from the mausoleum she currently lived in. Not till a few seconds later did recognition transfix her. That, of course, had been Kendrick's Georgian.

Chapter
32

Back at home Susan examined the contents of the mail basket, bored and thinking she'd have to teach Mrs. Trask to open and discard a lot of junk. But as she feared at the bottom lay one of those stiff envelopes. She carried the missive to a window. Vergil's scribble, of course. His inexcusably bad penmanship. But the message, longer than the others soon imprinted itself in her consciousness: "Isn't it a pity to part with bad blood between us when we've had so many good times together? Please see me, and let's patch things up." A civilized and rational—even a generous move. In all decency she couldn't refuse. She called his secretary and arranged a date for Friday.

Once done, the deed left her confused, unable to decide whether to anticipate or dread the day. She bought a new silk suit for the occasion, fashionable but not overtly high style.

They met at Hutton's, Vergil an intimidating presence even far off across the room. He treated her with consideration, helping her with her jacket in an almost gingerly way, avoiding that possessive handling that she'd so objected to.

He could amuse her, she confessed inwardly, more entertained by their conversation than she'd felt in months. He never once mentioned the ring nor her failure to reach a decision. They laughed over dinner and went on laughing at one of Philadelphia's night spots where a famous comedienne convulsed the audience with a satirical commentary on the joys of aging.

Joslin drove all the way to her office where she'd left her car (now delivered from Memphis) and opened the door for her with gallantry. Before driving away she looked back to where he sat behind the wheel of his own vehicle. For an instant his face seemed to express the closest to a pleading look she'd ever seen on it and his lips formed the words, "Three weeks?"

She maneuvered skillfully but mechanically out of the parking area, her mind made up. She'd wait no longer than one week, had kept Vergil on the string too long, owed it to him to say yes or no speedily.

All the way home she smiled at his restrained behavior. What reason had she to imagine she couldn't control him? Even if they married, she could always walk out if he displeased her. In this life, nothing is forever.

As if she didn't have enough on her mind the following week, the office handed her a whole series of disagreeable problems. On Tuesday one of her agents came in with a sob story and made a totally impossible request. Susan was appalled by his unrealistic attitude. After all, he'd worked for her for ten years, starting at age twenty-five when he'd needed a lot of direction. He'd developed into a good, though never brilliant operator. And surely he'd know her by this time. She contemplated his familiar good looks, his pale but healthy face, his slightly rumpled sandy hair.

Susan already knew that his third baby had been born blind. Now he was talking about a cure. At age thirty-five there was still something so youthful and naïve about the man that people called him Bimmy, though his name was Benjamin. The doctor, he said, had told him there were only three surgeons in the world who could perform the operation that would restore his child's sight. He'd contacted one in Sweden who had agreed to do it, but Susan wouldn't believe the fee that doctor charged! Yes, she would, Sue thought. And there was no way Bimmy could afford it on what he was making.

"So," Bimmy wound up, "in light of the circumstances, I thought I'd ask for another one or two percent on my commissions. Then I could get a loan and pay it back with the extra money."

Sue marveled at his evident sincerity. "I'm afraid the situation isn't all that simple," she returned, carefully impassive. "Percentages are set by policy, not according to need. I'd have to raise everybody's take across the board."

Bimmy actually looked hopeful. "I'm sure they'd all be mighty glad—" he began, seeing himself as something of an office advocate.

"No, no. What you're suggesting would make

me the outcast of the real estate community. Percentages are—sacrosanct, so to speak, and quite remarkably consistent. Frankly, I couldn't and wouldn't consider changing the system."

Bimmy's face fell. "But gee—my baby. What am I going to do?"

It occurred to Sue that in his shoes she'd be mightily motivated to sell more houses, but she realized that the man had long since hit his stride and couldn't conceive of ways to generate more business.

"Does your wife work?" she inquired, casting about for some way to answer his question.

"No, of course not. She has to stay home with the kids." He rose with an injured air. "I just don't know what I'm supposed to do."

"I'm sorry," Sue remarked, regretting her feeble response.

He paused a moment at the door. "Well, I guess you can't help it," he mumbled, but she could see that he didn't believe that.

All day she had to keep reminding herself that she had taken the only course open to her and need not feel guilty. Somebody was eternally there with his hand out. She couldn't afford to get a reputation as a soft touch, could she? She'd be cleaned out in a year!

Still, though she wasn't responsible for the world's woes, wasn't there some anonymous way she could address those that fell directly into her path?

Her conviction that she had to avoid becoming

a charitable organization strengthened on Wednesday when the local chapter of the Heart Association contacted her about purchasing one acre out of a twelve-acre plot that she'd bought fifteen years ago. They needed it to build their new headquarters. "That deserted stretch," the man had called it, thinking he'd get it cheap. And his almost ludicrous dismay on hearing the price half amused, half angered Susan. She didn't have to and would not explain that she was currently negotiating sale of land in that area for a light industrial park. She didn't intend to drive down the price by selling part of it for a song, just because the would-be buyer bore the name of charity.

Finally, on Thursday, to continue her lousy week, Susan's executive secretary, Miss Pierce, recommended with agitation and regret that Sue fire a clerk-typist who produced smudged, inaccurate copy.

Firing anyone had grave consequences, so before making a decision, Susan interviewed the lady, a small, neatly dressed person with a discontented face. "How do you like it here, Mrs. Veneable?"

"Pretty well. Better than I like being home. My daughter built an addition on her house for me. But her kids are always sick, she worries. I took this job to get away."

"I see. You're a widow?"

"Yes. My husband was a judge. Those were the days! Going out, and entertaining, even renting a hall for a big party!" The woman glowed, subsided, and inquired, "Anything in particular you wanted to see me about?"

"No. I just like to keep in touch with employees." Susan realized that she was postponing the inevitable and didn't know why. Was it up to her to place this misfit in a more suitable job?

That night she dreamed that a blazing fire burned a line across her body and across her hand and she awoke clawing at the bedsheet in a crisis of nerves. For several seconds she could hardly convince herself that nothing flamed in her bed.

Shaking, she rose and walked up and down in the dark room. Outside a revolving security light put there to discourage thieves flashed across her and the brightness caught in her pink satin gown richly embroidered with a pattern of roses. Exercise gradually calmed her, but when she tried to lie down again she trembled and felt tears rising.

Up again she dressed in a pair of baggy cotton pants, a bulky shirt and sneakers. She let herself out of the house and walked down the long, curved driveway. By the time she reached the gate she had admitted the source of her malaise: panic over marrying Vergil, of course. And she would marry him. She understood him and he her. She reviewed her decisions and transactions of the week and knew that he'd back her up in every move.

If only she felt happier about it all. More like singing. She groped for a song and a fragment of a tune she'd played yesterday, an old tape she kept in the car, came to mind. She sang under her breath.

> *"Nothing comes from nothing.*
> *Nothing ever could . . ."*

"Off key," she muttered, and tried the words again. Pretty silly, actually, but she went on to the rest of it.

> *"So somewhere in my youth or childhood*
> *I must have done something good."*

Preposterous. Hadn't she always detested that ditty and its ridiculous assumption that for being a Goody-Two-Shoes one could expect to be rewarded with an advantageous marriage! And above all how absurd to suggest that these rewards stemmed from long forgotten deeds of charity performed in one's—youth? or childhood?

Well, she stopped dead in her tracks and began to laugh. How about--? She sang breathily.

> *"Somewhere in my age and decrepitude*
> *I still might do someone some good."*

She repeated the words still laughing, her voice ringing out on the deserted road.

Then she sobered, and while plodding onward, her mind worked. She could make an anonymous grant to Bimmy? A specific gift to the Heart Association? Why not? Other things occurred to her that Vergil wouldn't approve of. But he'd never have to know about them. Because she was sending his ring back. She'd get an express mail envelope from her secretary in the morning.

And while she was altering her thinking, how

about if she also surveyed the wondrous cross and poured contempt on her pride?

Her tension and distress ebbed away, and she began to take cognizance of her surroundings. She'd walked a mile away from home in darkness. On this stretch lamps hung as far as a block apart. Houses, few and far between hovered in blackness. The world slept except for thugs who always crept out at night.

Uneasy, she wanted to call a cab. No phone here. Then she remembered that all-night café that had to be close by. She strained to see what lay ahead. Up there, a block from her, a beam lay across the road and she hurried toward it. She knew that place—humble and commercial but clean and well-lighted. Within a few minutes she came out of the shadows and into the radiance that beamed from the windows.

Her Grenville estate sold for three times its purchase price. And a few months later, while preparing to move back into the old Georgian, Susan came across a battered little trunk at the back of a closet. It was some time before she finally identified it as the one piece of luggage with which she'd left the orphanage. She sank down beside it, laid her tired head on the rough surface and wept, while a whole lifetime of slavery to money and status slowly ebbed away.

ACKNOWLEDGEMENTS

I appreciate the help I received from staffs of the Rock Hill Public Library and the Winthrop University Library.

I'm indebted to the Rineharts, the Burnettes, and the Reules for their backing and invaluable support.

I'm grateful for the technical support of Ray Reynolds and his staff and for Susan Witherspoon.

. . . .

And a thousand thanks to my beloved family without whose ongoing love and encouragement I'd never make it from day to day: Wade and Louise Houston, Margaret Burnette, Lucille Reule and Fern and Bob Welch.